RAMSEY JUDD

A NOVEL

TINA SPENCER
with CINDY HIDAY

This book is a work of fiction. Names, characters, places, and incidents either are products of the author's imagination or are used fictitiously. Any resemblance to actual events or locales or persons, living or dead, is entirely coincidental and not intended by the author.

TS

This book is dedicated to Cindy Hiday, for always being there whenever I needed her, for all her good advice and hours of copy editing, for thinking *Ramsey Judd* was worth republishing. But most of all, for believing in me when I didn't believe in myself. My deepest and sincerest thank you.

CH

To my talented cousin, Tina Spencer, for writing a darn good story, for putting up with my constant nagging to bring it back for a second opportunity to entertain readers, and for entrusting me with the honor. You're the best.

Chapter One
May, 1863

The rain had been steady all night, but the sky was clearing now. A pale moon slipped out from between the clouds, causing specters of sickly light filtered through the breeze-stirred branches of oak trees to dance and jerk like creatures in the last throes of death. Up from the rain-soaked ground rose a sickening-sweet stink, the unmistakable smell of rotting flesh. Masses of black flies swarmed furiously, eagerly, their frenzied buzzing filling the eerie calm of the final hour before dawn.

Ramsey Judd and a youth he hardly knew made their way along Fourteen Mile Creek. Mosquitoes sang about their ears and necks, but the man and the boy could do little to defend themselves against the stinging attack.

Their hands were wrapped stiffly around the heavy Springfield rifles they carried, their fingers close to the triggers, tense, ready.

Large skulking birds, their ugly, rounded heads bent on long, skinny necks, feasted on the garish images that had once been men. Most of the images were boys, Rebel soldiers, rendered by grapeshot into shapeless masses of rotten meat.

Above the guttural chatter of the birds and the flapping of giant wings, an occasional moan, a plea for help, rose from the fetid carnage. Some barely recognized as humans, more dead than alive, clung to breath by pure grit, want of seeing their homes and loved ones again.

The Union troops pressed on without seeming to hear the cries of fallen men. They'd won their battle, collected their wounded. They'd held their ground, and the assault was successful. The Confederate Army – what was left of it – for the time, had been stopped.

General Grant's troops succeeded in crossing the Mississippi River at Bruinsburg twelve days ago, claimed victory at Port Gibson, then maneuvered inland to take Raymond. Now Grant was on his way to Jackson, Mississippi's capital, intending to cut the city and the railroads off from Vicksburg, where Confederates awaited badly needed supplies and reinforcements. Judd and the boy were bringing up the rear of a small detachment assigned to assure that Rebel soldiers didn't slip through the main lines of Union forces and regroup to wage an attack from behind.

Ramsey Judd was a tall man with a long swell of plow-hardened muscles in his forearms, across broad shoulders and chest. He was wiry, with more than an intimation of physical strength in his clean-built body. His face behind the week's growth of dark beard, usually easy to look at, weathered from time spent in the sun, was hardened now by experience of battle. A lock of dark curly hair hung wet and limp over his forehead from under the blue Union cap he wore. His severely carved mouth bespoke of a self discipline and firmness that was enforced by a strong jaw and intelligent brown eyes that seemed to harbor some dark, sad secret behind the intensity of their gaze.

Johnny Bowler was the boy's name. He came from Tennessee. That's all Ramsey really knew about him. That's all he wanted to know. Ramsey Judd was a solitary man, a thinker. He wasn't inclined to make friends of the men who fought by his side. It made it easier when they fell.

The man and the boy slogged through ankle-deep, sucking mud, made red by the blood of battle. The clothes on their backs hung damp and heavy, caked with mud. Ramsey's boots had holes in the soles. Slime oozed in and ground the flesh from his feet, left them raw and burning like fire.

He numbed himself to the sites and the smell of death around him, his thoughts focused on the hunger gnawing at his belly. They hadn't had a good meal in weeks, been cut off from the supplies that were promised. The hardtack and desiccated vegetables had given out. There was no place to forage, no farms, no sutlers' carts. Coffee was something they only dreamed about. Game was scarce, frightened away by the fighting. Some of the men had made soup from lizards before they crossed the river. Neither Ramsey nor Johnny Bowler had eaten any. They hadn't the stomachs for it. Yesterday, Ramsey found a sack beside a fallen Confederate. It contained a few pieces of hardtack. He'd shared them with Johnny, but it was so hard they couldn't eat it, stale and loaded with weevils.

What he wouldn't give for a plate of Ma's smoked ham and scrambled eggs. It caused his stomach to growl just thinking about it. A big helping of boiled spuds, thick milk gravy, and some of her fluffy white biscuits drizzled with sweet honey. He wondered if he'd ever taste his mother's cooking again, draw another clean breath of air. He wanted to wash the vermin from his hair, shave with warm water and soft soap, use a sharp razor, sleep in clean sheets scented with lavender.

Johnny Bowler was thinking of home, too. Thinking about his widowed mother and four younger brothers and sisters eating decent food with the three-hundred dollars he'd been paid to join the Union Army. He wished like hell he was sitting down at the table with them. It hadn't mattered to him which side he fought for. He came from poor stock, considered white trash. His family didn't own slaves, didn't care much about the U.S. Government's political problems, either. If the Rebs had got to him first, offered him more, he'd be over there on the other side. The Rebs had lost this battle, but Johnny would bet his last nickel they had full bellies. God, he was hungry.

He glanced at the tall, sullen man beside him. He liked Ramsey Judd from Cincinnati,

Ohio. Admired him. He was tough, with a cool head. If he was afraid, he didn't show it. Ramsey Judd reminded him of his pa. Zeb Bowler died of pneumonia when Johnny was seven, but Johnny couldn't remember him ever showing fear.

Johnny wanted to talk with Ramsey, get to know him better, make friends. It was good to have friends at a time like this, when a man didn't know if he'd live or die. Johnny didn't want to die alone, with no one to care. He cleared his throat. The man beside him seemed not to hear. He cleared his throat again.

"Mr. Judd?"

As if the sound of his name had shaken him awake, Ramsey Judd's body jerked. He straightened and glanced over at him. "What is it, son?"

"I ain't your son, sir."

Ramsey didn't take offense at the boy's words. The tall, blue-eyed, peach-fuzzed face of the youth at his side wore the same man's uniform as he did. He was fighting a man's war. He wanted a man's due.

"Ain't you just a little bit scared?" Johnny asked.

Ramsey didn't answer. He was twice the boy's age, but fear didn't restrict itself to the young. No matter how many battles he fought, he couldn't get use to it. He was sick from it.

"Why'd you join up, Mr. Judd?" Johnny persisted.

Ramsey had been asking himself the same question for the past ten months. It was right that he fight for the North – for what he believed. He tried to convince himself that it had nothing to do with Jarred. Nothing to do with the hurt on his father's face, the tears in his mother's eyes. "I might ask you the same thing," he said. "A boy's got no business being here."

Johnny squared his shoulders. "I'm eighteen."

"You're not a day over sixteen, if that old."

"I'm fit," Johnny answered.

How many boys just like Johnny Bowler had Ramsey killed? At Perryville? How many at Stones River? Thompson's Station? He didn't like thinking about it. The mothers at home waiting for their sons – the sons that Ramsey had put down – haunted him. In his dreams he could hear the weeping of widows, of children. It had to end. He had no grudge against these men in gray. He was a peaceable man. Live and let live, that was his philosophy.

"Ain't seen no Rebs since the shootin'

stopped," Johnny Bowler said. "S'pose it's over, Mr. Judd?"

Ramsey tried to ignore the persistent young soldier beside him. He kept his ears tuned, listened, watched in silence as the first gray light of dawn crept in about them. An owl swooped low on silent wings in front of them and disappeared into the gloomy darkness of the trees. A woodpecker hammered away somewhere over their heads, the steady rhythm echoing and bouncing through the false quiet above the din of familiar sounds Ramsey had grown accustomed to, tried to block from his mind. Moisture dripped from trees with a soft patter, and in the distance he could hear the soft sigh of the river.

A melancholy morning bird called from a low limb nearby, waited for an answer that didn't come, then called again. A muted fluttering sound and the bird was gone. Nothing now except the sucking slog of the men's footsteps, the buzz of the flies and blood-sucking mesquites, the never ceasing whines and bickering of the vultures.

A man must deal with himself, Ramsey thought. It's his own face he's got to look at in the mirror when he gets out of bed each morning. As long as a man can face himself, don't matter what people think of him. What kind of mark a man leaves in the scheme of things while he's on this earth is personal...as long as he don't wrong no one and no one wrongs him. Like that golden rule thing his mother tried to teach him when he was a boy. Do unto others –

"You married, Mr. Judd?"

Ramsey's jaw tightened. What was he going to have to do to shut the kid up? He didn't want to answer questions, especially that question. He tried to force the old memories out of his mind.

"Any younguns?" Johnny continued.

It was too late. The memories closed in on Ramsey. He could hear Martha's cries from the upstairs window, splitting the quiet night, as he paced on the front veranda of his parents' porch.

Or were those the cries of the poor wretches lying in the mud along the trail? For a moment Ramsey closed his eyes, tried to block out the memories the boy had brought to the surface: Martha's lifeless face, the motionless body of the baby lying on the bed beside her. He tried to sort what was real, what wasn't.

No, Ramsey thought. No wife. No son to carry his name.

"Sure am hungry," Johnny Bowler muttered.

Ramsey stopped. He couldn't take anymore. He glared at Johnny. "Anybody ever told you, you talk too much?" he said gruffly. "You chatter like a damn magpie. If there was a Reb within five miles, he'd sure know where to find us."

Johnny looked down at the ground.

Ramsey sucked on his teeth. He'd hurt the kid's feelings. Too damn bad. This Johnny Bowler was a pain in the ass. Ramsey was tired. His legs ached from the constant pulling at the deep mud. His feet were beyond sore. He needed to rest. He looked at the boy, at the dejected slump of his shoulders, and took a quick breath. Hell.

"I'm hungry too," Ramsey said in a low voice, almost apologetically. He looked around them. "I'm scared, too. Have been since I joined up. Just about as scared as I've ever been."

Johnny cast Ramsey a grateful glance. "Think it's much further?" he asked.

"Can't be. Best keep your voice down. Sound carries a long way this time of morning." Ramsey loosened his grip on the rifle and arched his aching back.

Sky's clearin'," Johnny said softly. "It's

gonna get hotter than Old Billy Hell."

"Probably," Ramsey answered, wrinkling his brow and looking up.

"Wish I had me some tobacco. You got any makin's, Mr. Judd?"

"Afraid not." Ramsey hefted his rifle again. "Best get moving. We should be joining the others in an hour or so."

The boy grinned. "Hope there's some good food."

Ramsey grinned back. "Me, too. Even a little skilligalee would taste good right now."

"That ain't rightly what I had in mind," Johnny said. "Hardtack is hardtack, whether it be fried in pork grease or boiled in muddy water."

"It don't give your tongue much to crow about," Ramsey agreed, "but it fills the belly."

"How about some molasses cookies?" Johnny said.

"With a good cup of strong coffee."

"And cream and short sweetenin'."

"Soldier, your tormenting me to death." Ramsey pushed ahead. "Quit chewing and start walking."

Talk was over. They moved on in silence, each lost in their own thoughts. Ramsey wondered what he'd do after the war. He'd been wanting to go West. He'd heard of a place called Oregon. Land was good, free for the taking. His pa wouldn't like it much, but Ramsey wanted something of his own. Maybe he'd find a good woman, settle down again, try another family before he got too old. Maybe –

"Hey, Yank." The weak, raspy voice came from the woods just beyond the trail. Johnny jumped and stiffened. Ramsey stopped. The hair on his neck prickled.

"Can ya spare a sip of water?" the voice asked.

Ramsey swung and stared into the dimness. It took him a few moments to spot the man sprawled on the ground, his back leaned against the trunk of an oak tree. A musket lay half buried in the mud some distance away. Ramsey hesitated. He had his orders. No assistance was to be rendered to the enemy. He started to turn away.

"Mr. Judd?" Johnny whispered.

Ramsey glanced from the man to the questioning eyes of Johnny Bowler.

"Ain't you gonna help him, sir?" Johnny's expression held something short of accusation.

"Just a sip, mind ya – before I die," the Rebel soldier pleaded.

Ramsey drew a deep, ragged breath.

Christ. What had he become? What kind of animal could leave a man in the mud to die? He took the canteen with the last of his water from over his shoulder and walked back to the wounded man. Johnny followed, stood nervously shifting from one foot to the other.

"You hurt bad?" Ramsey asked. He knelt, lifted the man forward and tipped the canteen to his lips.

"My leg. Feared it's been shot off." The Reb took a sip of the water. "My belly's on fire."

Ramsey could tell by the rotten smell that the man had been gut-shot. There wasn't much hope when that happened. Death wasn't easy, slow in coming.

The man took a longer drink, raised his muddy hand and wiped at his mouth. "Obliged."

Ramsey's gaze that he'd tried to keep in tight check ran down the length of the man's body. His stomach twisted at the sight of the mangled, maggot-infested limb half buried in the muck, the dark stain on the front of the man's shirt where the mini ball had entered just above his belt. He hurried his eyes back to the fevered face.

"I wish I could help more." Ramsey swallowed hard.

"You can...if you've a mind." The man's voice was no more than a weak whisper, breath sucked in with the pain of moving. He wiped his hand across his chest to clear it of the clinging Mississippi mud, reached into his shirt pocket and drew out a sealed white envelope. "If ya make it through...maybe you could mail this. I wrote it...before the fightin'. Never got the chance to send it."

"I'll do that." Ramsey took the letter and stuck it into his own shirt pocket. "Rest now. Someone'll be along in a while to get you." Ramsey knew it was a lie. That's what he and Johnny and the men ahead were there for – to make sure no one got through. Even if someone did get past them, this man wouldn't be alive to know it.

"I'll be okay, now," the Confederate said. He let Ramsey ease him back against the tree. "The letter's to my wife in Kentuck...it's important. Last I heard...they were sick...her and the baby."

"I'll see to it." Ramsey laid the canteen on the ground beside him, within the man's reach. "I hate to leave you like this."

"You ain't got no choice. Name's...O'Dell. Parker...O'Dell." The wounded soldier weakly raised his hand. "God bless ya, friend."

Ramsey took the man's hand and held it tightly for a few moments. "I'm Ramsey," he said. "Ramsey Judd. This here's Johnny Bowler."

The man closed his eyes and drew a long breath.

Ramsey released his hand and stood. "You rest now." He turned to Johnny. "Get going, soldier."

After they were out of earshot of the wounded man, Ramsey reached out and laid a hand on Johnny's shoulder. The boy stopped. "You speak a word of this to the others and I'll have your hide."

"No sir, Mr. Judd. I won't."

It was full light now. Ramsey kept his eyes fastened to the back of Johnny Bowler walking ahead of him. It mattered little to Ramsey that he'd disobeyed orders. He'd broken his own rule, that's what bothered him. He'd felt something for the wounded Reb. The man weighed heavy on Ramsey's shoulders. Parker O'Dell. The name was a strange one. But it wouldn't have mattered if the man's name had been plain Bill Jones, Ramsey knew he wouldn't forget it for as long as he lived.

The large bloated carcass of a horse loomed up in the trail ahead, its legs sticking stiffly out from its ballooned stomach. A buzzard danced on top of it, its wings spread, its neck bowed. Johnny started to skirt the dead animal, his hand held over his mouth and nose. He stopped and looked down. Ramsey heard him gasp, then gag.

"Oh my God!" Johnny choked. "Mr. Judd, do something!"

Ramsey stepped in beside him, looked down. He groaned, the gorge in his throat rising. A Union soldier knelt behind the beast. With his knife, he'd laid the hide away from the backbone and was carving away at the tenderloins.

The soldier looked up, a crazed expression on his face, his eyes bright and shiny. Scraps of raw flesh clung to his lips. "Fresh meat." He grinned. "Ain't eatin' no more lizards."

"Lord, man," Ramsey breathed. "That meat'll make you sick. It's putrefied."

Johnny Bowler gagged and wretched. Ramsey felt his own belly roll. His mouth watered uncontrollably.

"Ain't you ever eat horse meat?" the soldier on the ground asked.

"It's rotten. You'll have the Virginia quickstep." Ramsey took a step toward the man. "Come on, let's get the hell out of here."

"No!" The man rocked back on his heels, his knife poised in front of him. "You just want it for yourself."

"I'm telling you, the meat – " Ramsey didn't have a chance to say more. The soldier lunged at him. Ramsey jumped back in time to miss the sharp edge of the knife as it sliced the air inches from his kneecap.

Johnny Bowler moved back, his eyes wide, mouth open.

"Go on ahead, soldier," Ramsey said to Johnny. "Catch up with the others."

Johnny stumbled backwards, then turned and hurried away up the trail.

"Sherman's bringing supplies," Ramsey said to the man, who had returned to his carving. "They're probably up ahead by now."

"That's what they told us three days ago," the soldier answered. "Sherman's not coming."

Ramsey shook his head. The poor bastard was probably right. Reinforcements were long overdue. Maybe they weren't coming at all. "You'll die of the screaming shits, you eat that."

The man glanced up from his work. "There's enough for both of us."

Ramsey knew it was useless to argue. "You can have it all," he said in a shaky-sick voice. He turned on his heel, left the trail and stumbled into the woods as the man put another piece of the stinking flesh into his mouth.

Ramsey was sick. That bastard back there was stark-raving mad! The war was mad! He rested his hands against the rough bark of a tree trunk and heaved, but his stomach was empty and nothing came up. He heaved again and again, doubled over in pain, felt like he was being turned inside-out.

The whole damn country had gone bloody...killing...mad...

Ramsey raised his head at the long rattling sound that suddenly commenced somewhere in the distance. It was followed by brittle reports. Gunfire. It was starting again. He heard the clanging of metal against metal, the sound of running footsteps, brush snapping. He had the urge to leave it all behind. Run. Never stop.

"Rebs!" someone shouted.

Ramsey stepped behind the tree for cover. The woods ahead were alive with sounds: men running, men shouting, more gunfire. "Johnny!" he yelled. Where in the hell was that boy? Did he get through?

Ramsey bent and tried to run. The mud tripped him. He started to fall, caught his balance. He moved, keeping his head down, his rifle ready, from one tree to another, found the trail, the dead horse. The crazed soldier lay in a lifeless heap next to it, his eyes sightless, a grimace that resembled a smile frozen on his lips.

He won't be hungry anymore, Ramsey thought. He turned away and moved on.

The sound of battle halted as abruptly as it had begun. The smell of gunpowder hung in the air. Nothing moved. Was it over? Ramsey stopped and listened, straightened.

A small skirmish, he thought. A few Rebs must have slipped through the lines. The main unit took care of it. He breathed a sigh of relief. That's where Johnny probably was now, up with the main unit.

A rustling in the bushes ahead caused him to stop.

Johnny?

A cold finger of fear brushed the back of Ramsey's neck. He tensed and crouched, pulling his rifle to his shoulder, his finger poised on the trigger. He saw the Confederate soldier step onto the trail. The man stood in the shadows, looking at Ramsey.

Ramsey froze to the place where he stood, his breath held, a caged cat feeling clawing away at his insides. The Confederate raised the barrel of his rifle.

He had no choice. It was kill or be killed. He didn't want to die. Not yet...

Ramsey stepped back. A twig snapped under his boot. The sound ended the silent standoff between the two enemies. They stood, ready. Ramsey could almost read the other man's mind. Who'd have the guts to shoot first?

Ramsey prayed. He didn't want to shoot. He didn't want to kill this man – another mother's son.

The enemy soldier lowered his weapon.

What in the hell? Ramsey watched as the Reb stepped into the light. A grin quirked across his familiar face. "Ramsey, that you?" he called.

Ramsey lowered his rifle. The voice was familiar. It couldn't be. Could it? Jarred? The man moved closer.

"Jarred?" Ramsey took a step forward. By God, it was! Ramsey let out a whoop. Jarred Judd dropped his rifle and closed the distance between them. The brothers embraced.

"What in the hell are you doing out here?" Jarred asked, as he released Ramsey and stepped away from him.

"Fighting a war, big brother."

Jarred grinned. "You don't look too bad in blue."

"More than I can say for you in gray," Ramsey replied.

"How's Ma and Pa?" Jarred pulled makings from his shirt pocket, rolled a cigarette, then handed the bag of tobacco and papers to Ramsey.

Ramsey glanced around. They should take cover. He leaned his rifle against the tree. What was he supposed to tell his brother? The folks are fine? Happy? Missing you? A momentary anger rose inside him. His hands shook as he fought with the tobacco and paper. Finally, he twisted the end tightly and stuck the cigarette between his lips. How in the hell did his turncoat of a brother think Ma and Pa were?

He looked at Jarred through narrowed eyes, and said, "Confused."

"I suppose."

"Pa couldn't figure out why you joined up with the South. Why, Jarred? If you were going to fight, why the Confederacy?" Ramsey handed the pouch back to his brother.

Jarred produced dry matches, lit his smoke. He cupped his hand around the flame while Ramsey lit his.

Ramsey drew deep. "Damn near broke the

old man's heart. Ma's, too." He blew the smoke out. It drifted away on the breeze.

Jarred's brow furrowed for a moment. He leaned toward Ramsey, like he had something important to say, hesitated, then straightened and grinned. The lines in his forehead smoothed. "It seemed like the thing to do at the time," he said, walking to where his rifle had dropped. He retrieved it, rested it in the crook of his arm, the barrel pointed to the ground in front of him. He laughed. "What in the hell was I thinking? You Yanks have been kicking our asses."

"Yeah, well." Ramsey's anger was gone. He grinned into the face so much like his own. "You Rebs been kicking back."

"Stand where you are, Reb!" The voice came from behind the two brothers. They whirled at the same time to see a Union soldier standing a few yards away. The bayonet attached to the barrel of his rifle was pointed at Jarred's chest.

"Johnny, no!" Ramsey yelled.

Jarred brought his rifle up. Ramsey reached for his. Johnny Bowler pulled the trigger. Flame belched from the barrel, followed by a cloud of black smoke.

Ramsey turned to his brother. A surprised

expression slid over Jarred's face as he stumbled backwards, his rifle landing at Ramsey's feet.

The rifle blast seemed to silence the countryside. Even the leaves on the trees ceased to rustle. A sick feeling formed in the pit of Ramsey's stomach. He felt like a band was being tightened on his head. He stood, dumbfounded, couldn't move. He saw the form of his brother lying motionless a few feet away, but he couldn't focus. Jarred was playing a joke – like he did when they were boys.

"Mr. Judd..." Johnny Bowler was crying. "Mr. Judd..."

Ramsey heard the boy above the roaring in his ears. His mind began to clear. "Jarred?" He walked to where the oldest Judd lay sprawled on his back. It wasn't a joke. A dark stain spread over Jarred's chest. Ramsey knelt, cradled his brother's head in his lap. The reality hit him like he'd been kicked in the belly. "Nooo..." His shoulders began to heave.

Jarred opened his eyes. His mouth moved but it was seconds before words came out. "Tell...Pa..." Jarred coughed and a pink froth formed at the corner of his lips. "...Yank at heart." Jarred tried to speak again, but it came out in a gurgle that started from deep in his chest.

"Oh, no...Jarred..."

Jarred shuddered and the light faded from his eyes. He stared somewhere beyond Ramsey toward the dark pressing clouds that had gathered again, hung heavy and low in the sky above the spreading limbs of the trees.

A sob bubbled up inside Ramsey. He stared down through a blur of tears at the remains of the man he'd grown up with, admired, loved. "Ah, shit." What in the hell happened? How could this be?

There was a soft sound behind him. He wiped a hand down the length of his face, then moved his head slowly. Johnny Bowler stood shaking, the gun still in his hands.

"You son of a bitch," Ramsey said in a dull, almost calm voice. His stomach was shaking inside. There was a kind of ringing in his ears. "Christ." He rose, raised his rifle.

"Mr. Judd, I..." Johnny stared at him, his face filled with fear. "I come back when the fighting started. I had to make sure you were okay. The Reb was going to shoot you. He had his gun pointed at you – "

Rage swept through Ramsey like a cyclone. He saw the soldier through a haze of red fury. For the first time in his life, Ramsey Judd wanted to kill.

The boy had no time to reload. He threw the rifle at Ramsey like a lance. Ramsey sidestepped and the bayonet struck a tree trunk, bounced off. Ramsey heard the blood rushing in his head. He saw the gray shadow move in the trees beyond the boy. He took his breath in slow and easy, fighting for control.

"You stupid son of a bitch," he whispered. You just killed my brother."

Slowly, deliberately, Ramsey aimed the muzzle of the rifle and squeezed the trigger.

Chapter Two
Salmon River, Idaho, 1884

A restless breeze creaked the tall tops of the evergreens on Lacey's Mountain, bringing with it the pleasant smells of pine and sun-warmed earth, the smell of springtime. Buttercups bloomed along the narrow creek that babbled down from higher up, its banks full from the last of the melting snow. A flock of starlings rose from the lush green grass that grew in the small clearing and swarmed like bees for the protection of the timber.

The man who called himself Parker O'Dell stood ankle-deep in the icy water of the creek, his broad, hairy chest and muscled shoulders bare, several shades lighter than the sharp, tanned vee at his neck. The face behind the shaggy, silvered beard was serious, weathered by time, his eyes keen and dark below the deep creases that worried his brow. A shock of water-dropped hair that matched his beard and hadn't seen a barber in months glistened in the sun.

He nervously contemplated the tall, slender woman on the creek bank in front of him. She was dressed in brown linsey-woolsey, and a man's canvas coat hung almost to her knees. A single braid of dark hair laced with strands of white hung over her shoulder. Clamped on her head was a shapeless, wide-brimmed hat. And pressed against her cheek was the smooth stock of a double-barrel, 16-gauge shotgun.

O'Dell's rifle lay twenty feet away, under the pine tree by the creek, along with his boots and hat. He glanced at the spot where he'd left his horse. It was gone.

The woman stood unmoving, except for the skirt flapping in the breeze against her legs. A knot twisted in his gut, and the hair on the back of his neck stood up. If that blasted thing went off, it'd knock her into the next county and blow him to kingdom come.

His suspenders draped about hips narrowed by years in the saddle, and his denim jeans, open at the front, were beginning to slip.

If she were a man, he'd come out fighting – trust the odds. No shame in bucking out in smoke. At least he'd die with his dignity intact. But a woman? That was another can of worms. How did a self-respecting man fight a woman?

"Hello, Hannah," he said softly.

She didn't answer, stood still as a statue, her blue eyes cold, calculating and steady, her arm rigid under the weight of the large weapon.

O'Dell wasn't use to being on the receiving end of a shotgun – or any other damn gun, for that matter. In all his years, he hadn't done anything this dumb, letting someone get the drop on him, especially a woman. He wanted to laugh, but it wasn't funny.

"Hannah, don't you remember me?"

She stared down the long barrels, her finger resting on one of the triggers.

She must recognize him, for Christ's sake. She wouldn't shoot him, would she? "How's your pa?" he asked, keeping his voice steady.

Hell yes, she'd shoot him. That was Hannah Lacey standing there. The set of the little pointed chin and the mouth, thin-lipped and tight as the closed jaws of a bear trap, told him she wasn't bluffing. She'd shoot him in a heartbeat, and she'd smile while she did it.

"Put that darned thing down, Hannah, before you hurt someone."

She still didn't speak. She hadn't said a word since he'd turned around and saw her standing there.

"Mighty good to see you again," O'Dell said. "It's all I've been thinking about – getting back to see you."

Hannah Lacey's eyes narrowed. The shotgun wavered slightly. She chewed her bottom lip, then spoke, her voice bone-cracking cold. "That's bull crap, Parker O'Dell. Save it to shovel around rosebushes. What're you doing here?"

"I come to see you, Hannah...honey..."

"You're a little late," she said.

"I can explain...if you'll just let me get my feet on solid ground."

Christ Almighty Christ. She wouldn't need to aim. At this distance, all she'd have to do was pull the trigger. She damn sure couldn't miss. He swallowed hard.

"I was washin' myself in the creek," he said. "Then I was going up to the house to see you...and Pete. Didn't want to go knocking on your door, sweet Hannah, after all these years, with fifty miles of trail dust sticking to me."

She didn't appear fazed by his sugar-dipped words. The shotgun steadied.

A cold finger of fear brushed the back of O'Dell's neck. "Jesus, Hannah. This ain't no way to greet a man you ain't seen in twenty years." His pants slipped a little further down his hips. "Especially a man you was fond of once." He started to reach for his trousers.

Hannah tensed. "Oh no you don't. Get your hands up."

Ah hell. "Please. Let me hike my pants."

He chewed on the bit of shaggy mustache that had slipped between his lips. Perspiration dampened his forehead and chest, trickled from his armpits. If the damn pants fell down, it would purely pile on the agony. He tried another smile.

"Hannah, please, let's talk."

Her finger tightened on the trigger. He stepped back, almost losing his balance on the slippery rocks under his feet.

Hannah's expression changed suddenly. Her eyes lost some of their steadiness. O'Dell held his breath. She was starting to give in, softening. For a moment she looked confused, like she was waging a war within herself. Should she or shouldn't she? She blinked.

"There's nothing to be said," she replied, composing herself, "except get off my property."

By God now, Hannah Lacey carried a grudge. She was still mad after all these years. No one could carry a grudge like her. "No need to be sore." He shifted his weight. "Just let me get to my boots. My feet are froze. I can't go anywhere without my boots – and my gun."

She blinked again, ran her tongue over her bottom lip, and pressed the stock of the gun tighter against her cheek.

"Okay, I'll go." He wiggled his fingers nervously above his head. "Can I pull up my pants and fix my suspenders?"

Again the rapid flutter of her eyes. Her brows knitted. "No..." Again the confused look on her face.

What was going on inside that pretty head of hers? She was doing a lot of backing and filling. That spooked him even more.

"Real slow." She motioned him out of the water with the tip of the shotgun. "And no funny business. I've got two barrels here. If the first one doesn't get you, the second will."

He moved slowly, deliberately, slipped the suspenders over his shoulders, fumbled with the buttons on his pants, moved his numbed feet. He eyed his boots and the rifle leaning against the tree.

"Please, Hannah, just my gun. I need my gun."

She hesitated. Then she shook her head as if to clear it. "Get it. Pick up your boots while you're at it and make tracks." She motioned again with the end of the gun. "And be quick about it, before I change my mind."

O'Dell edged toward the tree, his eyes not leaving her. He reached down and felt for his hat, found it and jammed it hard onto his head. He retrieved his other belongings and started down the trail before the wind changed. The sharp rocks bit into his bare feet with every step. The boots dangled by their tops in one hand, the rifle in the other.

"That damn horse," he muttered to himself. "Where'd he take off to? Probably half way to town by now."

He felt a little burning sensation in his back and glanced over his shoulder. Hannah was still standing in the same place, the toes of her men's boots wide apart and that shotgun still aimed right at him.

"I mean what I say, Parker O'Dell," she called after him. "Don't step foot back on my property."

There wasn't a doubt in his mind. She meant what she said. "I'm going, Hannah. I'm going." He quickened his pace.

After he was around the bend in the trail and well out of her sights, he set the boots down, being careful to keep his rifle within easy reach.

Crazy damn woman.

He glanced over his shoulder, pulled out the shirt he'd stuffed into one of the boots and put it on, then reached in the other and took out a pair of dirty socks. He'd learned a long time ago to keep things tidy. A man never knew when he'd have to grab his grip and run. He wouldn't put it past her to follow him, chase him all the way to the river.

She was the same old Hannah, aged a little, but she could still whip her weight in wildcats. Just as pig-headed and unreasonable as he remembered. He pulled on his boots, picked up the rifle and proceeded down the trail.

The jingle of tack coming from around the corner caused him to pause. He stepped cautiously into the trees, out of sight, made his way in the direction of the noise. Under a big bull pine tree stood the blaze-faced chestnut gelding grazing on bunch grass like he hadn't a care in the world.

"You old son-of – " The man grinned and walked toward the horse. "I ought to whip your tough hide, leaving me like that when the chips were down."

The horse looked up and rolled its eyes, walked to where the man was standing, and snorted. It rubbed its head on his chest.

O'Dell stroked the animal's shoulder and felt its muscles shiver under his hand. "That's okay, Hoss. It's not your fight is it? I'm glad we understand each other. I wouldn't hang around either, if some crazy filly was holding a shotgun on you."

He straightened the reins and mounted, the leather saddle creaking under his weight. He nudged the horse's sides, gave one last glance over his shoulder as the horse tossed its head and broke into an easy trot.

He'd expected Hannah to be mad. He'd prepared himself for a tongue-lashing. He probably had one coming. He hadn't expected her to be quite that mad – to aim a shotgun at him. What in the hell was she so riled up for? It wasn't like they'd been betrothed. He hadn't made any promises to her.

At the end of the trail, where it left the timber and joined the rocky bank of the river, he paused and took a bag of Bull Durham and papers out of his shirt pocket. He rolled a cigarette with a practiced hand and struck the head of a wooden match on the saddle horn.

"That's Hannah, Hoss," he said putting the flame to the twisted tip. "She's everything I told you she was. Maybe a bit hard around the edges, ornery as cat-dirt, but she let me have my Justins."

He wiggled the toes of his left foot and felt the familiar bulge of the twenty-dollar gold piece wrapped in old paper wedged tightly into the end of his worn boot.

"Don't rightly know why she acted like that, Hoss. She gets right notional sometimes, but that's Hannah." He smiled and nudged the horse's flanks. The horse began picking its way along the rocky trail.

~~~

Hannah watched the man go, the shotgun still pressed against her cheek. Her finger remained on the trigger.

Parker O'Dell, the voice inside Hannah's head said.

Hannah trembled. She tried to push the voice away, block it out, but it wouldn't go.

You'll be sorry, Hannah.

The man disappeared around the bend in the trail. Hannah heard the sound of light footsteps on the rocky creek bank behind her. She knew it was Sharon and didn't turn
~~~

around, continuing to stare in the direction the man had disappeared.

You should have shot him, the voice whispered.

No, Hannah answered silently.

You should have shot him.

I couldn't.

You could have. You should have.

Go away.

You'll be sorry, Hannah.

"Mama, are you okay?" Sharon asked, stepping up beside her.

Hannah didn't answer. Her head ached, and she squeezed her eyes shut.

"Who was that man?" Sharon asked. "What did he want?"

"Just a drifter," Hannah answered.

What did he want? Did you know him, Mama?"

Send her away.

Leave me alone, Hannah thought.

Send her away.

"Mama?"

Was it Sharon talking? Or was it the devil that lived inside her head?

Hannah...

"Leave me alone!" Hannah said out loud.

"Mama! I have your breakfast ready."

Dazed, the pain in Hannah's head increased. "He was...washing....in the creek," she said.

"Did you know him?" Sharon asked again.

Make...her...go...away.

"Mama?"

Hannah squinted through pain-slitted eyes at the beautiful young woman standing beside her, into the face so much like Parker O'Dell's, the brown eyes, the strong mouth. It hurt to look at her.

"What is it, Sharon? What are you doing here? What do you want?"

"I came looking for you," Sharon said. "Breakfast is ready. Who was that man?"

"He worked for your grandfather a long time ago," Hannah snapped. "Now, please, leave me be." She turned and started up the wooded trail toward the house.

"Is your head hurting again?" Sharon asked as she followed behind. "Are you having one of your spells?"

Hannah shivered in the warm spring sun.

"Are you ill?" Sharon continued. "Can I help?"

Hannah, send her away.

Hannah wanted to stop and sit on the fallen log beside the trail. If she could just get to that log. She forced herself onward.

"Mama."

Hannah moved faster. Her head thumped with each step.

"Mama, slow down. Please. I can't keep up with you."

Hannah was almost running. All these years. Not a word. Why now?

You should have shot him, Hannah. You should have shot him.

"Stop it!" Hannah staggered, stumbled.

Sharon stopped, her breath coming in short gasps. "What is it? What's the matter?"

Hannah sat on the log and put her hands over her face.

Hannah!

"Go, Sharon. Leave me be."

"But Mama – "

"Didn't you hear me, girl?" Hannah was on the verge of screaming. "I said I don't want you here."

Sharon let out a little sob. She lifted her skirts and started running up the trail.

Hannah breathed deep, held it for a few seconds, let it out slowly, did it again. Sweat-beads formed above her lip. The tightness in her chest eased, but her head still throbbed. She hated the headaches. She couldn't think clearly when they came. When had they started? She couldn't remember. One day...before her father died...when she'd given in to the voice inside her...did the devil's bidding. When the devil came to live in her, took possession of her.

You're afraid, Hannah.

"Go...away."

The voice laughed.

"Go away."

It use to be easy to send the devil away. It only came when Hannah needed it, wanted it there. But not now. Hannah breathed deeply again, took off the old hat and wiped her brow with the sleeve of her coat.

You're a coward, Hannah. Do I have to take care of this, too? Like everything else?

"No!" Hannah said out loud. "No. He's gone now."

The voice laughed again, a cruel mocking laugh. And then it was gone and all was quiet.

Chapter Three

The man called O'Dell rested his horse at the top of the hill and looked down on the sleepy, dusty little town of Indian Bend, crammed in between the elbow of the Salmon River on one side and empty, rock-scabbed hills on the other. He wondered why, out of all the places on Earth he'd ever been, he'd decided to come back here.

Maybe it was because of Hannah.

"There it is, Hoss, the armpit of Hell. It hasn't changed much. Maybe a little older, a little dustier, but it's the same hole it was when I left – hotter than the hubs of Hades in the summer, colder than a well digger's ass in the winter."

A dust devil picked up and whirled down the almost deserted main street like a ghost, and an unexpected twinge of anticipation slipped through him. He felt something next to kinship with the town that had endured time and change, kept its secrets well through the years, though he'd spent precious little time there. It wasn't as lively as it had been in its wilder youth, but, like himself, surviving.

He patted the horse's neck. "I'm getting old and tired. I must be. The place is looking good."

The horse stood stomping its feet, tossing its head, its withers flinching under an assault of biting flies.

"It'd be a good place to settle for a while, don't you think, Hoss? A place for a man to rest and gather himself."

The horse responded with a long sigh, sides heaving, blowing through its nostrils.

"I'd like a warm fire come winter," O'Dell said, "and a glass of whiskey and a woman sitting beside me. A woman who'll keep me warm, maybe even fetch my slippers and pipe – if I smoked a pipe." He thought of Hannah Lacey and chuckled. "I ain't ever owned a pair of slippers, Hoss." He straightened. "I'm just plain tired. Time to put it behind me, boy. I've almost forgot who I really am."

A flick of the reins and the horse picked its way down the rocky hillside toward Indian

Bend.

O'Dell flexed his left arm as he rode. Rheumatism, he thought. Damn, it was awful getting old. He'd seen his fifty-second birthday six months past. The years weighed heavily on him. That was old for a saddle tramp. He struggled with the thought. "Guess it ain't so bad, Hoss. Dyin', I mean. But I sure would like to do it in a real bed with someone to mourn my passing."

He rode into town, down the long street, between two rows of one-story buildings made of rough lumber and polished to a smooth patina from wind and weather. Several had their fronts boarded up, paint-peeled signs squeaking on rusted hooks, barely identifying what they'd housed in their heyday. O'Dell had forgotten, too.

He tipped his hat at a woman coming out of Henry's Mercantile carrying a large bundle and followed by three young children. The clinking of iron on iron could be heard coming from the blacksmith shop tucked in beside the livery. A dog lifted its hind leg on the steps to the sheriff's office, and some boys played mumbley-peg on the boardwalk in front of the bank. They stopped and watched the stranger for a few moments, then went back to their game.

O'Dell tied his horse at the empty hitching rail outside the Lucky Lady Saloon and loosened the cinch. He patted the horse's neck and stepped up onto the boardwalk. The smell of cheap whiskey, sour mop-water, and stale tobacco smoke greeted him as he pushed the swinging doors wide and stepped in. He stood a moment, letting his eyes adjust to the dim room after the bright sunshine outside.

It didn't look too lucky to him. The bar was empty, and it gave him a lonely feeling. No noise and confusion to clear his mind of the thoughts he'd been thinking on the hill a while ago. No loud friendly drunks to jolt the sense back into his thick head. He knew it was too late for him. His settling down years were long past. He'd wasted his prime running until there was no turning back. The double eagle and the paper in his boot reminded him of that every time he took a step.

He looked around the small cluttered room: rough board walls with pictures of half-clothed women, low ceiling, brass spittoons crusted with tobacco juice. Rickety wooden tables sat along the far walls, with wooden chairs, the backs broken off some. A dilapidated piano occupied one corner, and a billiard table sat in the middle of the room, an unlit lantern hanging overhead. It was just like a hundred other saloons he'd been in over the past twenty-odd years: dingy, stinking, familiar. The familiar gave him a downhearted kind of comfort and a lonely kind of welcome. It made him feel depressingly at home.

He walked across the room, his boot heels dragging and making a hollow scraping sound on the dusty plank floor. He wanted more from life than this.

The man behind the bar looked up through watery blue eyes rimmed in wrinkles of loose flesh. His black hair was streaked with yellowish gray, greasy looking and slicked back away from his pale, puffy face. He laid the dingy towel he'd been polishing glasses with on the bar and wiped his hands on the once-white apron around his bloated middle.

"What'll it be, friend?" he said in a smoke-graveled voice.

"A shot of whiskey and a glass of beer," O'Dell said, sliding his tall frame onto a wobbly barstool.

The bartender drew a mug of beer from the wooden spigot and set it in front of him. He reached under the bar and brought out a new bottle of whiskey, pulled the cork and grabbed a shot glass from a rack over his head.

"Leave the bottle," O'Dell said.

"Put your money on the bar." The bartender filled the glass and shoved it forward.

O'Dell dug deep into his pocket for the small wad of money he'd saved from his last lucky poker hand. "Kinda quiet," he said.

"Won't be along towards evening."

"Where can a man get a room? A bath – maybe a haircut?"

"Ain't no barber in town." The bartender picked up a few coins from the pile on the bar, slid the bottle toward him. "Old Harry used to cut hair. He kicked off last winter. Best place for the rest would be down at Pleasant Smith's roomin' house, clear to the end of Main. Rooms are clean. She fixes a pretty decent meal." The bartender rubbed his bristled chin. "But I could fix you up for less. I got a room in the back I rent and a pot of venison stew on the stove in the kitchen."

O'Dell wrapped his fingers around the glass, lifted it halfway to his mouth. "How many other men rent this room?"

"Unless someone else comes in lookin' for a bed tonight, which ain't likely, you'll have the place to yourself. The sheets were changed last week, been slept on twice, and there's a room back there with a tub and shavin' gear. You'll have to haul your own water."

O'Dell pushed the bottle toward the bartender. He wanted information. "Have a drink," he said, then lifted his glass and downed its contents in one swallow. He closed his eyes and shuddered as the hot liquid seared his throat and hit his empty stomach like a lump of molten lead. "Don't know where a man could find a few days' work, do you?"

"Not off hand, Mr..." The bartender produced another glass and filled it. "What did you say your name is, friend?"

The man called O'Dell refilled his glass, braced himself. The name on the tip of his tongue was alien to him now. He hadn't used it in over twenty years. Was the wanted poster still there on the post office wall, like it had been twenty years ago? The day Pete Lacey sent him to town for supplies, he'd seen it. He'd hightailed it back to the ranch, and that's where he'd stayed.

Not that anyone would have recognized him by the picture, one of those artist sketches. Damn poor artist he was, too. But then there hadn't been any photographs to go by – only someone's memory. Whose? He'd always wondered.

But the name on the poster wouldn't be easy to forget. He downed the whiskey and his stomach tightened in rebellion. He chased it with the beer.

This was it. It'd be all over as soon as he opened his mouth. He'd made his decision. He was tired of running. "Judd," he said as if testing the sound, tasting it on his tongue. "Ramsey Judd." He watched the bartender, waiting for signs of recognition.

"I'm Jake Kelly." The bartender extended a soft, white hand.

Ramsey hesitated, then extended his own. The man's handshake was flaccid and damp. Ramsey released his hand and poured himself another drink.

"What kind of work you looking for, Mr. Judd?"

Ramsey massaged at the aching muscle in his left shoulder. "Ranch work, I suppose. That's what I do most. Worked horses some years back for a man named Pete Lacey. Do you know him? He use to hire a lot around here."

The bartender raised an eyebrow and his glass at the same time. "You been gone for a spell. Pete Lacey died twelve years ago."

Ramsey nodded toward the bottle still

sitting on the bar. "Have another. Sorry to hear about Pete. He was a good man." Ramsey waited until Jake Kelly poured a second measure into his empty glass and slugged it down.

"He had a stroke a couple of years before he died," the bartender said. "He was helpless as a kitten at the last. Heard tell he couldn't say a word. Couldn't even go to the john by hisself, so he just laid there and messed in the bed."

A cold chill slipped up Ramsey's spine. He didn't want to die that way. A man had to keep his dignity. "Didn't Pete have a daughter?" he asked.

"Hannah? Took care of her daddy right up 'til he died."

Ramsey tried to put Hannah in the roll of nursemaid to her father. It didn't work.

"Must have been a blessin' from God when the old man died quietly in his sleep one night," Jake Kelly added.

"You suppose she's hiring?" Ramsey asked.

"Don't rightly think so. Reckon the widda's got about all the help she needs. Sorry lot they are, too. Bull Brenner has been with her since before Swede died. He's a worthless cuss. The rest, well...the only one that amounts to a hill of beans is Joe Keys, and he's a half-breed."

"Widow you say?" Ramsey's stomach tightened again. This time not from the whiskey. He poured himself another drink. He hadn't given much thought to Hannah marrying. Of course she would, a fine looking woman like that.

"Swede's been dead for near ten years now." The bartender finished his drink, then eyed Ramsey's bottle. "Injuns. The uprisin' of seventy-seven."

Ramsey remembered the big Swede. He was foreman at the Lacey ranch twenty years ago. Hard worker. He'd been sweet on Hannah.

The bartender toyed with his empty glass. Ramsey nodded toward the bottle. Jake poured another for himself and then topped off Ramsey's. "Funny about the injuns killing Swede. Shot him in the back. Didn't bother the woman or girl. Didn't bother nothing, just shot Swede and rode away. Wasn't the way the injuns usually did things." He pulled at his earlobe and gave his head a quick shake, then lifted his glass. "The widda sold the horses – bought sheep."

"Sheep!" Ramsey almost choked.

"Sheep," the bartender repeated.

"Old Pete would roll over in his grave."

"She ain't done too bad," the bartender

said. "She's made a livin' for her and the girl. Course, I don't think the sheep's where Mrs. Larken gets most of her money."

This time Ramsey poured. "Girl?"

"Hers and Swede's daughter. Name's Sharon. Don't know how the Swede done it, but she's sure a looker. Swede was big and blond – kind of a homely cuss. The gal is dark like her ma, with big brown eyes. Must be about twenty years old now, give or take. Don't see much of her. Once in a while, she comes to town with her ma for supplies. Hear tell," Jake continued, leaning across the bar and speaking in an almost whisper, "the widda has a gold mine up there in those mountains somewhere."

Ramsey didn't answer. Jake Kelly had more to say. Ramsey lifted his glass to his lips and waited.

"Of course, it's just rumor. But I got it from a man that works in the bank at Grangeville. She brings a poke in ever' so often to change into cash." He grinned. "Thought a few times about riding up and getting close to that widda Larken and her gold mine. Must get kinda lonely up there."

Ramsey stiffened.

The bartender chuckled. "But if I know old Bull Brenner, he's probably tapping into that his own self. Know what I mean? Course, any man in his right mind would think twice. Hear tell she has a shotgun and she's damn willing to use it."

Ramsey wanted to reach across the bar, shake the man, tell him to keep a civil tongue. Hannah had been through enough, by the sounds of things. She didn't deserve to be talked about like that. He tightened his grip on the glass, held his tongue. This wasn't the time for trouble. He didn't like trouble.

He finished his drink, picked up the change on the bar and stuffed it into his pocket, grabbed the half empty bottle by the neck and eased himself off the stool.

"What about the room?" the bartender asked.

Ramsey didn't answer. He started toward the door.

"That Pleasant Smith is gonna cost ya," the bartender said.

Ramsey didn't look back. He'd learned what he came to learn. Time for talking was over. He pushed through the doors and stepped outside.

~~~

The air was filled with the warm smell of baking bread as Ramsey rode to the end of the
~~~

street. There were other smells too, but he couldn't quite put his finger on just what they were. His stomach grumbled as he dismounted and tied his horse to the rail in front of the large, two-story, white house. He was hungry.

The gate of the white picket fence that surrounded the well-kept yard squeaked pleasingly as Ramsey let himself through and walked up the path between two rows of bright yellow flowers to the house. He stepped up onto the vine-covered veranda porch, lifted the heavy brass knocker on the door and gave it two hard raps. He waited, listening for signs of life from inside, tried to peer through the etched glass window on the door's front. Maybe no one was home. He rapped again.

A flock of goldfinches so thick they looked like yellow blossoms chirped from the willow tree in the front yard. Ramsey turned and watched them. He'd never seen so many birds in one tree in his life. A feeder made from a glass canning jar and wood hung on a lower branch. He smiled, turned back to the veranda. A porch swing hung from hooks in the roof, shaded by the vines, dappled by sunlight. Just like the one his ma had hanging on her front porch in Cincinnati, where he and Martha had sat in the evenings. Before the baby came.

But that was thirty years ago. No sense dwelling.

The aromas were stronger now. It almost made him feel lightheaded. Some kind of meaty broth, rich, with the smell of carrots and potatoes. He lifted his nose and sniffed. What was that other smell – the spicy one? It brought back pleasant memories of his childhood.

Ramsey was about to knock again, when the door opened.

"I'm sorry, I was baking bread and I couldn't – " The rosy-cheeked woman before him broke the words off mid sentence.

Ramsey was speechless. He'd never seen anyone quite like her before. She was short; the top of her gilded head barely came to the first button of his shirt. But what she lacked in height, she made up for in bounteous proportions. A frilly white apron covered her large bosom and swathed the rest of her full figure over the pink calico dress she wore.

She didn't speak another word for several seconds, while she assessed him from his head to his toes, tilted her chin back and lifted large green eyes fringed in dark lashes up to meet his gaze. Ramsey knew she was the most beautiful woman he had ever seen.

She lifted a floury hand to her face and

brushed it with the tips of her fingers, leaving a white smudge on her scarlet cheek. Ramsey liked it. When was the last time he'd known a woman who could blush like that? Or was it the heat from the kitchen that put the roses in her cheeks? It didn't matter.

"I'm..." Ramsey cleared his throat, pulled the sweat-stained hat from his head, worried the brim between his fingers as he twisted it around in both hands. "I need a room," he said.

The nostrils on Pleasant Smith's little nose flared slightly. She continued to stare up at him for several more long seconds before she spoke, then her full mouth twitched into a rather shy smile. "How long will you be needing the room?" she asked in a voice that reminded Ramsey of sunshine and music all rolled into one.

"Don't rightly know, ma'am. Could be a while."

"I have a room. It lets for two dollars a week."

Ramsey looked down at her, wanting to tell her he'd take it, but unable to form the words.

"The room includes three meals a day," she added.

Ramsey wondered how old she was. Her pale, silver-blonde hair was piled loosely on top of her head in a curly kind of do. Wisps as soft as silk thread fell out and hung down from her temples, framing her heart-shaped face. Not a trace of gray, that he could see. It didn't have the frizzled look of hair that had been dyed. There were few lines in her face – just around her mouth and eyes when she smiled. The woman could have been thirty-five. And then again, she could have been forty-five. Hard to reckon.

"You're allowed the privilege of the bathing room," she went on, "in the shed off the kitchen, as often as you like. There's a cook stove in there with a water tank on the side. You have to chop your own wood."

She paused and Ramsey swallowed. He felt as gawky as a schoolboy standing there. He couldn't think of a thing to say. The tips of his ears felt warm. He could look down the barrel of a 16-gauge shotgun and keep his cool, but melted like lard on a warm griddle at the first sight of a soft, fluffy woman with flour on her cheek. He'd been on the trail too damn long.

He nodded and waited for her to go on with her rehearsed speech.

"I do laundry on Fridays," Pleasant Smith said. "It'll cost you twenty-five cents extra. If you chop enough wood for the kitchen, I'll do your laundry for nothing." She paused again. "No women in the rooms," she said, dropping her gaze, then raising it to meet and hold his. "I run a respectable house. You have to be quiet in the evenings. I have five other rooms. Mr. Skomp, the schoolmaster, lives in number three, and Reverend Maudlin lives in five. Old Major Griswell is in number four. He's lived here for five years now. Number two is empty. I keep it for travelers passing through from time to time."

Ramsey nodded again.

"I clean the place on Monday morning," Pleasant continued. "I don't pry or snoop, just clean." She looked past him to the hitching rail. "Do you have a horse, Mr...."

"Judd, ma'am. Ramsey Judd." Ramsey cleared his throat again. "Yes ma'am, I have ol' Hoss." He hooked his thumb over his shoulder.

"Cost you fifty cents more. Tommy, that's my boy, keeps the barn clean and feeds the animals twice a day. He'll exercise him if you want. He charges a dime a day. It's his to keep."

Ramsey fished in his pocket for the last of his cash and carefully counted out enough for one month's rent and board for him and his horse. He pushed two silver dollars back into his Levis.

"There's an outside stairs in back," she said, taking the money he handed her and slipping it into the pocket of her apron. "You can use that. Meals are served in the dining room. Times are posted in the hall, along with the rules we've just discussed. You can come through this door for meals. I open it first thing every morning."

She smiled beautifully and Ramsey's stomach did a little flip.

"I'm home most all the time," she said, "if you need anything – except for Wednesday morning when I do my marketing. Your room is at the end of the hall, Mr. Judd. Number one, directly across from the downstairs door. The room is unlocked. You can pick up the key at supper. I hope you like it here."

That was all. She stood in the doorway looking at him for a moment longer, then took a step back, her hand on the door jam.

Ramsey bobbed his head, pulled his eyes away from her, and turned to leave.

"Oh, yes. Mr. Judd?"

Ramsey spun on his heel. "Yes, ma'am?"

"I expect all my guests to come to the table fully clothed." She blushed again, deeper than before. "You understand...shoes, shirt..."

"Yes, ma'am."

"Wipe your feet before coming in. And no hats in the house."

"Yes, ma'am."

"The noon meal is over, but if you're hungry, I have some soup left. Do you like apple pie?" She didn't wait for him to answer. "Put your horse away, Mr. Judd. Wash up and come to the kitchen door." She bit her bottom lip and tilted her head to one side, studying him. "I cut hair, too," she said, eyeing the mop on his head. "Twenty-five cents." Pleasant Smith stepped inside and closed the door.

Ramsey stood for a moment staring at the place where the woman had been, a smile drawing at his mouth. He donned his hat and walked back down the path to the hitching rail and his waiting horse. "I'll be go-to-hell, Hoss," he said, untying the reins. "Soup and apple pie. With my feet under a lady's table. I feel like I've purely died and gone to heaven." Ramsey grinned. "And, Hoss, I'll be darned if the lady don't cut hair, to boot. This is our lucky day."

~~~

Pleasant closed the door and leaned her back against it. She shut her eyes and held her breath. My-oh-my, how utterly wicked of her. Had he noticed how she'd stared at him like a brazen hussy? What must he think of her?
~~~

She couldn't help it. He was the handsomest man she'd seen since her Tom died seventeen years ago. Why, she was absolutely twitterpated. She laid a shaky hand over her thumping heart. It just wasn't like her to act this way. It wasn't like her at all.

It had been more than Ramsey Judd's good looks that made her heart beat in her chest like a butterfly trapped in a Mason jar. There was something in the way he looked at her. The heat rose to her neck at the memory of his eyes. It crept to her cheeks. She fanned herself with her hand. It had been a long time since a man looked at her that way. It had been a long time since a man had looked at her at all.

"Ma?" Tommy stepped from the dining room to the front parlor, where Pleasant stood. "Who was at the door?"

"Oh, Tommy." Pleasant breathed deeply, composing herself. "We have a new border. His name is Ramsey Judd. He's on his way to the barn with his horse right now. Will you please see to his needs?" She hurried past her son to the kitchen.

Tommy followed, a puzzled expression on his face. "You okay, Ma? Your face is red."

"I'm fine, son. Must be the heat." She was already taking a deep dish from the cupboard.

She took silver from a drawer under the counter and placed it on the kitchen table by the window.

"What are you doing?" Tommy asked.

Pleasant glanced at him, pushed a stray hair that had fallen over her forehead back into place. "Fixing lunch for Mr. Judd, of course. Please, Tommy. See to his horse."

Tommy stared at her for a moment longer. "You sure you're okay?"

Pleasant nodded. She took pie out of the warming oven above the stove. "Shoo," she said, fluttering her hand at him. "Do as I say."

"In here?" Tommy asked.

Pleasant looked up. "What?"

"You going to feed him in here?"

"What's wrong with that?"

"Nothing," Tommy answered. He turned to leave. "Just never knew you to feed borders at the kitchen table, that's all."

"Tommy, don't slam the – "

The door banged shut behind him.

~~~

Ramsey entered the dark barn and looked around. The stalls were well kept and clean. The place smelled of fresh hay. "Anybody here?" he called. His voice echoed through the large room. No one answered.
~~~

He walked his horse to an empty stall and lifted the stirrup, loosened the cinch and pulled the saddle from the animal's back. He placed it over an empty sawhorse. An array of curry combs hung from hooks on the same wall. Ramsey chose one and began scraping it across the horse's back. The animal shivered and leaned into the metal teeth.

"Feel good, Hoss?" Ramsey said softly. "Been a long time, hasn't it, boy?"

The horse blew contentedly.

"Are you Mr. Judd?" a voice called from the open door.

Ramsey grinned and turned to the sound of the voice, then stopped short, the smile dying on his lips. The curry comb clattered to the board floor. He stared at the blonde, blue-eyed youth in his late teens standing a few feet from him, his face illuminated by the shaft of light coming through the only window in the room. A soft shimmer of silky down brushed the boy's upper lip and cheeks.

An old ache flourished deep inside Ramsey and something twisted in his stomach. His fists clawed at his thighs. He took a step forward, the haze of anger beginning to blur his vision. The air trembled between them. He could almost smell the warm blood, hear the gunfire

"Johnny?" he said in a grating whisper, realizing even as he spoke it wasn't possible. Johnny would be older now.

"Sir?" The boy stepped back.

Ramsey stopped. What in the hell was he doing? He saw the question in the boy's face, the hint of fear. The tightness went out of Ramsey. He shuddered, backed up.

"Name's Tommy, sir," the boy said. "Ma told me we have a new border. Are you Ramsey Judd?"

Ramsey took a long breath, let it out slowly, nodded. "I am." He swiped his hand over his face, trying to wipe away the memories.

"Is something wrong, sir?"

"Sorry," Ramsey said. "You look like someone I knew a long time ago."

"I'll finish taking care of your horse for you. Ma's got your lunch ready." The boy took a step forward. "She don't like it much when her guests are late for meals."

Ramsey could feel the cold sweat beneath his clothes. His hand shook as he stooped and picked up the comb, handed it to Tommy. He hesitated a moment, wanting to say more to the boy, then turned and slowly started for the barn door, his legs heavy as lead. He glanced over his shoulder at the tall, young man that looked so much like Johnny Bowler. Tommy Smith was watching him.

"Go to the back door, Mr. Judd. Ma's going to feed you – in the kitchen."

Ramsey nodded and looked away, stepped out into the sunlight.

What in bloody thunder had come over him? He held no grudge against Johnny Bowler. Not now, after all these years. Johnny Bowler was gone. He'd reckoned with that a long time ago, put it behind him.

He thought.

Chapter Four

The cave was shallow, only a few feet back into the side of the mountain, and barely high enough for Hannah to stand up in. A shower of rock fragments, loosened from the wall by the sharp-nosed hammer she wielded, tinkled to the rocky floor. She knelt and examined the fragments, picked up two small pieces and dropped them into the coffee tin sitting beside her.

The vein of color had dwindled over the past two years and had almost petered out. Hannah kept up her daily toil, working and chipping, hoping it would reappear. It hadn't.

A sheen of perspiration dampened her skin. Dust sifted down onto her face, into her eyes and mouth. Her armpits and the valley between her breasts were like tiny rivers of sweat; sweat trickled down the sides of her head from under the brim of her shapeless old hat. She wiped her brow with the back of a grimy hand that ached from her work. Her knuckles bled where they had scraped the rough, rock surface, and her fingernails were worn to the quick. She kept pounding and jabbing and hacking.

The sound of footsteps on the rocky ground beyond the cave entrance caused her to stop. She listened, breath held, body rigid. She eyed the shotgun leaning against the wall of the cave.

Who is it? the voice in her mind whispered.

No one knew about this place except Hannah. Her father and Swede had found it years ago, but they were both dead now. She hadn't been followed, she was sure. Bull was in town. The rest of the men were up in the high country with the sheep.

Her pulse quickened as she heard the sound again, moving away. Then nothing. All was still except the gurgling of the creek beyond the cave's entrance and the hammering of her heart inside her head. She let the breath she was holding out. It must have been an animal passing, probably a deer coming for water.

Could be him, Hannah, the voice said.

Why should he come here? she answered silently.

He followed you.

No. Just a deer.

It was time to quit. Her head hurt. She'd been at her task since sunup. Hannah bent and picked up the coffee can with its few meager chips laying in the bottom, her lantern, her gloves and picks. She stepped from behind the great red fir tree that stood guard in front of the entrance to the cave, into the sunlight, squinted, hesitated a moment, studied the clearing and the trees that edged it. Nothing.

The mine's petered out, Hannah. The gold is gone.

No. It's there. I have to find it again.

There's gold in the stream.

It would mean sluices, digging. The whole world would know.

Hannah.

She walked to the creek, removed her hat and splashed cold water onto her face, soaked her aching hands, splashed more water onto the back of her neck. She stood and stretched, tried to loosen the tightness in the small of her back and across her shoulders.

Damn the throbbing in her head.

She gathered her tools, slipped them into an old burlap bag and poured the contents of the can into a leather pouch at her waist. Wearily, she started toward home. A breeze stirred through the trees and whipped a strand of hair from beneath her hat and across her face. She shook it away with a toss of her head. A twig snapped in the brush and she stopped. Someone was there.

It's him, Hannah.

Hannah laid the bag down and hefted the shotgun level with her waist. She turned in a circle, her eyes watching, her breath held. Nobody had any business up here.

It's him, Hannah.

Quiet!

Hannah listened. Only the breeze through the trees, the chirping of the birds, the loud chatter of a squirrel scolding from deeper in the woods, and the beating of her heart.

A squirrel scolding? Scolding what?

Her finger tightened on one of the triggers. "Parker O'Dell. Is that you?" she called in a half-whisper. "Show yourself."

Silence.

She picked up her bag and started walking again, watchful of the brush on either side of the trail. She was edgy, that was all. There was no one out there. It was her imagination. Just her mind playing tricks on her. Parker O'Dell hadn't been back for nearly two weeks. Maybe he wasn't coming back. Maybe she'd scared him off for good.

No. He'll be back.

Around the bend in the trail, Hannah stopped. Sharon was sitting on a fallen log, her hands folded quietly in her lap. She looked so pretty, oddly vulnerable, sitting there. Hannah stilled. There was something shiny about her daughter – the way the sun shown on her blue-black hair, the paleness of her skin. She had an innocence and a faraway look in her eyes. Hannah had never seen such a look on her face before, a dreaminess she didn't want to disturb. She lowered the gun. It had been Sharon she'd heard.

Why didn't the girl identify herself when you called out?

Hannah ignored the voice, stepped behind a tree and watched for a few more moments. Something deeper than motherly love washed over her, filling her with warmth. Sharon was hers. No one could take her from her. Sharon was the only thing in her life that belonged to her completely.

She smiled. Her headache was gone. She

stepped into the open, started toward Sharon. Sharon still hadn't notice her, her face turned toward the woods, watching the trees beyond.

Hannah heard a noise in the bushes across from Sharon, the snap of twigs under heavy feet. She moved back behind the tree and peered around it. A man stepped into view. Hannah shrank back further, pressed her body against the trunk, so as not to be seen.

She needn't have worried, the sun was in their eyes, but it was more than the sun that blinded them.

Sharon stood and walked to meet him. There was a hurting kind of glory on both their faces as they looked at each other. Their fingers met, entwined. The man leaned forward, drinking her up with his eyes.

An instant knot formed in the pit of Hannah's stomach. A tiny pulse at the base of her throat throbbed. For a moment it was twenty years ago.

I told you Hannah. It's him.

Hannah watched. Pain sliced through her brain like a knife.

Shoot him, now – while you have the chance.

I can't, Hannah thought. She clutched the shotgun. I can't. Sharon's too close.

Look at him, Hannah. Look at him!

The man moved. Hannah could see him clearly now. He looked like Parker O`Dell, somewhat. The same build, tall, muscled. His hair was like Parker O'Dell's, too. Dark, curly. But it wasn't Parker O'Dell in the clearing.

Shoot, Hannah. Shoot while you have the chance!

It's Joe Keys.

Hannah's head began to throb. She knew she'd regret the day she hired that man. Why had she hired him? He was everything she despised in a man: young, wild, reckless. Half Indian and all renegade. Just like –

What is Sharon doing with him?

Hannah fought to remain calm, remain hidden. She was too far away to hear what was being said between them, but the look in their eyes –

Joe Keys embraced Sharon, put his arm around her and lead her into the trees.

He'll take her away. He'll take her away from you, Hannah.

"No." There was a roaring in Hannah's ears. She felt dizzy.

You'll be all alone.

A familiar feeling as old as her daughter formed in the pit of Hannah's stomach. Anger that burned like fire flared up inside her. She surged ahead.

Sharon was in the man's arms and Hannah charged toward them, her thoughts all on the scene before her. "Sharon, get away from him this minute!"

The couple separated instantly. Sharon jumped back, startled. "Mama." Her eyes were wide and dark. "What are you doing here?"

"I should ask you the same question." Hannah glared at her daughter and then shifted her hot, angry gaze to Joe.

A look, quick as a flash of lightning, passed between the man and the girl. Sharon stepped forward. "Mother, I – "

Joe Keys stepped between them. "Mrs. Larken – "

"Shut up. I'm speaking to my daughter."

Joe's bold features tightened, hawk-like, and he started toward Hannah. Sharon laid her hand on his arm. He stopped.

"How could you do this to me, Sharon? After all I've done for you?" Hannah's hands clenched into fists at her sides. "I ought to whip you." The pain pounded in her head. She squinted at the couple, forcing her eyes to focus through the round hole of light at the end of the dark tunnel of her vision. "How dare you!" she screamed.

"Mama, I haven't done anything wrong." Sharon gave a trembly smile and took a step toward her. "Joe and I are – "

Pain gripped Hannah. "I know what you are. I know what he is. I...won't...let him hurt me again."

A shocked, confused expression came over Sharon's face.

Hannah's anger gained momentum with each pulsing throb of her head, thundering, like a locomotive down hill, out of control. She groped for the shotgun, but she'd dropped it when she charged into the clearing. "He's no good...like your father."

Sharon's mouth opened.

Hannah was like a drunkard with too much whiskey, ranting, not caring, not knowing what she said. "He'll leave you just like he left me. I forbid it, Sharon. Go home!" She turned to Joe, her hands still fisted at her sides. "I want you off this place. Do you hear me? I'll give you one hour. Pick up your pay at the house." She shoved her finger at him. "Stay off. Don't ever come back, or I'll – I'll – "

You'll kill him, Hannah.

"Shut up!" Hannah threw her hands to her head. "Shut up! Shut up!"

"Mrs. Larken. Please – "

"I'll kill you! Stay away from Sharon. Do you hear me? I'll kill you!"

"Mama!"

Hannah didn't speak. She stood, her eyes clamped in pain, her hands clasped like a vice at her temples.

Sharon sobbed. "Those awful things you said about Papa. How could you?"

"Get home," Hannah croaked.

"I will not."

"You heard me, child." Hannah's throat ached from screaming. Her head felt like it would split.

"Go on, Sharon," Joe said.

Hannah heard her go, the twigs snapping under her feet, the swishing of her calico dress. She slowly opened her eyes. The dark tunnel closed in, narrowed. The roaring in her head grew louder, more intense. She turned back to Joe.

A muscle twitched in the man's jaw and there was flinty fire in his black eyes. He glared at her for a full minute before he turned on his heels and strode away.

~~~

Hannah sat motionless in the old rocker in front of the fire she had built in the stone fireplace. The evening seemed chilled despite
~~~

the heat of the day. She watched the flames leaping and licking at the log she had just put on.

Her chest tightened at the memory of the scene that had taken place earlier in the woods. What had come over her? She had no right to rail at the child like that. It wasn't Sharon's fault. The girl was so innocent – like Hannah had been at her age.

It was *him* that made Hannah act this way. Parker O'Dell. Why had he come back after all these years? Hadn't he hurt her enough?

She heard the soft creak of the stairs and straightened, braced herself. The gentle rustling of skirts told her Sharon had entered the room and was standing behind her.

"Mama?"

Hannah sat rigidly silent, staring into the fire.

"Mama, Joe and I were going to tell you."

Hannah set the rocker into motion. She couldn't answer, didn't know what to say.

"I'm sorry, Mama. I didn't mean to cause you pain."

The room was quiet except for the creaking of the chair, the loud ticking of the clock on the mantle, and the crackling of the flames on the hearth. Hannah didn't want to talk about it now. She wanted it to go away. She wanted things to be like they were before. Before Parker O'Dell came back. How could she explain to Sharon? How could she tell her how dangerous men like that were? She breathed a long sigh. No. She couldn't talk about it now. She had a headache.

"Not tonight, Sharon. I'm very tired."

"I love you, Mama. I'm sorry."

In a rush, Sharon was around the chair and kneeling at her feet. Hannah's heart lurched as she gazed into the lovely face of her daughter. She was touched by the pain in the girl's eyes, the creases in her brow. She reached out and cupped Sharon's chin in her hand. "It's I who needs to apologize," she said softly. "I should not have carried on so."

Relief showed in Sharon's face. She took Hannah's hands in hers and squeezed them.

Hannah smiled. "That was no way for a grown woman to act. I should have dealt with it differently."

"Oh, Mama, you do understand."

"Of course I do, my dear." Hannah raised a hand and stroked Sharon's hair, like silk beneath her touch. As soft as baby hair. She wanted to pull her daughter to her lap, cuddle her close, like when she was small. "We all make mistakes," she said. "It doesn't matter, he's gone now."

"Mama?" The relief in Sharon's eyes wavered.

"He won't be bothering you again."

"No. You don't understand." Sharon's eyes widened.

"He's no good, child," Hannah continued. "Believe me. I know his type only too well."

"I love Joe. He loves me."

Hannah chuckled warmly. "You're too young to know about love."

Sharon stiffened, pulled away. "We plan to marry."

"No. It will pass. You won't see him again and you'll forget this silly notion."

"It's not a silly notion, Mama. Joe and I – "

Hannah cut her off. "I was young once too, remember? I know these things."

Sharon got to her feet. "You talk like I'm a child."

Hannah was taken aback slightly by the tone in her daughter's voice, the sudden defiance in her eyes.

"You talk like I don't know my own feelings," the girl continued.

"You are a child, Sharon. My child."

"Look at me, Mama." Sharon held her

hands in front of her, palms up. "I'm nineteen years old. I'm not a child anymore. I'm grown. I'm a woman old enough to know her own mind."

"It's a mother's duty to protect her daughter from things that could hurt her. I know what's best for you, Sharon. Believe that."

"You know what's best for you, Mother."

This was a side of her daughter Hannah hadn't seen before. She didn't know how to deal with it. It made her head hurt more. She wouldn't deal with it. "We can talk about this later," she said firmly, "when you're feeling more rational."

Sharon straightened. "We'll talk about it now. I'm quite rational."

I'm tired." Hannah's voice sharpened. "Go to bed."

Sharon took a long breath. "You always tell me what to do and when to do it." The words came out in a rush, like there wouldn't be time to say what she had to say. She bit her lip, studied Hannah. "I – I've felt like a prisoner up here on this mountain."

Hannah watched, speechless, as Sharon turned and walked to the fireplace, rubbing her hands together nervously. Then she retraced her steps, stopped in front of the rocker and faced her. "I haven't been to a party. I haven't been to a dance. I didn't have children my own age to play with. You even schooled me here, Mother. I have never been off this mountain without you with me." She choked on a sob, and tears pooled in her angry eyes. "When you do take me to town, you practically hold my hand like I was five years old. You choose my clothing – "

"That will be all." Hannah couldn't believe this was her daughter ranting on in this way. She'd never allowed sass. She'd always demanded respect.

"No!" Sharon cried. She stamped her foot and wiped at her cheek with her fingertips. "I've something to say, Mother."

Hannah couldn't abide tantrums. Never could. Never would. She braced her hands on the wooden arms of the chair, started to raise herself, opened her mouth to speak. This had gone quite far enough.

Anger blazed in the dark walnut eyes that locked with hers. The tears were gone. "If a man on this ranch smiles at me, he's gone the next day. If someone in town tips his hat, you glare at him with that silly shotgun in your hands until he runs off like a whipped dog. You watch me like a hawk."

Hannah felt the pain worsen behind her eyes. She fought against it. This was no time for one of her spells.

"You suffocate me, Mother."

Hannah stared at her daughter.

The girl needs a thrashing.

No, Hannah replied silently.

Don't let her get the upper hand.

I'll never strike Sharon. Never.

"Sit down, Mother, and listen to me for a change!" Sharon's eyes were hard and cold. "I will marry Joe. I will and you won't stop me."

Hannah crumpled back into the chair. The room seemed much too warm.

You'll be so sorry, Hannah.

"You...can't...stop...me," Sharon repeated through clenched teeth. "I'm of legal age. You can't stop me ever again."

There was a long silence. Hannah's shock turned to anger. She could stop her. She would stop her. She *had* to stop her.

Sharon took another breath. "I will marry Joe. Do you hear me, Mother? Get use to the idea."

Anger turned to rage. Hannah rose suddenly. Her open palm made a loud *smack* as it hit Sharon's face.

Sharon stepped back, mouth open, eyes

wide. Her own hand came to rest on the red welt already forming on her cheek.

Shocked with herself, Hannah wanted to say something, but words wouldn't form for the tightness in her throat. She stared at her daughter for several seconds, saw the surprise in her eyes, then something completely alien to her. Could it be...? Yes, she was sure of it. There was hate in Sharon's eyes.

What have I done? Hannah thought. Oh, what have I done?

Sharon sobbed once, whirled on her heels, lifted her skirt and ran from the room. Moments later, Hannah heard the door to the kitchen slam. She stood where she was, trembling so hard she felt she'd shake apart. She had never hit Sharon before. She had never thought of hitting Sharon before. She wrapped her arms around her stomach tightly, tried to stop the shaking inside her. She walked to the window.

You had to do it, Hannah.

"No," Hannah whispered out loud. "Go away." She leaned her head against the window frame and gazed out at the night.

There was a light in the bunkhouse. Bull Brenner was back. Another light appeared in the window of the cabin behind the bunkhouse.

Sharon had always been a good child, an obedient child. What had come over her?

A slender shadow passed in front of the cabin window as Sharon pulled the shade.

All this is happening because of...him.

Parker O'Dell.

As for Joe Keys? The envelope containing his pay still lay on the table in the kitchen. He hadn't the guts to come and collect it, Hannah thought. He was a coward. He was gone, she was sure. She drew a deep breath and dropped the curtain back into place, sat down in front of the fire and huddled there like a child.

They're just alike, Hannah.

Parker O'Dell and Joe Keys.

They would take Sharon from you.

The way Swede had tried to take her, send her to a finishing school in the east. Make a fine lady of her. Hannah hadn't stood for it then. She wouldn't stand for it now.

Everything Hannah had ever loved had been ripped from her. Her younger brother, William, had died on the trip west – buried and left in a lonely grave somewhere near the City of Rocks.

"Boys grow to be men, Hannah," her mother had said as they stood looking down on the mound of freshly turned soil. "It's best this way."

Hannah's insides knotted as another memory flashed in her mind. Her mother, limp and lifeless, dressed in a shimmering, emerald-green evening gown, laying on the barn floor. Pete Lacey stood over her, his eyes dry, his face void of expression, a knife with a long blade clutched in his hand.

Hannah shuddered, laid her head back and closed her eyes.

Go to sleep, Hannah.

Yes. She needed to sleep.

We'll fix it tomorrow.

What can we do? How can we fix it?

Bull Brenner, Hannah. Bull Brenner will help.

Hannah relaxed. Yes, she thought. Bull Brenner will help us. He's helped us before.

Sleep, Hannah. Sleep.

"Yes," Hannah said out loud. "Sleep."

Chapter Five

The half-empty whiskey jug and the glass sat on top of the chest-of-drawers across from Ramsey. He thought about getting up and going after them. If he did, he'd never find this exact position again. His arm and shoulder had been hurting him all day, and there was a heaviness in his chest that made him feel winded. The way he was lying eased the pain, helped his breathing. He was too comfortable to move, too tired to get up.

Tired. And he hadn't done a damn thing today except split a little wood for the landlady and help Tommy clean the barn. There was a time when he could work all day and drink all night, and work again the next day, and never even call up a sweat. Now he was as weak as a kitten. Old age was catching up with him, fast.

He sure could use a drink. A shot of whiskey might even help the aching in his joints.

A breeze fluttered the lace curtains and slid in through the open window, bringing with it the smell of rain. It was a hot, airless day, but thunderheads had been boiling up in the east all afternoon. Ramsey knew they were in for one hell of a lightning storm later.

He could hear Pleasant bustling about downstairs, preparing the evening meal: dishes clinking, hurried footsteps. It gave him a sense of well being he hadn't felt in a long time. Along with the well being, however, came a healthy share of hopelessness. He didn't quite know why.

The sounds below mingled with the scents of lavender, clean lye soap, and beeswax, reminding him of the room he'd shared with his brother, Jarred, in the house they lived in with their parents in Cincinnati.

Ramsey closed his eyes; his mind started conjuring up thoughts of those times. His mind had been doing that a lot lately, conjuring up thoughts that he just as soon it didn't. Memories of when life was simpler. Unencumbered. Where had the time gone?

The sound of Major Griswell's wooden leg

thumping down the hall brought Ramsey out of his thoughts. It was almost suppertime, but he wasn't particularly hungry.

There was something about the major that bothered Ramsey. Maybe the familiar, faded-blue cap he still wore, or the way the old man watched him whenever they were in the same room together. It made him uneasy as hell.

Probably his conscience, he thought. Old demons come home to roost. Ghosts in gray and blue come back to haunt him. They did every so often.

God. He needed that whiskey jug across the room. And his makings, too.

Ramsey wondered about his folks. Ma and Pa. Were they still alive? If they were, Pa would be pushing eighty, and Ma…? Close behind, he reckoned. Who'd be taking care of them in their old age? Not Jarred. Not Ramsey. Guilt yanked at him, hard. He had thought of going home often, but he couldn't. He'd brought enough shame on the folks. He and Jarred both. Wouldn't do to bring on more.

It was hard not having family. He'd acquired a few friendships along the way, but they were about as lasting as the dust on his boots when it rained. Except for Hoss, of course. Best friend a man could have, a horse.

Horses listened, seemed to understand, and never said a word of what they'd heard to anybody. But horses weren't family.

Ramsey would like to have settled down. Tried for another family. He'd thought about it a couple times, met a couple women that might have had him. But he didn't. It was too late for all that now. He'd hoped Hannah would be glad to see him, just because they shared something a long time ago. Maybe sit down and talk. He could explain, tell her about the past. They could catch up. Maybe –

It hadn't worked out that way. She didn't want to talk to him. She made that pretty damn clear. Ramsey had been in Indian Bend for two weeks and he hadn't gone back to see her. Why? Afraid? He didn't think so. Not really. Not of Hannah. She had her ways, but he didn't think she'd really shoot him. He recalled the day at the creek on the mountain. The look in her eyes. Maybe she would...

His thoughts stalled on Pleasant Smith. As fine a woman as a man would ever want to meet. Her house was the kind of home men like him could only dream of: spotless clean, comfortable, with enough of those doodads women like to make it right cozy.

Yes, he thought. A man could settle in here

and be as happy as a moth in a wool sock.

But women like Pleasant Smith were just a little out of reach for a saddle tramp with a price on his head.

A bit reluctantly and with some difficulty, Ramsey swung his feet over the edge of the bed and sat up. He put his shirt on and pulled a comb through his freshly cut hair. He ran a hand over his chin. There was a little stubble there, but he decided it was okay. He left his room, walked down the hall to the back stairs. He'd best make an appearance at least.

~~~

The smell of dinner changed Ramsey's mind as he entered the dining room. He was hungry after all. The table was covered with a white crocheted tablecloth and set with china bowls with a pretty rose pattern. Isaac Griswell sat on one side of the table, next to the paunchy, portly schoolmaster, Jacob Skomp. The major's faded blue Union cap hung from the knob on the back of the dark, polished wooden chair he sat on. His long gray beard twitched as if in anticipation of the meal to come.

The tall, elderly, beak-nosed and balding Reverend Josiah Maudlin, dressed in a rusty-black suit over a frayed white shirt, sat on the
~~~

other side. Tommy sat next to him. Ramsey's place was at the end of the table, opposite Pleasant.

Everyone looked up as Ramsey entered, but Major Griswell's gray eyes – one lighter than the other, almost white, milked over with cataract – followed Ramsey as he took his seat.

Ramsey glanced at the major, then to his bowl, and cleared his throat. "Evening," he said.

"Evening," the major answered, not taking his eyes off him.

The preacher and the schoolteacher were watching him now too. Ramsey wished he hadn't come down. He hated eating in front of everyone. It made him feel...like he wasn't wearing any clothes.

Pleasant Smith came through the door carrying a large, lidded tureen made of the same china as on the table. Ramsey forgot the major and the others...and his naked feeling. His eyes were on the landlady and the way she was looking at him. She was beautiful in her pale green dress with tiny pink flowers. Her white apron had a ruffle of stiff lace that lay perfectly on her bosom. Her face was pink from the heat of the kitchen. A tendril of damp hair clung to the side of her dimpled cheek.

She smiled a bright smile.

"Mr. Judd," she beamed. "I was afraid you weren't going to join us."

"Judd..." the major said as he always did when Ramsey's name was mentioned.

Pleasant sat the soup tureen on the table.

"Name sounds familiar," the old man continued. "Do I know you, boy?"

"Don't think so, sir." Ramsey shifted his gaze from the landlady to the elaborate pattern of the silver spoon lying next to his bowl.

The clean smell of Pleasant as she stood close distracted him. Her breast brushed his shoulder as she leaned over and picked up his bowl. She filled it, and set the dish in front of him. He wondered if the brush was deliberate. He doubted it. She moved away, filled Tommy's dish, then went around the table.

"I could swear we met somewhere. Don't usually forget a face." The old war veteran narrowed his eyes, studied Ramsey. "Did you fight the war? North or South?"

"Now, Major," Pleasant Smith said, picking up the elderly man's dish and ladling the heavy stew into it. "Quit bothering Mr. Judd. Eat your food." She sat down and smiled at Ramsey. "Forgive the major, Mr. Judd. He lives in the past, rambles sometimes. Reverend, would you please ask the blessing?"

Everyone bowed their heads and the reverend delivered a mercifully short prayer. When Ramsey raised his head again, the major was still staring at him.

"I fought for the North, myself," Major Griswell said, lifting a spoonful of stew to his mouth. "That's where I lost my leg – "

"Yes, Major." Pleasant passed a plate of hot biscuits to Tommy, who passed it to the reverend. "You've told us about that."

"The battle of Chattanooga," the old man continued, chewing his food, his chin and nose almost meeting for lack of teeth.

Ramsey's hand hung for a moment over the biscuits. He felt the panic rise up in him, the scared feeling squeezing his chest. He'd been at the battle of Chattanooga. He wanted to leave the table but couldn't, had to stay and see it through. He steadied his shaking hand, took a biscuit and passed the plate to the teacher. He didn't remember Major Griswell. There was no major in his unit with that name. Ramsey was sure of it. There were other units there. The major could have been attached to one of them.

"No, sir. I don't usually forget a name," the major said, "just can't always connect it with a time or face anymore. Judd does sound mighty familiar."

"Have you found work yet, Mr. Judd?" the reverend asked, looking at Ramsey over a pair of wire-framed glasses that perched crookedly on his long skinny nose.

"No, sir." Ramsey hadn't looked for work. He was tired; there was time. He'd spent the past two weeks roaming the countryside, when his body felt up to it, idling away his days, chopping firewood for the landlady, helping Tommy with the chores, and resting in his room.

"It'll come to me," the major said, oblivious to the rest of the conversation, "it always does."

"They need a freight driver up at Grangeville," Tommy said between bites. "Mr. Tobias, the owner of the freight company, had to bring supplies himself last week. His usual driver accidentally shot himself in the foot. He's going to be laid up for a spell. Mr. Tobias said he didn't know if he'd let him come back when he was healed up or not. Kind of a greenhorn."

"Thanks, Tommy," Ramsey said. "I may check into that." He glanced at Pleasant. A frown worried her brow for a moment, then she smiled her pretty smile, picked daintily at her meal.

Ramsey finished eating, excused himself and stepped out onto the veranda. It was beginning to get dark. He lowered himself into the swing, set it into motion with the toe of his boot, breathed the damp air. The lightning had stopped. He figured it was just resting for another good start.

The freight job didn't interest him much. He should at least check into it. It was work, after all. But freight drivers had to come in contact with a lot of people in a lot of towns. He didn't know if he was ready for that. Someone might recognize him.

Ramsey took a bag of Bull Durham from his pocket. Something was sure the matter. He felt almost urgent sometimes, like there were things he had to take care of, set straight. Unfinished business. He just didn't know how to go about it. He had to make things right with Hannah. He didn't want to die with her hating him.

A distant rumble of thunder broke the stillness. The evening felt muggy-warm, but Ramsey shivered. There was a tension in the air, like the night was waiting for something.

Waiting. Like Ramsey. Waiting for what? A chill slipped up his spine. The thunder rolled again, closer now.

Did a man have a way of knowing when his time was near? He'd been obsessed with the thought of death lately. Why? He felt alright, except for the aching in his left shoulder and arm from rheumatism. He was more tired than usual, but after all, he wasn't getting any younger. There comes a time when a man has to face his own mortality. The future gets a little more worrisome with years.

The preacher and the schoolteacher passed by without seeming to notice him sitting in the swing on the deeply shadowed porch. They went down the steps and around the side of the house. Ramsey finished his smoke. He'd like to sit here awhile. Maybe Pleasant would come out and sit with him. He drew a long breath. That wasn't too likely. She'd be in the kitchen fussing over the dishes, and he didn't want another encounter with the major tonight. He rose stiffly. It felt like every part of his body was being pulled down, like he had lead weights holding him back. What in the hell was the matter with him?

~~~

Hours later, Ramsey stared at the ceiling, still dwelling on the things that bothered him. He hadn't tried to sleep, wasn't ready for it.
~~~

The shaded lamp by his bed cast shadows about the room, and his gaze shifted back to the rose-pattern paper on the walls. The bright flash of jagged lightning dancing beyond the window illuminated the room briefly.

It was good being here, he thought. A man shouldn't be alone at the end.

Impatient with himself, Ramsey sat up and took a deck of cards from the nightstand, shuffled them and laid out a hand of solitaire. He tried to concentrate on the game, but his worrisome thoughts pounded at him.

He tossed the cards down, raked his fingers through the silver-streaked black curls on his head – the curls Pleasant had fussed at and admired as she carefully clipped and fluffed them. He'd sat on a chair in her bright, homey kitchen with the lace curtains at the windows and the matching tablecloth, a white hobnail vase full of violets in the middle of the round table, while she ran her delicate little fingers through his hair. He'd gloried in it.

Damn-it-to-hell. He had to get a grip on things. It was purely making him crazy, all this thinking. He thought again about the freight job Tommy told him about at supper. He had too much time on his hands, that was the problem. Maybe he'd best go up and check it out tomorrow.

First, he needed to go see Hannah. Maybe tonight. What excuse could he give for showing up on her doorstep unexpected in the middle of the night? Would she let him in? Offer him a drink? Would they laugh over old times? The scene at the creek?

Ramsey thought of the beautiful, wide-eyed woman-child he'd known so many years ago. Quiet, always within herself, dreamy, as though she knew secrets no one else knew. Sometimes sad secrets. Ramsey had been bewitched by her eyes always following him about the ranch, watching him work, always there at the edge of his vision. She spoke few words to him, but her eyes said what she was thinking, what she wanted. She'd wanted him.

There had been another side to Hannah Lacey, too, a dark side. She could change in a heartbeat, become riled over little things, almost loco. Like a wild mare, unbroken and uncontrollable. She liked having her own way. Her fits of temper could cower even the biggest and toughest of Pete's wranglers, Pete himself. Everyone stayed clear of her, gave her room.

Could Hannah laugh? Had he ever heard her laugh? He couldn't remember.

Ramsey scraped the cards off the bed,

straightened them, left his room and walked across the hall to the door that lead down to the kitchen. The floorboards creaked under his feet. Maybe Mrs. Smith would like to play Hearts, or Rummy.

He stopped. It was late, for God's sake. She'd be sleeping. What had he been thinking? He turned back to his own door.

He heard movement from below, the lowering of a lid to the top of the cook stove. Maybe she was making tea. He'd never thought much about tea, couldn't say if he really liked it. Hadn't drank much of the stuff. But there was something intimate in the thought of sharing a cup of tea with Pleasant Smith. And a slice of her spicy apple pie would sure taste good. He grinned, opened the door, and hurried down the narrow stairway to the kitchen.

~~~

Pleasant wasn't sleepy. She sat alone at the kitchen table, staring out the window, watching the lightning and listening to the thunder. She heard his footsteps above her, held her breath when she heard him cross the hall and then pause. She jumped up, ran to the stove and dropped the lid. Anything to let him know she was here. She pushed the tea kettle into place.
~~~

Every time he came close to her, something happened inside her. He made her feel things. The smell of his shirt as she held it to her nose before placing it gently into the steaming tub of boiling water woke the sleeping desires inside her, made her ache with wanting. Like the first blossoming on an old vine that she thought had died a long time ago with Tom's passing. She knew she wasn't the kind of woman who could easily attract another man. It hurt her deeply. She had a passion inside her.

Tom had been good to her, a good provider. They'd met on the wagon train west, married and settled in Idaho during the gold rush. Tom had worked hard, made his strike. He'd built this house for her. Nothing outlandish – Tom wasn't like that – a modest house with lots of rooms for the children they planned on having. Tommy was born, and her husband died of influenza before any more babies could be made.

Pleasant never thought of herself as pretty. Maybe when she was younger. Even then she'd leaned toward overweight, but it was okay. She'd been considered rounded, well built, shapely. Perfect for childbearing. The years since Tom's death hadn't been kind to her. She was lonely and she'd compensated for that loneliness by over-indulging in rich foods. She'd put on too many extra pounds, and she couldn't take them off. She was fat, she thought, hopelessly fat. Men like Ramsey Judd weren't attracted to fat women.

She waited in anticipation, listening to the sounds coming from the top of the stairs. Her lungs were full, and her heart beat against her chest like a little drum. She heard the door open and his heavy tread on the stair, the gentle rap on the door across the room from her.

Pleasant patted the light gold fluff at the top of her head, brushed at the little curls at her temples, let her breath out slowly. "Come in, Mr. Judd," she called softly.

She was taking the pie from the hutch when the door opened and Ramsey stepped into her kitchen.

He smiled and held up a deck of playing cards. "Thought you might like a game."

"I've just put the tea kettle on." Pleasant reached for the pie plates and china cups. She was fluttering so bad she thought they might clatter as she lifted them down. They didn't.

"Is that apple pie?"

"I baked it this afternoon from my own apples in storage in the cellar." She was babbling. She'd forgotten how to make pleasant conversation.

"I've never tasted pie like yours, Mrs. Smith."

A blush warmed her cheeks as she put a measure of tea into the little fob at the end of a chain, dropped it into the china teapot on the work counter, poured hot water from the kettle on the stove over it. She sliced the pie, aware of him watching her. It made her feel weak all over. She filled the plates and carried everything to the table.

Pleasant smiled as Ramsey picked up the fork and bent over his pie, but a worry she'd been feeling for days closed in on her. The man was ill. She could see it in the grayish tinge of skin around his eyes and mouth, the tiredness on his face.

He smacked his lips, glanced up and winked at her. "Good," he said. He picked the cup up, holding it by the dainty handle with a large thumb and forefinger that were obviously unaccustomed to such things, his pinky sticking out like a broken branch on a tree, stiff and straight. He took a sip.

There was something besides illness in his eyes and in the lines of his face after the smile had gone. There was a sorrow in him, a deep hurt. Pleasant could only imagine what it might be. A lost love, perhaps? A woman? Whatever it was frightened her.

"Where's your family, Mr. Judd?" she asked softly.

He looked up briefly, then back to his pie. "Right here in front of you, I reckon."

"No kin?"

He looked up again. His expression had hardened slightly. He chewed and swallowed. "Don't rightly know, ma'am." He laid his fork beside his plate.

"Where are you from?" She knew she was pushing. She couldn't help it. She wanted to know more about this man.

Ramsey pushed his chair back from the table. Pleasant had the feeling she'd gone too far.

"It's late, ma'am. I best be letting you get to bed."

"Wouldn't you like more pie?"

"No, ma'am." He rose.

"Mr. Judd, I am sorry. I'm just a meddling woman sometimes. Do forgive me, please. It is really none of my business."

"Nothing to forgive, ma'am." He walked to the door that lead upstairs and turned.

"Mrs. Smith," he said, "I ain't good at small

talk. Someday maybe I'll tell you all you want to know. Right now, I just ain't ready. Good night." He pulled the door behind him.

There was an emptiness in Pleasant's chest as it closed.

Chapter Six

Last night's storm had passed and the morning promised sunshine, but by noon a fresh bank of black clouds rolled in and camped low in the sky over the Larken ranch. The wind rose and the day turned prematurely dark. The first roll of thunder sounded far off when Hannah saw the horse and rider pause at the gate that led to the house. The man reached down and opened it, let it swing shut behind him.

Hannah clutched the shotgun. She watched him ride slowly toward her. A raindrop fell cold and wet against her cheek.

Is it him, Hannah?

It's him.

He'd shaved. His hair was cut. His clothes had been washed. But he was the same. All she remembered. Just older. Now she raised the weapon, aimed it at him.

The man reined his horse to a stop a few feet from Hannah. The horse turned its side into the storm; the man's gaze swept over her and rested on the shotgun. He reached to his hat, tipped it, shoved it hard onto his head to keep the wind from blowing it off. He flexed his arm as though it were stiff and leaned forward, resting it across the saddle horn.

The rain was coming down harder. It plopped off the brim of Hannah's hat. She stared up at him.

"Hello Hannah," he said, and almost grinned. "I see you still let your sidekick there do your talking." He nodded toward the 16-gauge.

She tightened her grip on the gun. "I told you not to come back."

"Wasn't going to." He kept his eyes steady as they gazed into hers. "I had to see you one more time before... There's things I want to tell you."

"I should have shot you, Parker O'Dell, when I had the chance."

"You've got the shotgun in your hand," he challenged.

Her skirt felt heavy and wet against her

legs. She tilted her head slightly and the water ran from the brim of her hat like a waterfall, washed over the front of her shirt where her coat was open. She shivered. He was calling her bluff. It caught her off guard.

"It isn't loaded," she said.

Hannah!

Hannah bit her lip.

"I'll give you time." The man kept his gaze level. "Go ahead, Hannah, load it. Let's get this thing over with."

She stared at the face she thought she'd forgotten years ago. All the anger and bitterness, all the hate, everything she'd been feeling for the past twenty years rushed up to meet her.

Load it, Hannah.

"Load it, Hannah."

There was a tired quality to the man's eyes, pain, Hannah thought, but they were cool.

Load it, Hannah.

She ran her tongue over her lips. Why was he doing this? Did he think she wouldn't?

She reached into her coat pocket and took out two shells and pushed the lever on the barrel. The shotgun broke open. She tried to stuff the shells into the empty chambers, but her hands shook. The rain blinded her; the wind shoved at her. She reached up and pushed the water from her eyes and tried again. The man sat quietly watching her, waiting.

Load it, Hannah.

Lightning jagged across the darkened sky. Rain fell like shards of glass against her skin. Thunder crashed the silence. Hannah felt it quiver the air, felt it in her head. Darkness swirled in at her from both sides.

It was hopeless. Her clumsy fingers wouldn't work.

You should have loaded it, Hannah.

Why hadn't she taken time to load the damn thing when she'd finished cleaning it?

One of the shells dropped onto the ground and Hannah bent to pick it up. Her hat blew from her head, caught on the string under her chin, tugged at her neck. Soft, gentle hands covered her wet ones. The shotgun was lifted away. Hannah looked up through a shimmer of rain and tears into her daughter's face, saw her eyes through the bright tunnel. Eyes that matched those of the man sitting on the horse. She felt so weak she thought she might faint.

"Stop it, Mama," Sharon whispered.

Hannah shifted her gaze to her own feet, watched the raindrops splatter on the toes of her boots. She didn't want to look at the man or the girl. She was terrified. She hoped they wouldn't look at each other, because she knew what would happen if they did.

It's too late, Hannah.

Her worst nightmare had come true. She waited, breath held. The silence seemed endless. Why didn't he speak? He must know.

When he did speak, his words were almost a whisper. "My God, Hannah."

Hannah didn't raise her head, didn't look at him. She wanted to. She wanted to look him right in the eye, spit on him.

"I didn't know. Why didn't you tell me?" he asked.

Again the silence. Hannah trembled, could feel the shaking clear to her bones. Go away, she thought. Go away.

"I'm sorry, sir," Sharon said softly. "I think my mother would like it if you left."

Hannah felt the rain beating hard against her head and shoulders, felt the wind buffeting her body, heard the rushing in her head, like the storm, beating and hammering against her brain. Pain gripped her head like icy fingers, and through the pain she heard the jingle of the bridle and the creak of the saddle. She heard the slow slog of the horse's hooves in the wet mud of the dooryard, the squeak of the gate and the thwack it made as it swung shut. Then nothing but the constant sound of the raging storm and the voice inside her head, laughing. Laughing at her like Parker O'Dell must be laughing at her, like everyone laughed at her. All her life, the laughing –

"Come on, Mama. You're soaking wet. Let's get you out of the rain and into something dry."

~~~

Realization burst over Ramsey like a Roman candle. It paralyzed his chest, and his head throbbed. He clutched the saddle horn and drew in deep, painful breaths.

Sharon Larken was his daughter. He knew the moment he laid eyes on her. No wonder Hannah hated him. No wonder she wanted to kill him.

The pain in his chest twisted tighter. It gripped his arm like a vice, felt like it would rip it from the socket. He'd never felt pain like this before.

Ramsey was aware of the thunder rolling out of the west, crashing over his head, of the rain beating down on him, of the crippling pain that seized his body. He slumped forward as the gelding continued faithfully down the side of the mountain.
~~~

"Ramsey?"

It was Pleasant speaking to him. What was she doing up here?

"Oh dear Lord, Mr. Judd."

The rain had stopped. He could smell fresh hay and horse dung. It was dark, a different kind of dark than anything he'd ever seen. Voices drifted in and out of his consciousness. The pain was killing. He felt something soft and warm break his fall as he slipped like a corpse from the back of his horse.

The throbbing ache in his chest and arm weighed him down, held him immobile. He tried to wiggle his toes, to feel the gold eagle in his boot. He tried to tell her it was there. He couldn't speak.

"Tommy," Pleasant called. "Tommy, help me."

Ramsey floated and whirled in the strange darkness. And then nothing.

A while later, he stirred. The hurting in his chest had gone. He moved his arm. What in the hell happened to him? Slowly, he opened his eyes and gazed into Pleasant Smith's frightened face.

"Lie still, Mr. Judd," she said.

"What happened?" Ramsey's throat strained against his words. "Did she do it? I felt like I'd been hit with both barrels."

"You've had a heart attack. The doctor will be back in a little while. He wants you to rest."

Ramsey ran his tongue over his dry lips and looked around. He was in his room at the boarding house; he breathed a sigh of relief. What did Pleasant say? Heart attack? "I'm thirsty as hell," he said. When would it happen? How much time did he have? "Can you hand me the bottle sitting on the dresser?"

"No," Pleasant answered. "You can't have whiskey. Not until I ask the doctor."

"Damn it, woman." Would she deprive a dying man a drink of whiskey before he went? "I'm thirsty."

She took a cup from the stand beside the bed and put her arm behind him, lifted him gently. "Here, you can drink this."

"Water?" He supported himself on one elbow, wrinkled his nose and lifted the cup to his lips, rolled the first sip around in his mouth and swallowed. It tasted good. He tipped the cup again and downed every drop.

Pleasant stood and fluffed the pillow. She pushed him gently back against it. He didn't resist as she pulled the quilt up to his chin. "If you need anything," she said and smiled kindly, "ring this. I'll leave the doors open so I can hear you." She lifted a little silver bell and shook it. It jingled disgustingly.

Ramsey groaned and closed his eyes. He didn't want to die while she was gone. "Please, don't go..." He felt her soft, cool hand on his brow. And fell asleep.

When he woke a while later, he stared up into the face of a tall, older man, with gray hair, gray eyes, wearing a black coat and white shirt.

"I'm Doctor Cobb," the man said. "How are you feeling, Mr. Judd?" He put his stethoscope into his black bag and snapped it shut.

"Give it to me straight, Doc." Ramsey closed his eyes again. "I can take it."

"You've had a heart attack," the doctor answered.

"I know," Ramsey said. "Mrs. Smith told me. How much time do I have?"

"You need to take better care of yourself, sir. Avoid any unnecessary excitement."

What did it matter now? Ramsey thought. It was kind of like closing the barn door after the horse had gotten out.

"You were lucky this time, Mr. Judd," the doctor continued.

Ramsey opened his eyes.

The doctor was half smiling. "This one was mild. You'll make it – if you do what I say. If you don't, the next one could get you. I've left medicine with Mrs. Smith." He stepped to the door. "Rest now. I'll check on you tomorrow."

"Doc, don't go." Ramsey pulled himself up, tried to sit. But he was too tired and slumped back onto the pillow. Dr. Cobb stepped closer to the bed.

There were questions Ramsey needed answered. Things he needed to know.

The doctor anticipated his concerns and smiled. "You have a lot of good years left, Mr. Judd, providing you take care of yourself. You'll need to slow your pace a bit – "

"God, Doc. If I slow any more, I won't be moving at all."

The doctor chuckled, sat on the chair beside the bed. "Mr. Judd, you seem to be in pretty good health, otherwise. You're strong."

"How long would you say I got left, Doc?"

"Oh, I don't know, Mr. Judd. I'm a doctor, not a fortune teller, but I'd give you at least twenty years...give or take, if you take care of yourself. Be a little moderate with your lifestyle. Don't drink too much. Don't get too tired. I'd recommend bed rest for a while."

"Bed rest." Ramsey groaned. "For how long?"

"You let Mrs. Smith tend you and you'll be

back up and around in a couple of weeks. Don't rush it." The doctor stood. "I have to go make a few house calls. I'll check back with you tomorrow." Doctor Cobb left the room.

Ramsey breathed a sigh of relief and relaxed onto the plump pillow under his head. He'd had close calls before, but this was the closest. He stared up at the ceiling. He was one lucky mother's son. He wasn't going to die. Not yet. He had time.

He had a daughter he wanted to get to know.

~~~

"Please, Mama." Sharon set the teacup on the low table beside the wing-back chair where her mother sat in front of the fireplace. She pulled the crocheted lap robe over her mother's knees and knelt onto the hooked rug in front of her. She gazed up into her far-away eyes. "Who is he? Why are you so afraid of him?"

"I'm not afraid of Parker O'Dell," her mother whispered. Her voice was barely audible above the crash of thunder and the rattling of the rain against the window. She stared deep and hard into the fire on the grate. Outside, the wind keened under the eves and around the corner of the house. She twisted the fringe of the cover on her lap around and
~~~

around in her hands. "I hate him," she said softly.

Sharon laid her hand on her mother's knee. "Why do you hate him?"

"He's an evil man," she replied, not shifting her gaze.

"Is he the same man that was at the creek that day?"

"The devil always returns when you sell your soul to him, Sharon." Her mother's gaze shifted to her. "Remember that. The devil always returns."

The look in her mother's eyes made a shiver slip up Sharon's spine. Who was he? Why wouldn't her mother tell her? He looked so familiar somehow, like she had met him somewhere. It was the eyes.

"He didn't seem like the devil," Sharon said. "He looked so lost and...lonely."

"Men like Parker O'Dell don't get lonely, and they don't get lost. They don't have anywhere to get lost from, because they don't stay in one place long enough. They take what they're wanting and then they ride away."

Sharon sighed. Poor Mama, she thought. How could she help her? Was there any help for her? Grandpa Lacey told Sharon when she was young, before he got sick, when she didn't understand her mother's moods, that it wasn't all her mama's fault. She'd been born to it. Grandpa had told her a lot of things that Sharon hadn't understood then. But she did now, and it made her sad and a little afraid. Had she been born to it too?

Would it be right marrying Joe, knowing what she knew? Would their children be born to it?

How could she leave Mama alone now? The spells were getting worse. Should she tell Joe? Let him decide if he still wanted to marry her? Would he take the chance?

"Stay away from him, Sharon."

Sharon started at her mother's words. Could Mama read her thoughts? She couldn't stay away from Joe.

"No matter what, don't go near Parker O'Dell."

Sharon blinked up at her.

"Do you hear me, daughter?"

"Yes, Mama, I hear you."

"Good." Her mother leaned her head against the back of the chair. Sharon watched her face until it relaxed and her breathing became steady. She wanted to reach up and brush the stray strand of hair from her mother's cheek and touch the strong chiseled face. The face without humor, without laugh lines, without expression. Not a hint of softness in her, except now, in sleep. She looked so pretty. Childlike. So...vulnerable. Sharon dared not touch her. She did not want to break the spell.

She rose, added another stick to the dwindling fire, then walked to the window and watched the rain wash against the glass as though someone were throwing it there by the bucketsful. The same questions rolled over and over in her mind. Parker O'Dell. What was it about him? She'd looked into his eyes and she'd seen something there. It had given her an uneasy feeling. Why was he here? And what kind of a hold did he have on her mother?

~~~

It was late when Hannah woke. Her headache was a dull throb behind her eyes. She glanced at the time. Seven o'clock. She didn't feel rested, but she had the chores to do. She grabbed her hat and coat from the hook by the kitchen door, took down the lantern and lit it. Retrieving her milk bucket and egg basket from the back porch, she walked through the rain-chilled bleakness of early-evening twilight.

Hannah fed the chickens and gathered the eggs, then made her way to the milk shed
~~~

attached to the far end of the barn. Had Sharon put the cow in? Hannah hoped so. She didn't want to go looking for the animal in the rain this time of night. That had always been one of Sharon's chores, finding the cow and putting her in the shed.

Hannah glanced at the cabin as she passed. There was light in the window. Sharon hadn't yet moved back to her bedroom in the house. She was still pouting, Hannah thought. How long was this going to go on?

The milk shed was warm with the smell of hay. The cow waited patiently, her head in the stanchion, eating the fresh hay that Sharon had put there. Hannah took oats from a barrel against the wall and put it in the cow's feed box. Rain hammered on the roof over her head, and the steady swish-swash of the milk hitting the inside of the bucket made her impatient. She was tired and wanted to go to bed. That man's visit had taken all the strength from her.

Why had he come back? There was no reason for him to be here. Had someone told him about Sharon? No. That was impossible. No one knew Sharon was not Swede's daughter. No one except Swede and her father and Hannah.

Why was Parker O'Dell doing this to her?

Hannah yanked hard on the cow's teats and hit her head against the animals stomach. The cow jumped and tried to sidestep, brought its hind foot up and kicked at the stool Hannah was sitting on. Hannah slapped the cow's belly with her open hand. The animal bawled.

"Settle down, you old rip."

The cow gave one last futile kick, then stood nervously and let Hannah continue.

Ironic, Hannah thought, that Sharon should take refuge in the cabin, the very place she'd been conceived.

Hannah softened a bit, remembering. She had wanted Parker O'Dell. She had loved him, and she knew he loved her and wanted her too. She could tell by the way he smiled and winked at her when he saw her watching him from a distance.

There wasn't room in the bunkhouse and Parker was sleeping in the cabin. It was a hot summer night and Hannah couldn't sleep for thinking of him. She had slipped from her bed in the house and gone to him. The cabin door wasn't locked and she'd gone in, removed her night dress and slid under the covers.

She remembered the warmth of his naked body as she pressed close to him, the smell of him, the soft rise and fall of his chest as she put her arm over him. The firmness of his stomach as she moved her hand down his body, and the hardness of the desire she provoked with her caresses.

He'd mumbled something. Martha, she thought. Then he awakened, startled at having her there, and moved away. But Hannah moved closer. He told her to go, but she wouldn't. He tried to rise, but she held him back with her kisses. He finally groaned and pulled her to him, buried his face in her hair, whispered her name, explored her body with his large rough hands.

Hannah shivered with the memory. Before he made love to her, Parker O'Dell told her he had to leave, but Hannah was sure he'd stay...after.

He hadn't. When she woke the next morning, he was gone. He'd ridden out and left her. She'd hated him for it. A month later she discovered she was with child. It was Parker's child, she knew. He was the only one she'd ever laid with. She'd given herself, her innocence, to him, and he'd gone away.

Oh, the humiliation she had suffered. She'd gone to her father, told him she was with child. He'd been angry. She thought he'd go after Parker, bring him back, but he hadn't. He gave her to Swede Larken instead.

Hannah drew a long breath and leaned her head against the cow's belly. She'd hated Swede Larken.

And she'd hated Pete Lacey, too.

She finished her task, then rose and moved from the milk shed to the main part of the old building, hung the lantern on a hook from the ceiling, lit a second lantern and climbed the ladder to the darkened loft. An old, rickety wooden crate sat in the middle of the hay-filled space. Hannah set the lantern on it and took the pitchfork from the corner. She threw fresh, loose hay down to the two horses in the stalls below.

A scuffling sound from the far corner of the loft caught her attention. She looked up as a small gray and black animal peered out from under a mound of hay, its masked eyes glittering in the lamplight.

"Silly raccoon. What are you doing up here?"

The curious animal sniffed the air and slipped back out of sight.

Hannah returned the fork to the corner and backed down the ladder. She heard the scuffling of the raccoon as it ventured again from its hiding place. She'd have Bull get rid of it tomorrow.

She took up her milk bucket and basket of eggs, removed the lantern from its hook, and made her way through the darkness back to the house. After taking care of the milk and eggs, she drew warm water from the tank on the side of the cook stove and washed thoroughly. She changed into her night clothes and returned to the comfort of her chair before the fire.

How long she had been sleeping, she didn't know. When she stirred and opened her eyes, the room seemed dark, but a strange glow lighted the window, flickering orange. It wavered in a soft pool in front of the dead grate of the stone fireplace. She could smell the smoke that lingered.

Still fuzzy-headed from her sound sleep, Hannah forced herself to full wakefulness. Something wasn't right. What had wakened her? The rain? She listened. The wind had stopped. A peculiar snapping sound penetrated her mind, like feet on dry twigs, or —

Fire!

Her bare feet hit the floor running. She flung open the kitchen door and ran out into the yard. One end of the barn's roof was engulfed in flames, and her heart stalled. "Oh my God!"

Slippery mud squished between her toes as she ran, nearly fell once, but kept running. In seconds her clothes were soaked. Her body was chilled, but the heat from the blaze was hot on her cheeks.

Where was Bull Brenner?

Worthless man. Probably down in Indian Bend swilling whiskey.

From out of nowhere, Sharon appeared beside her.

"Mama!"

"The cow, Sharon! Get the cow! I'll get the horses!"

Sharon darted off in the direction of the cow shed. That part of the barn wasn't burning yet. A few moments later, the cow was bawling, running out of the building to the safety of the trees at the edge of the yard.

Hannah stopped at the large barn door. She could see smoke curling out from around the edge and heard the roar of the flames above, the screaming of the animals inside. The heat was intense, scorching. She looked up. Fire shot from the loft window and a billow of black smoke hung heavy, weighed down by the rain. She brushed the back of her hand across her eyes.

You have to go in, Hannah.

Hannah tried to push out the awful sensation in her stomach. She fought against her panic.

The box, Hannah. Go in now.

A fresh rush of adrenaline surged through her. She pulled the barn door open and rushed inside.

Blinding smoke choked her, the heat like a wall against her body. She coughed and wiped the stinging tears from her eyes with the cuff of her sleeve. She tried to peer through the smoke to the stalls and horses across the room. She could hear them stomping and the terrible sounds they made, almost like crying. Hannah started toward them.

No Hannah. The box. Get the box first.

Hannah ran deeper into the burning building, lifted a trap door in the floor and

withdrew a heavy, wooden box. She clutched it to her breast, ran back to the door, her chest heaving under the weight of her burden, to fresh air, and left the box lying in the mud of the barnyard. She filled her lungs and let the breath out, did it a second time. Taking one last great gulp of air, she held it and dashed back into the barn.

From somewhere behind her, she heard Sharon. The girl was there beside her, but Hannah couldn't yell at her, couldn't tell her to leave. Together, they ran blindly to the stalls. Their fingers fumbled with the latches until the gates opened. The horses bolted for the open door. Sharon and Hannah followed.

The night was thick as a blanket around them, the air moist and hot, heavy with smoke and steam. Their clothes were like wet skin, itchy against their flesh, and falling ash burned their eyes. They stood together and watched the roof of the barn cave in with a great explosion of flames and sparks and rolling black smoke. Everything gone – except the wooden box and the animals. And all they could do was stand and watch.

"It was set," Hannah said, her voice raspy. It scraped her raw throat as she spoke. She swallowed hard, painfully.

"What?" asked Sharon.

"The fire was set."

"Who would have done a thing like that?"

Something niggled at the back of Hannah's mind. Something she should remember, but couldn't.

You fool, Hannah. The lantern.

"We'll put the animals in the sheep shed,"

Hannah said. "If we ever find them. We'd best get out of these wet clothes first." Without another word, she turned, hefted the heavy box with both hands and headed for the house. Sharon followed through the orange glow of the fire that still crackled behind them.

Chapter Seven

Pleasant rapped twice on Ramsey's room door before pushing it open with the toe of her slippered foot. Her heart beat a little faster, like it always did when she entered his room. She almost felt guilty the way she enjoyed taking care of him.

"Good morning, Mr. Judd," she said cheerfully. She carried a tray with a pitcher of warm water on it, set it on the low dresser, then raised the blinds at the open windows. "How are you feeling this morning?"

Ramsey raised himself to a sitting position, letting the covers fall away to reveal the white night shirt Pleasant had insisted he wear. She felt very uncomfortable looking at his bare chest every morning. He grunted.

"My, aren't we cheerful this morning," she

said as she crossed the room. She fluffed the pillows and propped them behind him, drinking in the smell of him, feeling the heat from his body. Her cheeks warmed as she smoothed the quilt that covered his lap, glanced up into his face.

He wasn't smiling. In fact, he looked downright ornery. She smiled anyway. His color was good. His mood had certainly not been good the past few mornings, however. He was like a caged cat. Impatient, she thought, and she didn't blame him. He wasn't the type to be shut in for very long. He'd start clawing his way out pretty soon, she knew. She hoped she could keep him down a few more days, but she had her doubts.

"Well?" she said, standing beside the bed with her hands on her hips, the smile still on her lips.

"Well, what?" he growled.

"I asked how you were feeling this morning."

"I'm fine, Mrs. Smith."

There was an edge to his voice. Pleasant tried to ignore it.

"You've got to quit fussing over me," he said.

"I don't mind a bit, Mr. Judd." Pleasant

returned to the dresser and poured water from the pitcher into the wash basin.

"It's been two weeks," Ramsey grumbled. "It's high time I was out of this bed."

"Not quite two weeks, Mr. Judd. Now you just relax." Pleasant placed the bowl of water on the tray beside the towel and soap. "We don't want to rush things." She carried the tray to the bed and set it on the nightstand. "I'll fetch your breakfast while you wash."

"You'll do no such of a thing." Ramsey pushed the tray. "I can get up to wash and I can take my meals downstairs from now on."

"Maybe at lunchtime," Pleasant said.

"Take this damn thing away." Ramsey gave the tray another push. Water slopped from the wash basin.

"Mr. Judd, please – "

"I have to use the thunder mug, Mrs. Smith," he growled. "You gonna bring that to me, too?"

Pleasant stared at him, mouth opened. She wanted to snap back at him, but what purpose would that serve? It would only make him worse. "Mr. Judd, I – "

"Just leave me in peace. I'm not helpless."

"I'll bring your breakfast while you...take care of your morning affairs." Pleasant lifted the tray away and set it back on the dresser.

"No, I'll come down for it. I won't be cooped up in this room. And I won't have you running and fetching and fussing over me like a banty hen one minute longer."

Well that did it. She didn't have to stand here and take this man's abuse. Pleasant started for the door. "All right," she said. "If that's the way you want it." She gave the door a push and it slammed shut behind her.

By the time she reached the bottom of the stairs to the kitchen, she was so angry she was crying. She'd been waiting on him hand and foot. Sat by his bed after he'd gone to sleep each night for the past week and a half, worried herself half sick over him, prayed he wouldn't die. And this was her reward. Not that rewards were always important to her, but didn't he know how she felt about him?

The dining room where Tommy and Major Griswell and the other borders had been having breakfast was empty. All that was left was the mess. She brushed the tears away from her eyes and started picking up the dishes. Mr. Judd had no right to talk to her that way. Who did he think he was? Well if that's the way he wished it, then fine with her. She would do no more for him.

Pleasant was carrying a load of plates to the kitchen when the stair door opened and Ramsey stepped in. She placed the dirty dishes on the counter without turning to face him. "You could knock, Mr. Judd."

~~~

Ramsey stood in Pleasant's kitchen, his hands thrust deep into his pockets. He watched the back of the woman who had been so good to him. He felt like a real heel. "I'm sorry," he said.

"From now on, you may take your meals in the dining room with the other men," Pleasant answered.

"I didn't mean to hurt your feelings, ma'am."

She was crying. He could tell by the way her shoulders heaved. Now what was he suppose to do? He'd never had a woman go all soft and weepy over him. What could he say?

"It's just..." he stammered, trying to think of a few words that would make everything all right again. He couldn't. "Ah damn, ma'am, don't cry."

"I'm not crying." She hiccuped, swiped at her cheek with the back of her hand, and turned to look at him with a chin-quivering smile. Her face was flushed, her eyes big and
~~~

round, rimmed with dark, wet lashes. She blinked.

Oh God. Just looking at her made Ramsey wish he could kick his own ass. He felt as low as a snake under a flat boulder. He took a step toward her. "I just don't like being sick, ma'am," he said softly.

She took a step back. "I understand. Now if you'll please excuse me, I have work to do."

"You are crying," he said, and took another step toward her.

"Lunch is at twelve o'clock sharp," she replied, pressing her backside hard against the counter. "If you'd like to go in and sit down, I'll bring your breakfast. After this, please be on time." She turned her back to him again.

Ramsey didn't move. "Mrs. Smith, I'm not use to being cooped up for very long. It purely makes me want to hunt bugs."

"I'm afraid I've made quite the fool of myself," she said, fussing with things on the counter. "I'm sorry, Mr. Judd."

"Ah, no, it's me. Ma'am, please look at me."

She didn't look at him. She continued her fussing. "I was very worried about you."

Ramsey scratched the back of his neck. He couldn't think of another thing to say. "I'm not hungry, Mrs. Smith. Please don't bother." He backed a couple of steps toward the stair door. "I'll just be taking my leave."

"You've paid in advance for your meals. It's no bother."

"I said I ain't hungry, ma'am."

"Fine," Pleasant said. "Then please leave."

Damn it to hell. Ramsey stood there watching her. He wanted to oblige her and leave, but he couldn't. He had to do something, even if it was wrong. He didn't want her mad at him. He crossed the kitchen and laid his hand on her shoulder. She stiffened.

"Mrs. Smith..." His voice caught in his throat. "I mean...ma'am..."

She turned, and before he knew how it happened he'd pulled her to him, put his arms around her and gave her a quick hug.

"I'm sorry," he said almost gruffly. He started to release her, but it'd been a damn long time since he'd held a pretty woman in his arms. She felt good. He just couldn't let go. He forgot himself.

Pleasant started to resist, but Ramsey held her tighter and she relaxed against him. Her arms slipped around his waist.

"I'm sorry," he repeated. "I'm real sorry."

"Oh, Mr. Judd," she whispered. "Do let me go."

Her head was against his shoulder and he kissed her sweet-smelling hair. The warm rise of her full bosom pressed against him. His body responded immediately.

What was a man to do? He lifted his hand to her chin and tilted her head back with a curled forefinger. Her eyes were round as saucers, green as emeralds, as he brushed a kiss across her forehead, then her cheek. Her lashes fluttered shut as he found her lips. Ramsey groaned and kissed her gently but firmly.

The kiss lasted only seconds. Her eyes were still closed as he stepped back and looked down at her. She was nothing like Hannah.

Hannah.

For a moment, he'd forgotten.

Ramsey released Pleasant, backed away from her. He had a daughter by Hannah, and he wanted to be part of the girl's life. He had a duty.

"Forgive me, Mrs. Smith. I had no right to do that."

Pleasant's hand fluttered to her throat, her eyes opened wide, lips parted. She didn't speak, just looked up at him.

He stood like a fool, staring at her, the room picture-still. No matter what he might say, it would only make it worse. It was already bad enough. He'd best go.

~~~

Pleasant watched the door close behind him. She wanted to call out to him to come back, but she was speechless. Not since Tom was alive had she ever felt so...sexual. So deliciously, wickedly, sexual. The experience made her feel swimmy headed and weak all over.

Ramsey Judd had kissed her.

She leaned against the work counter for support. A long deep sigh escaped from way down inside her. How many nights since he'd come to live in her house had she laid in bed and dreamed of just that...and more.

Oh merciful heaven, what kind of woman was she? Right now, she didn't know. She didn't even care. All that mattered was that she had very strong feelings for Mr. Judd. She hadn't had strong feelings like that for a man since... Well, since Tom died.

The memory of the kiss still moist on her lips caused another intake of breathless wonder. Could he possibly care for her too? Really care?

Tears weakened a man. Especially a man like Ramsey Judd. Was it, then, just a moment
~~~

of weakness?

Pleasant's heart sank. "Oh." She put her hand to her heated brow. What had she done? What a fool she'd made of herself, a mess she'd made of things. She'd practically leaped into his arms. Certainly, Ramsey Judd wouldn't be interested in someone like her. Ramsey Judd was a drifter. He was running.

From what? she wondered. The law?

Possibly. Maybe he was simply running from himself.

What caused the sadness in his eyes sometimes? A broken heart? Could it be a woman? Pleasant remembered the day of his heart attack. "Did she do it?" he'd asked. "I feel like I been hit with both barrels."

Did who do what? If there was a woman, where was she? Who was she?

What brought Ramsey – Mr. Judd – to Indian Bend? It was far off the beaten path. Was the woman here?

That must be. Pleasant felt terrible at the thought. She tried to remember every woman she knew that might fit her mind's description of the unknown love. Someone tall, slim as a willow, beautiful, dark hair.

Oh dear. It could be one of half a dozen. How silly she'd been. What a foolish dreamer.

No sense wanting what she couldn't have. The thought hurt her deeply.

Pleasant tucked the memory of the kiss away like violets pressed preciously between the pages of an old book. Nothing could come of it. She was being a ridiculous woman.

~~~

Ramsey hadn't planned to go see Hannah when he left Pleasant Smith's boarding house. Now it seemed the proper thing to do. He wanted to see his daughter.

The higher up the mountain he traveled, the cooler the air. He breathed deep. It felt good after his confinement. He stopped at the creek, drank his fill, allowed his horse to drink. Sitting under a tree, he leaned his back against the trunk and closed his eyes. He was tired. The doctor's words came back to him, "No unnecessary exertions." He'd rest a spell before going on.

Ramsey pulled the brim of his hat down low on his forehead, folded his arms across his chest, and squirmed until he was settled in comfortably. He could hear the horse chomping on grass nearby, the gurgling of the creek, the breeze through the trees. It was a good kind of quiet.

He knew what he'd have to do. The
~~~

thought had been mincing around in his mind since he left Hannah's ranch over a week ago. There was no other way around it. If she could come down off her damn high horse and...if she would have him.

A bee buzzed about his head. He raised his hand and brushed it away. He wished Hannah could be more like Pleasant. Pleasant's kiss was still vivid in his memory. The way she'd felt against him. The way she smelled. He'd grown real fond of that lady. A man could get the all-overs just looking at her.

What could he offer a woman like Pleasant, if he was free to offer anything, which he wasn't? What could he offer Hannah, for that matter, and what in the hell good did he think he could do for his daughter? All he had to show for fifty-two years of life was wrapped up in an old piece of paper and crammed in the toe of his boot. It was too late for him to amount to a hill of beans. But he had to try.

A noise from somewhere farther up the creek stopped his thoughts. It wasn't loud. In fact, he wasn't sure at first he'd heard anything. He listened. If it hadn't been so quiet where he was sitting, he would have missed it. The faint pinging of steel on rock. Ramsey came full awake. The horse was standing stock still, head lifted, nose pointing.

"You heard it too, Hoss?"

Hoss's ear turned toward him at the sound of his voice, but his attention fastened to the trail ahead. Ramsey straightened his hat and rose from his place under the tree. He walked to the horse, tightened the cinch and mounted.

"Let's go see."

The animal stamped nervously.

"Easy, boy. What's the matter?" Ramsey patted its neck. From his side vision, he caught a movement in the trees to his left. He swung his head just as a man on horseback came riding at them hard. Ramsey's horse squealed and reared.

"Whoa, Hoss! Whoa!" Ramsey pulled on the reins. The horse whirled, nearly throwing him off.

The other horse and rider swept past and galloped hell-bent down the trail. But not before Ramsey got a clear look at the man's face. He was big, with hooded eyes, a shaggy rust-colored mustache, and a deep scar across the bridge of his nose.

"What in the hell?" Ramsey kneed his horse gently and brought it around. "You okay, Hoss? That fellow was in a mighty big hurry. It looked like he was coming from the direction of that pounding. Let's get a closer look." Curiosity getting the better of him, he nudged the horse with his knees and they moved forward.

Ramsey came to the edge of a small clearing, in close to the rock wall of the mountain, and stopped. The creek ran to his right; a big red fir tree stood on his left. The hammering was coming from behind the tree.

He sat quiet and listened. Whatever it was had stopped. A figure stepped out from behind the tree, carrying a burlap bag in one hand and a shotgun in the other.

"Hannah?"

Hannah jumped and dropped the bag. A can she'd been holding in the same hand crashed to the ground. In the next instant, she had the gun leveled.

"Hannah!" Ramsey said. "Put that damnable gun down. I'm tired of looking down the barrels every time I get close to you."

"Stay where you are," she said. She was shaking all over and Ramsey could see the little hollow at the base of her throat pulsing.

"You missed your chance," he said. "You should have shot me when I told you to."

"The gun's loaded now," she replied.

This had to stop. She'd either shoot or she

wouldn't. He was just going to have to trust the odds. He slid down from his horse and closed the distance between himself and Hannah before she had time to think about what was happening. He grabbed the shotgun, twisted it out of her hands. "I said put it down, Hannah."

She lunged for it. He side-stepped. Hannah went sprawling onto the rocky ground. She laid there, the wind knocked out of her, gasping for breath.

Ramsey opened the gun and pocketed the shells, tossed the weapon away. It landed with a thunk a few yards from Hannah. He reached down and pulled her to her feet, held her away from him while she kicked and railed like a mad woman.

She was strong. It took all of Ramsey's strength to restrain her. Her body felt like steel under his fingers, muscled, work hardened.

Hannah's hat fell from her head. The hair that had been loosely pinned on top tumbled down around her shoulders, across her face. She looked half crazy, her eyes wild.

"Stop, Hannah. I'm tired of it. It's time you and me had a good talk."

She glared up at him through the curtain of hair. "Let me go, Parker O'Dell! I hate you!"

"There's a thin line between love and hate,

Hannah."

He pulled her roughly to a fallen log beside the creek and sat her down, hard, stepped back a couple of paces and stared at her.

"You aim that damn cannon at me again," he said through clenched teeth, "you better pull the trigger. Do you understand what I'm saying?"

Her only answer was a brief, angry, lifting of her lashes. Her eyes were glittering hard – icy cold. She flipped her hair away from her face with a quick toss of her head.

Ramsey hooked his thumbs in the waistband of his pants. He was afraid to touch her again. He had no experience with spitting-mad women. He was afraid he'd start beating her and never stop. "Now what's makin' you act so damn loco?" he said.

"Get the hell away from me, Parker. Get off my land." She closed her eyes and crossed her arms over her chest and breathed deep. "What do you want here, anyway?"

"My name's not Parker O'Dell," Ramsey said.

"Is it the gold?" Hannah asked. "The claim's petered out."

"What gold?"

"You know what gold. The gold behind the tree."

He glanced at the red fir and back at her.

"You been spying on me," she said.

"I haven't been spying on you."

"You burned my barn," she said.

"I what? Someone burned your barn? Hannah, I swear to God, it wasn't me."

Ramsey resisted the urge to recoil from the look of pure hatred on the woman's face, the fury that filled her eyes. He was scared of her, could feel his hands shaking. He wanted to walk away, leave her to herself, but he couldn't. He reached into his shirt pocket for his makings.

"That gal's my daughter, isn't she?" Ramsey tried to steady his hands as he rolled the cigarette and put the twisted end between his lips.

Hannah glared at him. "No. Her father's dead."

He struck the end of a wooden match with his thumbnail. It hissed as it burst into flame. "Quit your damn lying."

"You have no right to her, Parker. No right at all."

"I told you, my name's not Parker. I didn't know about her, Hannah."

"If you hadn't gone running off like the coward you are, you would have known."

He winced at the truth in her words. "Does she know?" he asked.

"No, she doesn't know. And she isn't going to know. If you've got it in your head to – "

"She's my daughter." Ramsey tried to control his voice. He hadn't come to fight with Hannah. He'd come to reason with her – help her if he could. Damn it to hell. "If you're having trouble – "

"I wasn't," she said. "Not 'til you showed up and burned my barn."

"I didn't burn your damn barn. Why in the hell would I want to burn your barn?" He tossed the cigarette to the ground, stamped it with the toe of his boot. Trying to talk to her in a civil manner was hopeless. What had he thought to gain by coming here anyway?

He stared at Hannah, studying her. She held the stare, glared back at him defiantly.

"Did Swede know?" Ramsey asked.

"Of course Swede knew." Hannah laughed. "Do you think I was going to let him have a say in her rearing?"

"What are we going to do about it, Hannah? About Sharon?"

"We're not going to do anything about it,"

she answered. "You're going to ride out of here and you're not going to come back. I'll shoot you before I'll let her find out, Parker."

"My name's Ramsey. Ramsey Judd."

She gave him a curious look, then her eyes hardened again. "I don't care who you are. It's too late. There's nothing she needs from you."

"We could – " Ramsey stopped and thought about what he was going to say. He didn't really want to say it now. He looked at her. He'd thought about her for all those years, but this wasn't what he remembered. He didn't know if he could do what he'd planned to do back on the trail.

He had to say it. He had to do the right thing, had to look in the mirror at himself in the mornings when he got up. And it was the only way he could be close to Sharon. His pa told him when he was still a fuzz-faced kid that if he ever got a girl in trouble, he should do right and marry up with her. That was the proper thing to do.

"We could..." he stammered, looked down at the toe of his boot, kicked at a pine cone, then raised his gaze once again to meet hers. "Ah hell, Hannah, we could get hitched. I could make it up to you."

A hush fell over the clearing. Hannah

stared at him, her mouth open, her eyes wide. He stared back.

Then she laughed, tipped her head back and held her stomach. It wasn't a nice laugh.

It stopped as suddenly as it began. She glared at him again, her face sober, her eyes hard. "I'd see you in Hell first," she said.

It was time for Ramsey to go. This was only making matters worse. "Okay, Hannah." He turned away. "Okay," he repeated. "But I want to know my daughter."

"There's not a chance," she replied.

"I'll be back." Ramsey strode off.

"Hey, you," she called after him. "Parker...or Ramsey...whoever you are. Why'd you lie about your name?"

He stopped, didn't turn. When he'd started up here this morning, he had every intention of telling her everything, hoping she'd understand. Now, it wasn't worth the effort. She wouldn't.

"Doesn't matter. It ain't important. I'll be seeing you, Hannah." He took a step.

"I thought you'd be dead by now," Hannah said. "I didn't cry thinking it. I hoped you were."

Ramsey pulled himself heavily into the saddle and reined his horse hard to the right.

Without looking back at the woman, he rode away.

Thank God, he thought to himself, as he put distance between them. Hannah didn't want to get married. He sure in the hell didn't want to spend the rest of his life with her.

~~~

Hannah was still in a fury when she reached the house. Her head hurt. Oh God, she hated that man! The nerve of him, thinking he could come back after all these years like nothing had happened. She had to get rid of him, whatever his name was – Parker O'Dell or Ramsey Judd. She threw her tools and her bag in a heap beside the sheep shed.

He was no good.

Even his name's a lie, Hannah.

Why? Why had Parker O'Dell...Ramsey Judd lied about his name? There must be a reason. She wanted to know what it was.

He's here to take Sharon away from you.

That wouldn't happen. She'd make sure of it. He was a threat, whoever he was. He could go straight to hell and she'd help him on his way, if she could.

You can, Hannah. You know you can.

It wouldn't be easy. Folks in Indian Bend were still wondering about Swede's death.
~~~

Even after all these years. Hannah could tell by the way they stared down their long noses at her when she went to town. The way they whispered behind their hands when she passed by.

That didn't matter either. Let them think what they would. They couldn't prove a thing. Nobody saw what happened. The hired hands had rode off that morning to help defend Slate Creek Stockade against the Indian uprising. No one was left on the ranch when the band passed through, except Swede and Sharon and Bull Brenner. And Sharon didn't see what happened.

The Nez Perce had no quarrel with Swede Larken. The only thing they'd done that morning was to leave enough tracks through the barnyard to prove they'd been there at all, and Hannah had used it to her full advantage.

A stiff smile tightened Hannah's lips. Swede was a fool. He'd questioned Pete Lacey's death. He actually accused Hannah. For two long years, Swede had held it over her head. She'd had her fill.

Pete Lacey was a rotting, stinking old man. He died of natural causes brought on by his stroke, as far as anybody was concerned. That's what the good Dr. Cobb had said. She was rid of them both – her father and Swede Larken – and glad of it.

Hannah, the voice whispered.

Yes, Hannah thought. She had to be rid of Ramsey Judd as well.

Hannah started for the house, then stopped and turned back toward the bunkhouse. Bull Brenner's horse was tied, saddle still in place, to the hitching rail in front. What was he up to? Why was he back at the ranch so early? The man irritated her. Right now, however, she was glad he was so handy. She hastened her step, knocked on the door.

"Bull, you decent?" Hannah called. She didn't wait for an answer and stepped inside.

Bull Brenner was sitting at the table, rolling a cigarette. He looked up briefly when she entered, then dropped his gaze back to his hands.

"Where have you been?" Hannah asked.

Bull grunted, lit his smoke, looked up at her from under heavy lids. He was an ugly man, dirty. The mustache below the scarred nose was stained and rusty looking, redder than the greasy brown hair that matted against his head, the indentation of where his hat had rested still clearly visible.

"High pasture," he answered.

That was a bald-faced lie. He hadn't been to the high pasture for over a week. Wiley Marker and Clive Henson were with the sheep. Hannah didn't confront him with the untruth. She stared at him, feeling a repulsion growing inside her. Bull Brenner was a cruel, ruthless man, without conscience. She would have fired him long ago, but he knew too much.

So be it, she thought. It was time he made himself useful. "I need your help," she said.

Bull looked at her now, a slow grin spreading across his face. "Pull up a seat, Mrs. Larken," he said, nodding toward the chair across from him.

Hannah didn't move. She'd never sit at table with this man, not for any reason. Never. "I have a...special job for you."

Bull scraped his chair away from the table, tipped it onto its back legs. "Will this special job bring me some...special considerations?"

She didn't like the look on his face, or the hidden meaning behind his words. Anger welled up inside her. She gripped the shotgun she still held in her hands, bit her tongue, kept her control. She glared at him for a moment before she spoke. "You'll be paid well enough."

"I'm interested, go on."

"The job must be done away from the

ranch. Away from Indian Bend," Hannah said. "I have a plan. If you agree to do the job, we'll talk about it."

"So just what is this job you want me to do?" Bull asked.

"I want you to kill the man called Ramsey Judd. The man who burned my barn."

Chapter Eight

It was well after dark when Ramsey returned to the boarding house in Indian Bend. He was bone tired, felt like an old rag wrung dry. Major Griswell's door was open when he walked down the hall. The old man looked up at him from a book he was trying to read through his half-blind eyes. Ramsey tipped his hat, walked on, hoped he could avoid a confrontation. He didn't feel like talking to the major tonight.

"Mr. Judd," the major called.

Ramsey stopped. Damn. He wasn't fast enough. "Yes, Major," he answered.

"Mr. Judd, I remember where I heard that name."

Ramsey turned and walked back to the old man's open door. He leaned against the jam, asked tiredly, "Where was that, Major?" He didn't much care right now.

"He was a special agent for the Union Army during the Civil War." The major eyed him. "Was that you, sir?"

Ramsey chuckled to himself. Not hardly, he thought. "No, Major. It wasn't me."

"You wouldn't be lyin' to me, would you, boy?"

"No, sir. You got the wrong man."

The major shook his head. "I'm not very often wrong about such things. That agent's name was Judd. Can't recall his first name right off, but it'll come to me."

"Good night, Major." Ramsey started back toward his own room. He'd decided some time back that there wasn't much to worry about regarding the major. He was just an old man living in the past, hanging on to his memories. Ramsey figured maybe he'd be just like him in a few years.

Ramsey was hungry. He'd missed lunch; supper was over. He couldn't go facing Pleasant now. He sure had a way with women.

Hannah was all horns and rattles. He couldn't blame her for being mad. But trying to talk to her, reason with her, was like barking at a knot or spitting into the wind – a waste of time. The best thing for him to do was pack his grip and git. His rent was coming due next week. He'd move along, maybe up to Oregon. There were a lot of horse ranches around Athena and Pendleton, some up near Enterprise and Joseph, too. He'd find work, hunker down for the winter.

There was still Sharon, though. He'd surely like to be a part of his daughter's life. She'd probably hate him, too, when...*if*...she found out.

Why in the hell when something good did come a man's way, it came too late?

Ramsey reached the door to his room, laid his hand on the knob and started to turn it.

"Mr. Judd, I was getting worried about you."

Ramsey turned. Pleasant stood in the stairway door. She was smiling. He was glad to see her. In fact, just having her standing there made him feel better all over.

"I'm sorry to worry you, ma'am. I had some business to take care of."

"You should take care of yourself. You look done in. Are you feeling well? Are you hungry?"

A grin spread across his face. A little of the heaviness around his heart lifted. "I'm tired,

Mrs. Smith. And I sure am hungry."

"Well, come downstairs. I saved you some fried chicken and fixings, and the greens are out of my own garden."

If that wasn't just like Pleasant. He grinned again, a little sheepish. "Do I have to eat in the dining room?"

She gave him a look over her shoulder as she descended the stairs. Everything was okay. He breathed a sigh of relief and followed her.

Ramsey sat and stretched his long legs out under the kitchen table. He was grateful. He watched her rounded behind bustling about the stove. It was a good feeling, her caring enough to wait up for him. She turned from the stove and his stomach did a little skip-and-swing dance at the radiant smile on her lips. There was a sparkle in her eyes and pink heat-spots on her cheeks. He liked looking at her.

"I have apple pie for dessert," she said.

"Now how did I know that?"

She kept up her bright chatter as he ate his meal. He'd upset her, but she'd gotten over it. That was a good quality in a woman. All the troubles of the day seemed to fade away. He relaxed, smiled up at her and accepted the cup of tea she poured him.

"Did you see my white lilacs in bloom? I

sent away for them last summer...and the petunias are so pretty and..."

As he finished his pie, Ramsey promised himself to take a long look at the yard she spent so much time in. "That was good, Mrs. Smith. I'm obliged."

"It was no trouble to save a plate."

He pushed his chair back from the table. "It's late. I've kept you up long enough."

Their eyes met, and he didn't miss the glint of disappointment in hers. She wanted him to stay. He thought about it briefly, but knew he couldn't.

The look disappeared and she smiled. "I'll see you at breakfast, Mr. Judd."

As Ramsey took the stairs to the second floor, he couldn't help wondering what it would be like to stay here with Pleasant Smith. Settle down. Belong. The thought brought the corners of his mouth up.

Then reality set in again. That was impossible. He could never stay in Indian Bend. Not with Hannah and Sharon so close. It just wouldn't do. He'd almost made up his mind not to bother Hannah anymore.

He entered his darkened room, fumbled with matches and lit the lamp. Major Griswell was sitting in the chair, looking at him.

"The door wasn't locked," he said. "I couldn't sleep. Figured I'd wait for you."

Ramsey was irritated. The old man was beginning to be a damn nuisance. "What do you want?" he asked.

"Well, sir," the major said, squinting up at Ramsey, "I thought about it long and hard. It drives me plum crazy when I can't remember somethin'..."

"And?" Ramsey sat on the edge of his bed and folded his arms across his chest. He wasn't going to get any sleep until he heard the old man out.

"Once I start rememberin'," Major Griswell said, "It all comes back. Like it happened yesterday." He paused, studied Ramsey.

"Go on," Ramsey said.

"That Union soldier...his first name was Jarred."

Ramsey felt like he'd been kicked in the stomach. He stared at the old man, unable to breathe. What kind of a bad joke was this? "Jarred?" he whispered. "He was a Reb."

"He was a secret agent for the North. Died down around Raymond, near Fourteen Mile Creek. Shot by a Union soldier."

That couldn't be, Ramsey thought. Jarred was wearing gray. A sick feeling formed in the pit of his stomach. He fought to keep his supper down. "You knew him?"

"Met him once," the major answered. "News that the Rebs had retreated to the rail center in Jackson and were receiving reinforcements needed to reach Grant before he and his troops got there. The only way to get the information to him was by special messenger. Someone who could sneak through enemy lines and deliver the papers to Grant personally. We knew Grant should be somewhere around Raymond. Judd was close by, holed up in the Rebs' camp. We got word to Judd..."

Ramsey listened to the old man's story. When he'd finished, the room was as still as a tomb. Ramsey shook inside; beads of sweat formed on his upper lip and brow. He swallowed hard, wiped his hand down his face, looked at the major. "You dead sure about this?" he asked in a quiet voice.

"Sure as I'm sittin' here," the major replied. "When they found him, the boy who shot him was guardin' his body. Course he'd mistook him for a Reb soldier, done up in that gray uniform and all."

"Johnny Bowler," Ramsey whispered.

Major Griswell leaned forward, looked

Ramsey in the eye. "The boy said Judd's brother had been there, shot a Reb soldier before the Reb shot the boy. Then he skedaddled out of there. The brother was never seen again."

Ramsey breathed a long sigh. That explained everything. He leaned his elbows on his knees and rested his forehead in his hands. Tears stung his eyes. He wondered if his pa ever found out.

"I'm thinking," the major said, "you're that soldier's brother."

Ramsey looked up at the old man. "Did the papers get through?"

"They were found on Judd's body," the major said. "A messenger got them to the general in the nick of time."

"Watching my only brother die that day took all the fight out of me, Major," Ramsey said. "I couldn't take anymore killing."

Major Griswell kept silent, just looked at Ramsey.

"All these years," Ramsey continued. "I thought Jarred was a turncoat."

"I was afraid that might be the case," the major said.

"And now that you know who I am, what are you going to do about it?"

"Ain't gonna do nothin'," the major answered, a toothless grin spreading across his face. "Figure it was a long time ago. I'd a done the same thing, I reckon."

Ramsey stood, held out his hand to the old man. The major hefted himself out of the chair and took it.

"Thanks," Ramsey said. "I appreciate you telling me."

~~~

In the two-room cabin behind the bunkhouse, Sharon removed her shoes and stretched out on the quilt covering the bed. She watched as dusk slipped dappled light through the lace curtains that hung at the window. Grandpa and Grandma Lacey lived here when they first came to Idaho, before the new house was built. Mama and Papa lived here after they were married, before Grandpa Lacey got so sick. Then it became hers to use whenever she wanted. She had hoped someday maybe she and Joe could live here.

Now she doubted that would happen. Mama would never give her blessing. But whether Mama gave her blessing or not, whether they lived here in the cabin or not, it didn't matter. She and Joe would be married. Mama wouldn't be able to stop that.
~~~

Sharon heard a noise outside, at the front of the house. She rolled her head toward the curtain at the bedroom doorway, held her breath and listened. Probably her mother coming to try to make her return to the house. Mama got lonely without her close by.

It was almost dark. She should have lit the lamp. She heard the front door open in the other room. It *was* Mama. She'd pretend she was asleep. Surely Mama wouldn't wake her.

What if it was Joe? Her pulse quickened. Maybe he'd come to take her away. She'd only seen him once since Mama made him go. He said he'd come back for her when he could.

No. Joe wouldn't come to the front door. He'd go to the back and knock at the window. It wasn't dark enough yet. It had to be Mama. Sharon closed her eyes as someone slipped quietly into the bedroom.

What was that wretched odor?

Sharon's eyes snapped opened. A hooded figure standing over her bed pushed a white handkerchief across her mouth and nose, stifling her scream. She struggled against the pressure of his gloved hand, but another hooded man held her feet. The suffocating smell overwhelmed her. Her eyelids closed against her will.

~~~

Hannah brushed a lock of hair back away from her face, stretched the freshly washed sheet across the line and secured it with wooden pins. She'd expected Sharon to be up by now. It was nearing nine o'clock.

Hannah turned to the basket for another sheet, paused and glanced at the cabin. She wondered how long this was going to last. They'd been getting along well since the day Ramsey Judd came to the house, but Sharon still hadn't agreed to move back where she belonged.

Leaving the basket, Hannah walked to the cabin and opened the door. Everything was quiet. "Sharon? Time to get up."

No answer.

"Sharon, you in here?"

Maybe she was sick. Hannah crossed the main room and parted the curtain at the bedroom doorway.

"Sharon?"

The bed was empty. The blankets were mussed, but it hadn't been slept in. Where could she be? Hannah sat on the edge of the bed and saw the folded paper laying on top of the pillow. A funny feeling unfolded in her stomach as she picked it up and read the words
~~~

written on it.

She crumpled the note into a wad, stuck it into her pocket and stood. It had started sooner than she'd expected. Good. She left the cabin, walked past the laundry basket under the line, hurried to the house. She opened the wooden box she had retrieved from the barn the night of the fire, lifted back the lid and gazed at the contents. Her life's savings, along with her father's life savings, and the savings Swede's father left to him.

She'd spend it all if she had to. Every last penny. Hannah counted out a sufficient amount of cash, closed the lid. She went to the kitchen and made herself a pot of tea, sat at the table and smoothed the piece of crumpled paper out before her.

Soon. Very soon. She would have her revenge on Ramsey Judd, and she'd have Sharon back. A smile tugged at the corner of her mouth. He would pay. Oh yes, he was going to pay dearly.

~~~

It was late afternoon when Pleasant, kneeling in her garden behind the white picket fence, saw Hannah Larken dismount. She rose, removed her gloves, touched the pretty white bonnet she wore and walked to meet her.
~~~

"Good day, Mrs. Larken." She smiled, but the smile was forced. Pleasant didn't like Hannah Larken.

"Mrs. Smith."

Pleasant could tell the stiff smile on the other woman's lips was forced too. It never quite reached her ice blue eyes. "Is there something I can do for you?"

"I hear Ramsey Judd is boarded here. Could you please direct me to his room?"

Oh! The truth hit Pleasant with a jolt. This was the woman in Ramsey Judd's life. How she knew, she couldn't say, but she did know. "No women allowed in the rooms, Mrs. Larken. I can tell Rams...Mr. Judd you're here. You can visit in the parlor."

"What I have to say is private. I'd rather speak to him in his room, if you don't mind."

Pleasant minded very much. She didn't want this woman alone with Ramsey.

"I assure you Mrs. Smith, my intentions are most honorable. I only wish to offer him a few days work."

Pleasant bit her bottom lip. She couldn't be wrong. Hannah Larken had to be the woman. She eyed her suspiciously, then forced another smile. "Up the stairs in the back," she said, "the last door to the left."

"Thank you, Mrs. Smith. I'll leave the room's door open if it would make you feel easier." A taunting smile played on Hannah Larken's mouth.

Pleasant felt the anger boil up inside her. Such a hateful woman, she thought. But she wouldn't be bested by her. Not entirely. "Please do, Mrs. Larken."

She watched the tall, slender woman round the corner of the house, then gathered her garden tools, put them in a watering can on the back porch, and entered the kitchen. Pleasant silently ascended the stairs to the second floor, opened the door a crack and pressed her ear to it.

~~~

The doughy bitch.

Hannah climbed the steps at the rear of the rooming house.

Watch out for her, Hannah.

She doesn't scare me, Hannah thought. Her heart thumped in rhythm with her boot heels as she walked down the hall and rapped on the last door on the left.

She's in love with Ramsey Judd, Hannah.

That was no concern of Hannah's.

She waited a few moments and then knocked again. She heard movement on the
~~~

other side of the door, felt a moment of breathless panic when she heard heavy footsteps cross the room beyond, saw the doorknob turn. She had to stay calm.

The door opened and Hannah was staring into the shocked, dark eyes of Ramsey Judd.

"Hannah!"

"Hello, Ramsey."

"Hannah, what are you doing here?"

"Can I come in?" She looked past his fuzzed, shirtless chest, his muscled arms, past the flat belly and trail of dark hair rising up from the opened waistband of his pants. Her stomach jerked.

He hesitated a moment, then swung the door wide to let her through. She strode by him with an air of self confidence she didn't quite feel. "Leave the door open," she said. "House rules." She turned to face him.

Ramsey was slipping into a worn shirt, buttoned it, tucked it into his faded Levis. He had a bewildered look on his face.

She took a deep breath, attempting to still the trembling that had started inside her. His nakedness unsettled her. She was a woman, after all. Twisting the gloves she'd removed on her way up the stairs, she cleared her throat. "I need your help."

He raised an eyebrow in what she knew was disbelief; a smile pulled at the corner of his mouth.

The stupid fool thinks you're giving in, Hannah.

He motioned to the overstuffed chair with a nod. "Sit down. Should I have Mrs. Smith bring tea?"

"No, thank you, I'll stand." Her gaze didn't leave his.

"You need my help?"

"Sharon's gone."

"Sharon?"

"Our daughter. She's been kidnapped," Hannah said in a controlled voice.

Ramsey stared at her. It took several seconds for her words to sink in, for realization to register on his face. He scraped his fingers through his hair. "Who in the hell would want to kidnap Sharon? Why?"

Silently, Hannah handed him the note. Ramsey read it.

He lowered himself slowly onto the edge of the bed. He reread the note, glanced up at Hannah. "Walla Walla, Washington?"

Hannah watched him, heard the blood pounding inside her head. He was looking at the note again.

"That's a lot of money," he was saying. "Surely you don't have that much money. Where would you get – "

"I have the money," she interrupted. "And the kidnappers must know it. We can ride to Lewiston and take the train to Walla Walla."

Ramsey let out a long breath. He was shaking his head. "We can't be sure they'll give Sharon back." He laid the note on the bed and gazed up at her. "Have you notified the authorities?"

Careful, Hannah.

"You read the note," she said curtly. "If I do that, they'll kill her. I have to do what they say." She tried to stay calm. Why was he hedging? The instructions were plain enough. She twisted the pair of gloves she was holding in her hands. "Help me find her, Ramsey, please."

"How did they get her?" he asked.

"Her bed was mussed, but not slept in. I assume they took her while she was resting."

"They took her out of her bedroom? Didn't you hear anything?"

Hannah's head throbbed. Her side vision was becoming blurred, the darkness closing in. She squinted.

Hannah –

Not now. Hannah forced the voice out of

her head. She had to think clearly, finish this discussion, get out of here. She couldn't breath.

"She stays in the cabin," Hannah said. "She has for a couple of weeks. We quarreled."

Cry, Hannah.

No.

Cry, Hannah.

"Why would they take her to Walla Walla?"

Hannah dropped her gaze to his bare feet, held her eyes open without blinking, keeping them that way until they began to sting. She covered her mouth with her fingers. Her chin quivered. She blinked up at Ramsey through a shimmering veil of forced tears.

Instantly, he was beside her, his arm around her shoulders. "Don't cry, Hannah."

It took all her effort, but she didn't resist him, leaned against him as he led her to the chair, eased her into it.

"Please, Ramsey, you must help me." Her voice wavered. Her words ended in a little choke. She clasped her hands in her lap and looked up at him.

"That's over two-hundred miles – "

"More like three," she said.

Ramsey returned to the edge of the bed, sat, knees apart, hands dangling between them. "Why in the hell clear to Walla Walla? It would be easier..." His voice drifted away. The room fell quiet.

Hannah held her breath, waited for him to speak. Her eyes were still tearing, and she made a sobbing sound.

Ramsey studied his hands. "There's a lot of country out there." His voice was low, more like he was talking to himself than her. He looked up. "I just don't get it."

Silence lengthened between them, Ramsey's eyes holding hers, searching her face. Hannah was afraid. What if he didn't believe her?

"Don't worry, Hannah. We'll get her back."

She breathed a deep sigh of relief that ended in a hiccup. "If anything were to happen to Sharon, I'd die."

"I have some loose ends to tie up." Ramsey rubbed the back of his neck with his fingers.

Hannah stood. "So do I. I have to let the hands know I'll be gone for a while."

"Do you need help?" Ramsey asked, rising from the bed.

"I can manage."

"It'll be dark in a few hours." He laid his hand on her shoulder and she stiffened under the touch. "We could leave first thing in the morning."

"Meet me at the ranch." She shrugged out from under his grasp and walked to the door.

"I'll be there at first light." Ramsey stepped out into the hall with her.

She smiled a tight smile.

"In the morning then," he said.

"In the morning."

~~~

Pleasant pulled back from her place at the stair door and eased down the steps to her kitchen. She slipped onto a wooden chair and laid her hands flat on the top of the table.

Sharon Larken? Ramsey's daughter? Pleasant felt almost faint. She didn't trust Hannah Larken. Sharon couldn't be Ramsey's daughter. She just couldn't be.

But she was. Pleasant knew the truth. The dark eyes, like Ramsey's. The hair. Oh my God! Did Ramsey love Hannah? He fathered a daughter with her. He must. That was twenty years ago – at least. Why had he left? If he really loved her...

She didn't want to lose Ramsey Judd. Not now.

But how could she lose him? She never had him. She was a stupid woman to think that one kiss, in a moment of weakness...

Did Hannah care for him? Did she want
~~~

him? After all these years?

Pleasant was being ridiculous. Selfish. The girl was missing. Kidnapped. Of course Ramsey and Hannah would be drawn together in such a crisis.

But still... Pleasant couldn't explain why she felt the way she did. There was something amiss. The woman was up to no good.

"Oh, Ramsey," she whispered. "My dear Ramsey."

~~~

Ramsey leaned his arms on the rail of the landing and watched Hannah disappear around the side of Pleasant's boarding house. She was desperate, he could tell. Worried sick. So was he. He was scared to death. What if they hurt Sharon? What if she was already laying dead somewhere?

An overwhelming feeling washed through him, consumed him. Something stronger than anything he had ever felt in his life. His daughter. Someone had kidnapped his daughter.

Damn it to hell! He'd get her back and he'd make the sorry bastard, or bastards, who took her pay for it. If one hair on her head was hurt, he'd kill them with his bare hands.

Ramsey pushed back from the railing and
~~~

walked down the hall. He felt older than he had a half hour ago. In his room, he put his hand inside his boot and took the wad of paper out of the toe and unwrapped the double eagle. He spread the paper on the bed and smoothed it with his fingers. It was barely readable after all these years. He looked at the picture that was suppose to be him. Could have been anybody in a Union hat, Ramsey decided. He read the words under the drawing.

$1000.00 REWARD
WANTED DEAD OR ALIVE
RAMSEY JUDD
For desertion from the United States Army and
stealing an officer's horse.

The date was worn away. On the other side of the poster, in a scrawly hand:

Friend,

If you're reading this letter it means I'm dead and you want my boots. Go ahead, you can have them, and the reward, too. But please, take this double eagle and see I'm laid out proper.

Signed,

Ramsey Judd.

He wadded the paper and threw it across the room, picked up the coin and weighed it in the palm of his hand. He had rent to pay, and a bottle of whiskey and tobacco to buy. Some provisions for the trail. There wouldn't be anything left for a coffin.

~~~

Ramsey couldn't sleep. He fumbled for the box of wooden matches on the stand beside him, lit one and touched it to the wick of the lantern, rose and pulled on his pants. He crossed the room to the bottle and glass on the dresser, poured himself a good measure of the amber liquid and walked to the window. He lifted the curtains and gazed out onto the moonlit yard below while he sipped at the whiskey.

Why Walla Walla? he wondered. Of all the places to take Sharon. It didn't make sense.

He dropped the curtain and lowered himself into the chair and leaned his head against the back. Something was purely wrong with this whole damn picture.

Could be, he reasoned, Walla Walla was just a diversion, to keep them moving. He had a strong hunch if they stayed to the main road, they'd meet up with the kidnappers long before they got to Walla Walla. In fact, he'd lay odds they'd be contacted before they reached Lewiston.
~~~

He heard the lightest footfall outside his door and then a gentle rap. Who in the hell could that be at this hour?

He padded across the floor on bare feet and jerked the door open.

Oh sweet Jesus!

Ramsey stared at Pleasant Smith. Her shiny yellow hair hung loose about her cheeks, spread out over her shoulders and down her back in shimmering waves of spun gold. The cottony whiteness of her high-necked nightgown spilled in graceful folds over a large bosom that stood up amazingly high without restraint. Ramsey knew she wore none, for he could see the points of her nipples pressing at the fine fabric as it draped over her, from her neck to the roundness of her hips, to the toes of her bare feet.

"I heard you pacing, Mr. Judd." One of Pleasant's hands fluttered nervously at her breast and the other held a heavy white mug. "I thought a nice cup of warm milk and honey might help you sleep."

Aw Christ! Milk and honey. How could a man think of such a thing at a time like this?

Her eyes were soft, with a hint of fear. Her cheeks glowed like rose petals. She was so damn pretty.

She nibbled at her bottom lip, her chin trembled. Ramsey knew what it had taken for her to come here, and he knew why she had come. For a moment he was sorely tempted to pull her inside the room, close the door and forget the rest of the world.

He forced a smile and reached for the cup. "Thank you, Mrs. Smith." His voice was husky and low. He set the cup on the stand behind him, took her tiny hands fringed at the wrists in white lace and pulled her closer to him, bent forward and brushed a kiss across her cheek, then her nose, and then her full lips.

Oh the softness of her, the sweetness of her. He held heaven in his own arms and he didn't want to let it go.

He stepped back and gazed into her eyes, shook his head. "Mrs. Smith, it's not because I don't want you. I do. But it just wouldn't be right. I have some business to tend to. I'll be leaving for a while in the morning."

A small smile trembled on her lips. "Yes, I know. I was eavesdropping, I'm afraid. Shameless of me."

"You know then?"

"You're coming back, aren't you, Mr. Judd?"

"I'll be back, Mrs. Smith."

"Please be careful. That woman..." Pleasant

bit her lip. "You aren't well yet."

"I'll be fine. Don't worry."

"I..."

Ramsey reached out and touched her face, brushed a strand of hair from her cheek.

"I care deeply for you...Mr. Judd," she whispered.

"I promise," he said. "I'll be back."

"Good night then."

His throat squeezed. He had to let her go. He wanted her to stay. "Good night," he said.

Ramsey closed the door and leaned his forehead against it. The promise he'd just made pressed heavily on his heart. It was one promise he hoped to hell he'd be able to keep.

Chapter Nine

Dawn was breaking as Ramsey and Hannah rode down the mountain trail toward the river. Hannah rode in front on her black mare, a fat pair of saddlebags tied securely behind her. Ramsey followed on the chestnut, leading a dun-colored packhorse loaded with their provisions. The early morning chitter of birds, the breeze in the trees, the clinking of bridles and creaking of leather filled the chilled air. The clear sky promised a warm day ahead.

Ramsey's mind was on a hundred different things, but could focus on not one completely. Daydreams, old memories and old regrets, the letter he'd left on his dresser along with the rent money. He hoped Pleasant would find it and mail it for him. He hadn't the courage to do it himself.

The trail widened and he pulled abreast of Hannah. She rode ramrod-straight next to him, her eyes ahead, the old hat pulled down low on her brow, a determined set to her face; a tight little muscle twitched in her jaw. Her lips moved slightly, like she was talking to herself, and he wondered what was on her mind.

"Hannah?"

She didn't answer, but he knew she'd heard him by the way her lips tightened into a narrow cut. He tried to think of something to say; he'd only spoken her name to rid himself of his own thoughts.

"Hannah."

"We should be in Grangeville by two o'clock," she said.

"I aim to do some checking when we get there."

"What kind of checking you going to do?"

"I still don't think they'd haul her off to Walla Walla."

There was an impatient edge to Hannah's voice when she answered. "While you're messing around doing your own thinking, they'll be gaining distance. There's a chance we could catch them if we keep moving."

"Just the same, I want to look around."

They crossed the bridge over the Salmon

River and followed the road toward Indian Bend. Ramsey took a wooden match from his shirt pocket, stuck it between his teeth and chewed on the end.

"I was surprised to hear you married the Swede," he said, for lack of anything else to say, "but he always was sweet on you."

Hannah didn't say a word.

"If I'd known about the girl – "

Her head snapped around. "What, Ramsey? If you'd known about the girl, what?"

He sucked on the match for a moment. "I'm just so damn sorry, Hannah."

"Sorry don't help." She shifted her eyes back to the trail ahead.

"A lot was going on back then," he said. "Things I couldn't change. I'd made a bad mistake, and – "

"I don't want to hear it. I'd rather forget it."

"Let bygones be bygones?" he asked.

"I didn't say that. Bygones be damned."

"I just wanted you to know."

"Shut up."

"Hannah, I'd like to make it up to you."

She pulled her horse to a stop, looked at him with a mixture of rage, hurt, and pure hate on her face. She leaned forward slightly and stared straight in his eyes. There was venom in her voice when she spoke. "I didn't ask your help to rekindle old feelings, Ramsey Judd. There's only one reason I brought you along. I want my daughter back. I'd have called on Satan himself to do that, and when it's done, you can go straight to hell. Now you don't lose sight of that and we'll get done what has to be done. But don't be trying to settle old scores, do you hear?"

"Christ, you're a hard woman."

"Don't forget it. I'd as soon shoot you as look at you. And there's a chance I might before this trip is over."

She whirled her horse away, kicked it in the flanks, and shot forewarn, leaving him staring after her. The wind blew her hat from her head. The chin-cord snapped against her throat. The pins came out of her hair and it blew free as she put distance between them.

Ramsey decided there was a little bit of bitch in Hannah. She reined her horse to a stop and it reared and pawed the air before settling onto all fours. She sat watching him watch her from where she had left him.

"Are you coming?" she called. Her words were nearly lost in the roar of the river flowing beside them, like the fury storming inside the woman. Neither could be controlled, Ramsey thought. No sense in trying. He kneed his horse and reined in silently behind her. They made their way along the rocky bank, and Ramsey wondered if he hadn't jumped right in the middle of hell, coming on this trip.

As they passed down the main street of Indian Bend, Ramsey glanced at Pleasant's rooming house out of the corner of his eye. He was sure he could see her standing at her kitchen window. He didn't tip his hat or wave, though he wanted to. He remembered the night before, her standing there in all her sweetness, and he wished things could be different.

They left the town and proceeded up the narrow, winding, seven-mile grade that lead from the river to the prairie above.

~~~

Pleasant stepped back from the window where she had watched Ramsey and Hannah pass by. Little tingles of fear prickled up her spine. Why did she feel such a sense of danger? Maybe because of the recent heart attack? Certainly a man shouldn't go riding out for God-knows-where right after a heart attack.

But it was more than his health. Something deeper. She felt like if he went with Hannah, she'd never see him again. She didn't know
~~~

Hannah Larken well. Nobody did. The woman lived up there on top of her mountain and rarely came to town, but there was something evil about her. And there were stories about her, too.

Oh for heaven's sake, Pleasant thought. She was being ridiculous. She simply didn't want Ramsey to leave. She was letting her overactive imagination run away with itself.

She tried to push down the fears inside her, lifted the watch suspended from a chain around her neck and looked at the time. Breakfast wasn't for another hour and a half. She took the large key ring from its hook beside the stair door, ascended the stairs and let herself into Ramsey's room. The scent of the man rose to greet her. A worn blue shirt hung on the bed post. Pleasant lifted it almost reverently and put it to her face, breathed him deeply into her nostrils.

A lump formed in her throat and pressure pushed at the back of her eyes. She sat on the edge of the bed, the springs creaking under her weight. A great sense of loss and loneliness swept over her. Would he really come back? Would she ever see him again?

She gave a ragged sigh and rose, pulled the bed covers up and smoothed them, then went to the window and opened it to let air in. That's when she saw the long white envelope lying on the dresser, next to the little stack of currency on top of a note that said *rent*.

There was enough money for a whole month. He was coming back! Beside herself with happiness, Pleasant crushed the envelope to her breast.

"Oh, thank you, Lord!" she said out loud. "Oh, thank you, thank you!"

And he'd written her a letter! She looked at the envelope and started to tear it open, then noticed it wasn't to her at all. Her heart fell.

Elizabeth Judd – Cincinnati, Ohio.

Strange, she thought. Who could Elizabeth Judd be? She'd never heard Ramsey speak of her.

A wife, perhaps?

No, that wasn't likely. If Ramsey had a wife, he wouldn't be here chasing after Hannah Larken and his long lost daughter. It had to be a sister, or his mother. But the letter was more evidence that he really did plan on returning. After all, why else would he have put Indian Bend for a return address?

There was a bounce in her step as she finished tidying the room, emptying his ashtray, dusting the furniture. She picked up a small wad of paper laying on the floor beside the dresser and slipped it into her apron pocket to dispose of later.

When she'd finished, she closed the door behind her and hurried down the stairs with the letter in her hand. She worried over it, but she would post it for him, for it must be important or he wouldn't have written it. Ramsey didn't strike her as the writing kind. Perhaps she was opening another passel of trouble. Oh well. She would deal with it when the time came.

Downstairs, she took the wad of paper from her pocket and started to throw it into the cook stove. She stopped, lowered the stove lid, spread the crumpled paper onto the table and read what it said, then turned it over.

Her pulse quickened. "Oh my word!" Ramsey Judd was a wanted man. She bit her bottom lip. Dear Lord in heaven. Desertion? Surely not! Ramsey was no coward.

Pleasant smoothed the poster with trembling fingers, reread it. Why, that picture didn't even look like him.

The paper was old. He was younger. It could be him.

She plunked down in the chair next to her. No. There must be some mistake. Not her

Ramsey. Not the man she loved. She was a better judge of character than that.

Or she was a fool.

She leaned her elbow on the tabletop, rested her chin in her hand and chewed the tip of her little finger. There must have been a reason. A very good reason.

"Surely...after all these years..."

A man could do a lot of changing in that length of time.

Pleasant looked at the paper before her again, closed her eyes and shook her head, breathed a deep sigh. She wanted to believe in him. She reached out and grabbed the paper and wadded it. Maybe she was a fool, but she was going to believe in him anyway. At least until he could explain himself.

When he comes home.

A terrible feeling rolled in the pit of Pleasant's stomach. If he *could* come home. Did Hannah Larken know? If she did, a thousand dollars was a lot of money.

Something had to be done. But what?

This could all be a trick. Sharon could be safe and sound at Hannah's ranch, and Ramsey Judd was out on some wild goose chase. Hannah could kill Ramsey and collect the reward. The poster did say *dead or alive.*

Pleasant considered going to the sheriff. But what evidence did she have of any bad intentions on Hannah's part? Only her woman's intuition, and sometimes even she doubted that. And besides, if she told the sheriff that Ramsey Judd was an...outlaw, he would surely take him away and put him in jail. Pleasant couldn't bare that thought.

There had to be a way. She couldn't just sit by idly and let the man she –

And then it struck her. There *was* something she could do!

Pleasant ran to her bedroom and grabbed her bonnet, ran back to the kitchen, picked up the letter and hurried from the house, a plan developing in her mind. A plan so completely unbelievable and so completely out of her character, her heart pounded loudly in her ears just thinking about it.

She had to do it. There was no other way. She had to save Ramsey Judd.

A few minutes later, Pleasant turned and started up the path to Olive Jensen's house. Her old friend had helped her out on several occasions, when she'd been called away on business.

She was breathless by the time she reached the door and knocked. She pulled air into her lungs and let it out slowly. The door swung open and she gazed into the surprised, bony face of her best friend.

"For land's sake, Pleasant. What are you doing out so early?" Olive swung the door wide. "Come in, come in. I'll make tea."

Pleasant stepped in, put her hand on her chest in an effort to slow her pounding heart. "Olive, I have no time for tea. I need you to take care of the boarding house for a spell. I'm being called away on the most urgent business."

~~~

The sun was up full now. It beat down on Hannah's back, and she and Ramsey slowed their horses. They stopped under a lone, scrubby pine halfway up the steep grade, where a spring trickled out of the side of the already sun-parched hillside.

They dismounted and splashed their faces, drank their fill and allowed their horses to refresh themselves from the little pool that formed beneath the cold, flowing stream of water.

"What's she like, Hannah?" Ramsey asked, wiping his wet hands over his face.

Hannah glanced at him from where she was sitting, twisting her long, loose hair into a thick braid and tying it with a scrap of
~~~

rawhide. The wistful quality of his expression gave her pleasure, and she thought of not answering. But the feeling passed. She had to indulge him a little, keep him going. It was the only way her plan could succeed. For a brief moment, second thoughts ambushed her. Would she be able to pull it off?

She had to, if she was to know any peace. It gave her some comfort knowing that Sharon was probably safe at home by this time. That had been the plan. Bull would take the girl back to the ranch as soon as Hannah and Ramsey left.

Where was Bull Brenner now? When would it happen? Would he fulfill his part? It made her uncomfortable knowing that she'd already paid him half of their agreed price. It was a sizable amount – enough to cause a man to ride away without having to work for it. The other half of his payment was tucked safely into her saddlebags. The ransom money, as far as Ramsey knew.

He'd better be where he was suppose to be, when he was suppose to be there, or she'd find him and roast him alive. But in her heart, she knew he would. This was one job that would be too much fun for Bull Brenner to miss.

She felt the smile pull stiffly at her mouth.

"She's a good girl, obedient and gentle. I don't understand why..."

"You don't understand what?"

Hannah shook her head to bring her mind back on track. She'd started to wonder why Sharon had been acting the way she had of late. The girl had been almost rebellious and a bit sneaky. That wasn't like her.

"Nothing," she answered. "I don't understand why anyone would want to hurt her."

Ramsey plucked a blade of dried grass from beside him, chewed the end and looked out over the valley at the town they had left below. "Money," he said. "That's what makes some men the way they are."

"What makes you the way you are, Ramsey?"

He didn't answer, continued to stare off into the distance, the lines of his face rigid, his eyes almost black in the shadow beneath the brim of his hat. What was he thinking about? Hannah wondered. Was he suspicious? Did he really believe her?

Or was he thinking of the landlady? She hadn't missed the look on Pleasant Smith's face yesterday at the boarding house, or the meaning behind it. Did Ramsey share those feelings? Something short of jealousy rippled through Hannah.

It didn't matter. Ramsey would never see Indian Bend again after today – or Pleasant Smith, either. That thought pleased Hannah.

But she resented Ramsey's private thoughts just the same. He had no right to them. She needed to bring him back to her, glanced at him and asked, "What do you care about Sharon, anyway?"

"She's my daughter too," he answered quietly.

"Fine time for you to feel so...responsible."

"If I'd have known before – "

"How was I suppose to tell you? I could have put an ad in the paper, Ramsey Judd, or perhaps, Parker O'Dell, come home, you have a bouncing baby girl."

"It wouldn't have done no good. I don't read the papers much." He tossed the grass away. "I could still make it up to you, a little, if you'd let me."

Hannah bit her tongue. "If we want to make Grangeville before midnight, we'd better get going."

"I aim to be part of her life, Hannah."

"We'll see about that." Her words were barbed, her temper on the verge of erupting.

She rose abruptly and brushed the dust off her brown split skirt, tightened the cinch, and hefted herself into the saddle. Not waiting for the man, she started up the grade at a brisk pace.

~~~

Ramsey rode hard to catch up with her.

The breeze was blowing on the prairie, the air cooler. Farm houses dotting the landscape looked farther away than they really were because of the vastness of the country. Horses and cattle grazed on the deep meadow grass behind barbed wire fences. From where they rode, not a tree was in sight, just little rolling hills and open space, blue blossoms of camas, and the deep pinks and purples of cranesbill and fireweed.

A hawk soared overhead, riding the wind, its wings stretched out, gliding and swooping. It screeched and dove behind a hill and out of their sight. Then all was quiet, except for the plodding of the horses' hooves.

Ramsey watched the figure on the horse in front of him. She rode with a firm, sure seat, as sure and straight as any man. He had to admire her. She was a brave woman, toughened by circumstances and what life had dealt out to her. It couldn't have been easy for her, losing
~~~

her father and husband, raising a daughter by herself.

He had quit thinking of a future for himself and her, but she was the mother of his daughter. He'd done his part in making Hannah the way she was. For that he was sorry. He couldn't change things. "She's a pretty gal," he said, breaking the silence that had stretched out between them. "Like her ma." He couldn't see Hannah's face, only the stiffening of her back at his words. "Does she have suitors?"

Hannah didn't answer.

"There must be a whole stream of young bucks just standing in line, beating a path to your door."

"Not so's you'd notice, there isn't," she said.

"She doesn't have...anyone special?"

"There was one no-good hanging around. She thought herself in love with him, but I put a stop to it before he had a chance to hurt her."

"No others?" Ramsey asked. He was abreast of her now, and Hannah shot him a cold look.

"No one's going to do to her what you done to me. I won't let it happen. Not ever."

The old guilt stabbed like a knife in Ramsey's guts. "Not every man's like me,

Hannah. What if she really falls in love?"

"She won't."

"You can't stop her."

"And since when have you been such an authority on love?"

"I'm not an authority on love, but she's not a little girl anymore."

Hannah glared at him. "You don't know a tinker's dam about little girls."

"You're right about that. I don't know much about little girls, but I know little girls grow into women, and I know a little about women, Hannah. Not much, except they fall in love and leave their mothers."

"Stop it, damn you!"

"You afraid to let her go?"

"I'm not afraid of anything."

"There's something you're afraid of."

"What would that be?"

"I haven't figured it out yet."

She shot him another withering look. "When you do, let me know."

~~~

They'd stopped for their noon meal in a small grove of cottonwoods. Hannah was washing the two tin plates and matching cups at the creek when Ramsey led his saddled horse into camp.
~~~

She eyed him coldly over her shoulder. "I'm not ready to go yet."

"Might as well make camp here tonight."

She stood and turned to face him, her hands on her hips. "There's hours of daylight left."

"I'm riding on into Grangeville to have a look around. I don't know how long I'll be. We'll camp here tonight."

"I'm goin' with you."

"No, Hannah, you're not. I'm not as well known as you are. I can ask questions, see if anyone's heard of Sharon, or seen her."

"And I'm suppose to sit here and keep the campfire burning while you're away? I don't take orders from you, Ramsey."

"Do you want Sharon back?" He was tired, and he didn't feel like arguing.

"Of course I do, but they're taking her to Walla Walla. I told you that. No sense in dilly-dallying along the way."

"And I want to know what makes you so damn sure. Do you know something I don't?" He watched her eyes; something changed in her expression.

She turned back to the creek. "Go then. But you'll be wasting your time."

"Maybe, maybe not." He mounted and

galloped off in a cloud of dust, not slowing until he was well out of sight of camp.

~~~

It was late when he returned. He could see Hannah sitting on the ground in the light of the fire, her hand resting lightly on the shotgun across her lap.

He called out, "Hannah, it's me," and wondered if it was his imagination, or if she really had tightened her grip and pulled the heavy end slightly around. He knew it wasn't. When he got closer, he could see the barrels aimed right at him. His gaze lifted to the sharp lines of her face, made sharper by the flickering flames of the campfire.

"If you're gonna do it, Hannah, do it now and get it over with." His voice was soft and controlled, but a sick feeling had developed in his gut. He waited.

Her grip relaxed. "Good thing you announced yourself. I could have shot you. Did you find out anything?" She lifted the weapon from her lap and laid it carefully on the bedroll beside her.

He rode into camp, eased his aching body from the saddle. "I talked to the man at the general store. He said two men and a woman fitting Sharon's description passed through
~~~

yesterday morning. Said the girl was real quiet. Like she was afraid."

Hannah's face whitened. Ramsey could see her hands begin to tremble.

"That's a good sign," he said, trying to ease her distress. "Means they haven't hurt her. She's alive and well."

Hannah didn't answer. She was staring off into the night, her eyes blank, her lips moving.

"Still don't mean they're taking her to Walla Walla," Ramsey said, pulling the saddle from the horse's back, along with his bedroll, and placing them near the fire. He removed the bridle and slapped the animal gently on the rump. The horse moved off beyond the ring of light, into the darkness. Hannah's mount and the packhorse needed to be hobbled, but Hoss wouldn't go far. Not without Ramsey. "Any coffee left?"

Hannah was mindless to his question. She shifted her gaze to the fire, sat there staring. What had gotten into her? he wondered. She should be happy as hell knowing Sharon was safe. For the moment at least.

He found his whiskey bottle in his saddlebag, poured a measure into the tin cup sitting on a rock, and filled it to the brim from the coffeepot sitting on the ground near the fire. He was hungry. He hadn't eaten since lunch, but it was obvious Hannah wasn't going to fix him any supper, and he was too tired to do it himself.

"Want some coffee?" he asked.

She ignored him. Ramsey sat on the ground on top of his bedroll, legs drawn up, arms across his knees, and watched the flames licking at the wood.

"We'll get an early start in the morning," he said softly.

It was like he wasn't there. The woman didn't budge. He looked at her.

"Hannah, is there more – something I should know?"

He watched her. Tried to read her face. She didn't look at him, her eyes fixed to the leaping flames.

"It doesn't matter, anything you might be keeping from me. It doesn't matter."

She said nothing.

Ramsey rolled a cigarette, lit it, and sat for a long time watching the fire, listening to the coyotes, wondering what she was thinking about, what kind of devils she battled.

He threw the butt of his cigarette into the fire and tossed the dregs of the coffee into the coals. They hissed, and a cloud of steam and soot rose up. Setting the cup down, he picked up the bottle, pulled the cork and let the cruel liquid spill down his throat and dribble off his chin. He wiped it away with the back of his hand.

How many times had he sat beside a campfire in some lonely place and listened to the coyotes yip or the frogs croaking beside a creek, or an owl hooting from some distant tree, and thought about Hannah Lacey?

How many times had he lay in his bedroll on a hard ground and looked up at the stars and wondered if she might be looking at those same stars, and if she was, would she be thinking of him?

How many times had he said her name out loud, just so he could hear the sound of it?

Ramsey took another long swig from the bottle and flinched as it punished his mouth and throat and hit his stomach with a smack.

He had thought himself in love with Hannah Lacey at those times. He could admit it to himself now. Or maybe it was just her memory he'd imagined himself in love with. Thoughts of her had kept him going when he would have given up if he hadn't had something good to remember. Things sure had a way of twisting themselves around.

He'd drank nearly all the whiskey in the bottle by now, and he watched the sparks shoot into the air through whiskey-blurred vision as the log in the fire fell. He tried to change the direction his drunken thoughts were taking him, but for the life of him, he couldn't.

Here he was in the middle of nowhere with a woman – with Hannah – the same Hannah he'd dreamed about all those years. And he couldn't get close to her if he wanted to because she'd sooner have him dead than alive. The funny part was, he didn't want to be close to her anymore. If it weren't for Sharon, he'd be back in Indian Bend. He'd be trying to clear up his past so he could pop a certain question to a pretty little lady with yellow hair and a ready smile that did care about him...cared enough to keep his supper warm.

What in the hell was he thinking? He wouldn't be proposing to Pleasant or any other woman. It wouldn't take long for the news to get out that Ramsey Judd had returned. The army would be all over him like stink on shit. He'd more than likely go to prison for a long time, if they didn't decide to hang him first.

His laughter broke the silence, but it wasn't funny. It was scary as hell.

Hannah jumped when he laughed, gave

him a blank look, then settled back into her trance-like state. She'd been mumbling to herself, but he couldn't make out what she was saying. She wasn't talking to him, he knew that for sure. Ramsey finished the bottle and gave it a toss. He heard it land with a plunk off somewhere in the darkness.

Every damn thing he touched turned to shit.

Maybe he shouldn't even go back to Indian Bend when this was all over. Maybe he should just keep riding. He remembered the promise he'd made to Pleasant last night. She'd be better off without the likes of him.

"Best be going to bed, Hannah," he said. "We have a lot of miles to go tomorrow."

She ignored him.

"Suit yourself then."

Ramsey took off his hat and boots and crawled into his bed. He lay on his back with his hands tucked on the saddle behind his head and watched the stars twinkling in the dark sky above until they flickered and went out.

~~~

Hannah sat in the darkness for a long time. Her head was splitting; she watched the flames in the fire through her tunnel vision burn
~~~

down low. Where was that son of a bitch, Bull Brenner? He wasn't suppose to drag Sharon all over the country with him. He was suppose to shoot Ramsey Judd. That was all. That was the bargain.

Ramsey Judd could be wrong, Hannah. Maybe it wasn't Sharon.

Oh be quiet, she thought. Of course it was Sharon. There wasn't a doubt in her mind.

Bull had Sharon out there somewhere. Why?

Shoot him now, Hannah, while he's asleep. You can do it. Then go find Bull and Sharon.

Hannah eyed the shotgun lying on her bedroll beside her. Yes, she could shoot Ramsey Judd. Her heart beat hard in her chest to the rhythm of the pulsing pain in her head. It would be so easy. And she would enjoy doing it.

You can rid yourself of Bull Brenner, too.

And she wouldn't have to give him the rest of the money. And she'd have Sharon back.

Do it, Hannah.

Hannah ran her tongue over her bottom lip. The pain in her head throbbed. Her finger itched as she slowly reached for the weapon.

Do it, Hannah. Do it now.

Chapter Ten

Ramsey sat bolt upright, every nerve in his body tense, his ears tuned, even through the haze of his whiskey-soaked mind. He hadn't been asleep long, he knew. He could still feel the heat of the fire. He listened. Something had wakened him.

Acute to the sounds around him, he reached out and laid his hand on the cold steel of the Winchester lying beside him and drew it closer.

He glanced at Hannah. She was still sitting in the glow of the dying embers, where she had been when he'd gone to bed. There was a frightened look on her face, and her hand rested on the 16-gauge beside her.

"Did you hear that, too, Hannah?" he asked in a soft whisper.

She didn't answer. Ramsey listened. There it was again. Somewhere beyond the fire. A foot-fall on dry twigs. Then a low snort.

The horses.

Ramsey rose swiftly. Without pulling on his boots, he took up the rifle and edged his way in the direction the sound had come from. Then he heard the jingle of a bridle, the soft thudding of horses feet dying away in the distance.

Ramsey hurried now, and was relieved to see the hobbled animals' silhouettes, two dark forms against the night sky. He gave a low whistle and Hoss came to him. He rubbed the animal's neck affectionately, then turned back to camp.

Someone had been there, watching. Who? And why?

"You'd best go to bed, Hannah. Whoever it was is gone now." No sense in chasing after the watcher tonight, he decided. Like looking for a pebble at the bottom of a well. He was still feeling the effects of too much drink to do much good anyway. Whoever it was had done no harm that he could tell. He settled back under the cover and relaxed his tense muscles, closed his eyes, his hand resting on the rifle next to him. He heard Hannah moving beside him and knew she was finally getting ready for bed. Now if he could just recapture the dream he'd been dreaming before he woke. Of Pleasant Smith in a white night dress, cheeks flushed, golden hair and green eyes aglow, standing at his room door, offering him apple pie.

~~~

The second day out, Ramsey and Hannah rode through Grangeville without stopping. In Mt. Idaho, they bought a few provisions at a well-stocked mercantile and inquired of a few locals if two men and a woman fitting Sharon's description had passed that way. They had, yesterday. When asked the woman's condition, it was learned that she seemed okay. Maybe a little tired.

They rode on, breaking down a steep grade into heavily timbered country, staying to the main trail until they reached Jackson Bridge Trading post, a low log structure set in beside the South Fork of the Clearwater River. It served as wagon stop and supply post for miners and homesteaders in the Idaho back country.

No one in that place had seen the trio. Ramsey and Hannah kept to the narrow river until it met the main Clearwater, where they
~~~

rested their horses and waited for the cable-drawn ferry to pull from the opposite shore through the swift current and take them across. They followed the river to Kamiah Station, an Indian village on the Nez Perce Reservation. The people watched from little groups standing quietly, or sitting on the dried grass, or clustered on narrow benches in front of shabby buildings, as the white couple passed.

The women wore bright shawls over printed cotton dresses, handkerchiefs tied about their heads. Some of the men wore flannel shirts, others dark linen coats, sitting apart from the women, all with the look of hopelessness on their brown faces, weary and troubled, seemingly dulled with the poverty of their world, finding no comfort in what might lay ahead. Several of the oldest men pulled blankets over their grim, weathered faces, not wishing to gaze upon the intruders in their midst.

Ramsey and Hannah rode through a mixture of board, log, and tepee dwellings. Village dogs barked about the horses' heels, causing them to shy and dance sideways. Hannah kicked at the dogs with the toe of her boot, caught one under the chin and sent it yelping back to a group of children standing nearby.

Ramsey grinned and waved at a beautiful little girl about four or five years old with long jet braids, wearing a dark cotton dress, standing motionless beside her mother. The child immediately stuck her finger in her mouth and slipped behind her mother's skirt, peeked around, her dark eyes wide. The mother showed no reaction, stared back with that blank faraway expression.

Hannah's eyes darted from one sun-bronzed face to another. "Filthy, heathen animals," she said, none too quietly.

"They're people," Ramsey replied.

"There's more trouble brewing. Wouldn't surprise me if we don't have another all-out Indian war. That bitch, Alice Fletcher, from Washington has been filling their heads with promises of land allotments, a full quarter-section for each head of family."

"Small price to pay for what the government has taken from them."

"Really, Ramsey! What would these lazy, red dogs do with land? Look at them, for God's sake, standing about, letting the government feed and cloth them. Seems a waste of food and blankets and good land, if you ask me. And if that Fletcher woman's promises don't come about..."

Compassion pulled heavily at Ramsey's heart as he looked around him. As if they had a choice, he thought. He was glad no one had asked Hannah. "Give them a chance," he said.

Hannah made a disgusted sound in her throat and said no more. They rode past a church and on to a trading post with a painted wooden sign that read *Kipkip Kapelikan* hanging over the door. Ramsey dismounted, left Hannah sitting her horse, and inquired within. Still no sign of the two men and girl.

The ferry was just pulling onto their side of the river as they rode up. They crossed over and camped in a clearing a few miles further along.

~~~

They had finished their supper of fried potatoes and canned beans and sat on their bedrolls near the fire, the flames whipping the darkness away from their faces. Hannah twisted her hair into a braid and watched Ramsey, who seemed to be in some deep, thoughtful place known only to himself.

He took his tobacco out of his pocket and rolled a cigarette, the heavy creases between his dark eyes deepening, the tight muscle along
~~~

his whisker-covered jaw twitching. The flickering light danced along the sharp planes of his timeless face and he breathed a deep sigh, as though she weren't there at all. He was keeping his own company.

He looked tired, she thought. They'd been riding hard all day. She didn't care. She hadn't wanted to stop for the night. She'd been sick with worry, wanted to keep going. She felt an urgency to find her daughter, to have this man sitting beside her in his grave.

"Why don't we just keep going and catch up with them and get Sharon back?" Hannah asked. She still didn't understand why Sharon would be with Bull. When she caught up with him, there'd be hell to pay. "They can't be that far ahead of us."

Ramsey stuck a twig in the fire and waited for it to catch. "Our visitor's back." He lit his smoke.

"Who?"

"I don't know. I think it's time I found out."

She shifted her gaze nervously toward the pines at the edge of the clearing. It could be very soon, now. Tonight even. It must be Bull out there.

"Indians?"

"Hell no."

"How do you know?" she asked.

"I can hear him," he said flatly. "I'm surprised you can't. He's stomping around out there like a wounded grizzly."

"What are you going to do?"

"Wait. Act like we don't know he's there."

"Maybe Sharon's with him," she said.

"No. It's one man and he's alone. Just keep a steady conversation, Hannah. Act natural."

Hannah couldn't think of a natural thing to say. She wasn't use to making casual conversation with anyone, especially Ramsey Judd. She cleared her throat. "What do you want me to talk about?" she asked.

Ramsey took a drag from the cigarette. "There's always the subject of you and me."

"That's the last thing I want to talk about."

"Do you really hate me so much, Hannah?"

"This is no time to talk about my feelings for you." Oh, she did wish she could have shot him last night. She would have, too, but he woke up before she could do it. If that had been Bull out there in the dark, he'd saved Ramsey's life without knowing it.

"No," he chuckled, "but it's conversation."

"Yes, I hate you that much," she said. "Why wouldn't I?"

"I've said I'm sorry. Can't we leave it at

that?"

Hannah gave a quick laugh, but there was no humor in it. "You're a fool, Ramsey."

"I've been called worse."

"No. I can't leave it at that. You got what you wanted. You knew you'd be leaving – "

"So did you. I told you that night. And it seems to me, you wanted it just as bad as I did. Anyway, you're the one that started it all." He tossed the butt of the cigarette away. "There were reasons I couldn't stay, if you're interested in hearing them."

"It's too late for explanations now."

"I just wish things had been different."

"Oh, God. Will you shut up? I'm tired of your worthless prattle."

"Just keep talking, Hannah," Ramsey said, lowering his voice. "He's far enough away that he can't hear everything we say. He's just watching us. Wonder what he's got on his mind?"

Hannah took a deep breath. Maybe it would be good to clear the air. Then when the time came, he'd know why he was going to die. "I loved you, Ramsey."

"Guess I must have loved you a little too, Hannah."

"You don't know how to love."

"I know how to love, I didn't know how to stay – "

"You didn't want to."

He didn't look at her, kept his eyes on the fire. "There's never been a thing, or a person, I haven't been able to walk away from in my life," he said, "if I took a good notion. I've had to do it more than once. But you were the hardest. I swear to God you were. When I came back, I hoped there could be something between us." He looked at her now.

Against her will, she let his gaze hold hers in a strong black velvet grip. There was a hurt in his eyes, a kind of lonely sadness. For a moment, she felt a tug at her heart and it frightened her. "I don't want there to be anything between us," she said.

"I don't either, now. But I did."

For some reason she couldn't understand, his statement felt like a knife in her chest. Then it passed. Her revenge would be sweeter somehow, if he still cared about her. "You don't give a care about me now, do you?"

"It's different, Hannah. I care about you. You're the mother of my daughter. But I've decided I'm not in love with you."

It didn't matter, she told herself. It would be sweet just the same.

But it *did* matter. She wanted Ramsey to feel for her. She wanted him to love her. "I thought you were going to tell me something important," she said, brushing his revelation aside for the moment.

"I'll answer any question you put to me. Just ask."

There was plenty she wanted to know. But she was afraid to ask. "What *are* you tryin' to do, Ramsey?"

"Make my peace. Nothing more. Do what's right." Again that wistful quality in his expression. "How can I make you happy, Hannah?"

His answer angered her. "Make your peace? After all these years? With me? It'd be easier to catch a weasel asleep. You can't make me happy. You could never make me happy...unless you were to keel over dead right now."

"And my daughter." He plucked a twig from the ground, put it in his mouth and chewed at it. "I want to do right by her."

"I meant what I said. She's never to know you're her father." It irritated Hannah how cool he could be, no matter what she said to him. What would it take to hurt him to the heart, like he'd hurt her?

Ramsey didn't answer. His joints creaked as he rose and pulled his bedroll away from the fire, into the shadows. He slipped under the cover with his boots on, pulled it up to his chin and tipped his hat down over his face.

"What are you doing? I thought we were talking."

"We are. You can say anything you want to. I'm listening."

"I thought you were going to find out who's following us."

"I aim to. When the time is right."

Hannah hated his rejection. He'd turned away from her while she was talking; she had something more to say. She stood and walked to where he was lying, stared down at him, her fists balled at her side. "I want you to know," she said, "that when you're dying like a gut-shot coyote twisting around and pissing all over the ground, I'm going to be standing over you, Ramsey Judd. I'm going to be watching and laughing until you can't move anymore. And you'll be looking up at me and I'm going to spit on you and leave you there for the ravens to eat. Then I'll be happy."

~~~

Ramsey's blood ran cold at her words. He knew she meant them. But he didn't plan on
~~~

dying like that. He pushed his hat back, looked into her cold hard eyes, his own expression, he hoped, hiding what he was feeling. She looked like a she-devil and he shivered inwardly, but kept his outward expression calm. "Is that all you have to say?" he asked.

"No. Plenty more, if you can take it."

"Good. Move back to the fire and keep talking." He slipped from the dark side of the bedroll, leaving the Winchester. A rifle could be cumbersome up close, and Ramsey figured on getting real close to whoever it was out there. He crawled on his belly to the shelter of the trees a few feet away. All the while, Hannah kept up a flow of threats and profanity. He closed his ears to what she was saying. They were just words to keep the man watching, listening. They meant nothing.

Once safely out of the glow of the fire, he rose and circled around the camp. The watcher was silhouetted against the light of the campfire, in plain view, leaning against the trunk of a cottonwood tree, a holster slung high on his hip.

Hannah kept talking. Ramsey could no longer make out what she was saying. It couldn't be nice, he knew. He slipped silently from one tree to the next, until he was so close to the man he could hear his breathing.

In one fluid motion, Ramsey jerked the revolver from the man's holster, put the barrel to his ribs, and circled the man's neck in the crook of his other arm. "Nice weapon," he whispered, pulling back the hammer with his thumb. "It's a Colt, isn't it? How does it work?"

The man cried out in alarm, "That thing has a hair trigger!"

"Then you'd better not make any sudden moves. What are you doing here?"

"Nothin'."

"Wrong answer." Ramsey poked him with the cold steel of the barrel. "I'll give you another chance. What are you doing here?"

"Watchin', that's all."

"Watching what?"

"Just watchin'."

Ramsey increased the pressure to the man's ribs. "Why?"

The man didn't answer.

"Damn it, you better talk. I've got my finger on your hair trigger."

"Because I was told – "

"By the man who has the girl?"

"What girl?"

"I think I'll just put you out of my misery." Ramsey tightened the grip on the man's neck.

"Ah! I don't know anythin' about no girl. Watch that damn gun!"

"Then why you been following us?"

"My boss...told me to keep an eye on you and the woman."

Ramsey released him and stepped back. He kept the revolver leveled. "Now turn around real slow."

The man did as he was told. The glow from the campfire lit up one side of his face. He was younger than Ramsey had expected, maybe in his early twenties, a dark growth of scraggly beard shadowing his jaw. He was tall, but not as tall as Ramsey, and he was bone lean.

"Who's your boss, and why does he want us watched?"

"I ain't sayin' a word."

"Would you rather die right here?"

"Bull. Bull Brenner."

"The same Bull Brenner that works for Hannah?"

"That's him."

"Did you burn her barn?"

"Hell no! I just started workin' for Bull a week ago. Don't know nothin' about no barn."

"And the girl?"

"I told you. I don't know nothin' about the girl neither."

"Why are we being watched?"

"Don't know. Bull just said to watch you."

Ramsey studied the man for a few seconds, contemplating his next move. "Where's Brenner now?"

"Don't rightly know."

"You're pretty damn dumb, aren't you? If you want to live to see him again, you'll get smart fast and tell me." Ramsey lifted the barrel.

"If I tell you, Bull will kill me, sure as not. Guess the odds are against me any way you look at it."

Ramsey lowered his aim, leveled it at the man's belly. "But this way, you see, you got a chance. You're a young man. Lots of life to live. You might be able to make a run for it, if you tell me what you know. Ever seen a man shot in the gut? It ain't pretty. Long slow death."

"Camped a few miles from here," the man said in defeat. "But don't you tell him I told you."

"Where?"

The younger man paused and Ramsey's hand tightened on the wooden grip.

"Other side of Jackson Bridge. There's an old miner's shack, off the main road a piece. That's all I'm sayin', mister."

"That's enough. You can go."

The man looked surprised, breathed a sigh of relief. "Can I have my gun?"

"I been needing me a nice Colt with a hair trigger. You must have a rifle, probably on your horse, right?"

"Yes, but – "

"Think I'll keep the Colt. Take off the belt and holster and drop them on the ground."

The man did as he was told.

"What's your name?"

"Cady. Jack Cady."

"Thanks, Jack Cady. Now git. Tell Brenner if he wants his money, bring the girl in and he can have it. If he has business with me, face me like a man. I'll be waiting. Tell him, too, that if he harms a hair on Sharon Larken's head, I'll kill him as sure as my name's Ramsey Judd. You understand me?"

Without another word, Jack Cady turned and hurried through the dark brush and disappeared. A few moments later, Ramsey heard the horse's hooves beating a steady tattoo on the hard ground. It echoed into the distance and died away. Ramsey stepped into the ring of light from the campfire.

"Is he gone?" Hannah sat wide-eyed by the fire. "What did he want?"

"He's gone." Ramsey put the revolver under his bedroll, took off his boots, slipped under his blanket and rested his head on the saddle. "We have a long ride ahead of us tomorrow. Best get some sleep."

He closed his eyes and listened to her moving about, putting another log on the fire, pulling her own boots off and slipping under her blanket.

"Your hired hand, do you trust him, Hannah?"

"Which one?"

"Bull Brenner."

"Of course I trust him. Why shouldn't I? He's been with me for years."

"Do you know a man by the name of Cady?"

"Yes. Bull brings him in every spring to help with the sheep during sheering. Why?"

"Because Bull Brenner's having us followed," he said, "and Jack Cady is the one following. Good possibility Brenner's got Sharon. And he isn't headed for Walla Walla."

There was something wrong with this whole damn picture he couldn't figure out. If Bull wanted the ransom money, why didn't he just make a move? Why all the cat and mouse?

Ramsey had made up his mind about one

thing. There'd be a change of plans come morning, no matter what Hannah had to say.

~~~

Hannah pulled the covers up around her. The fire snapped and an owl hooted from somewhere beyond the camp.

If Bull was following them, where was Sharon? And what was he waiting for? Why hadn't he shot Ramsey? He'd had plenty of chances. They were far enough away from Indian Bend now. She wanted it over with, wanted to be back home with Sharon.

She never could depend on a man to do things the way she wanted them done. But if she were to end it all here, shoot Ramsey herself, Bull would have one more thing to hold over her head. He wouldn't have the rest of his money coming, and he still had Sharon.

For now, her only choice was to trust Bull. Tomorrow. It would happen tomorrow.

Hannah smiled to herself. She could almost find it in her heart to be kind to Ramsey, on what could be the last night of his life. There were things she still wanted to know, questions she wanted the answers to. She gazed over at his quiet form and softly whispered, "Ramsey?"

~~~

Ramsey's eyes snapped open. Had he

dreamed hearing his name? A breeze stirring the trees was his only answer, and he closed his eyes again.

"Ramsey."

"Hannah? Is something wrong?"

"Why did you leave all those years ago?"

He drew a deep, sharp breath that caught painfully in his chest. He looked up at the dark, endless sky and wondered if it would do any good to tell her. "It was a long time ago." He'd wanted a chance to explain; now he wasn't sure. Maybe it was best to leave it be.

"Why, Ramsey?"

There was a softness in her voice that shocked the hell out of him after her spitting words earlier. She had a right to know, he guessed. He'd told her he'd answer any of her questions. "I'm a deserter from the Union Army."

Silence. Not a word from the woman.

"Hannah?" Her name caught in his throat. "Did you hear what I said?"

"Why?"

"My older brother was a Reb, or I thought he was at the time. I watched a Yank shoot him down not more than six feet in front of me. Guess I went a little crazy, watching him die like that. I'd had all the war I wanted. I walked until I found a horse, which turned out to be the company commander's, and rode away.

"Then that day at your pa's ranch, when a sergeant showed up to buy horses, he recognized me, and I recognized him. I'd been to Indian Bend a few days before and saw my wanted poster in the post office. I knew it was just a matter of time. I couldn't stay. I wanted to, but I couldn't." Ramsey paused, collecting his words. He wanted her to understand, but he doubted she ever would. "I'd already made up my mind to leave, that night you come sneaking into my bed. I'm sorry, Hannah."

She remained silent. Ramsey was glad. He had nothing more to say. He settled back against the saddle under his head. A lonesome breeze tossed the wood smoke from the fire into his face, then fanned it away again. From the woods, a night bird called. He could hear the perpetual rush of the Clearwater over the thudding of his heart.

"Who's Martha?"

The thud of his heart gathered; something old and lost stirred in him. "How do you know about Martha?"

"You called me Martha that night. Who is she?"

"She was my wife. She died before the war.

Along with the son she tried to give birth to."

Another long stretch of silence. Then, "The name, Parker O'Dell. Where'd it come from? Did you just make it up?"

"There was a Reb soldier, shot up pretty bad, not much chance of his making it. He gave me a letter to give to his wife in Kentucky. After I swiped some civilian clothes off a clothesline and got rid of the Union uniform, I rode up Kentucky way and tried to look her up. She and her little girl had died of the fever a week before I got there. I headed to Missouri and came across a bunch of Mormons getting ready to head West to Utah. Figured it was a safe way to get the hell out of the country, so I hired on as scout. I needed a name and borrowed the Reb soldier's. Parker O'Dell. It stuck with me until I came back to Indian Bend a month or so ago."

"Do you think the law's still looking for you after all these years?"

"Hard to say. There was a price on my head."

"How much is the reward?"

"Last I saw, it was a thousand dollars."

"Dead or alive?"

"Yes, Hannah, dead or alive." He was tired. It didn't matter that she knew. It had to end.

Maybe when this was all over, he'd turn himself in.

Hannah gave a little chuckle.

"What's funny?"

He heard her sit up. "Why, Ramsey, you could be worth far more to me dead than alive."

"I'll keep that in mind, Hannah, be watching my back when all this is over."

She laid back down. "Good night, Ramsey," she said in a voice that was way too sweet.

Ramsey rolled over to face where she was lying. He reached under his bed and brought the Colt out, tucked it in next to his belly. He didn't know if she was joking, but he wasn't taking chances. Hannah had a way about her.

He'd gotten it all off his chest. He figured it would help, but somehow, it hadn't made him feel one damn bit better.

~~~

"Hannah?"

She opened her eyes and looked up into Ramsey's face. It was still night.

"It's time to get up," he told her.

"What time is it?"

"The sun'll be up in a little while. We should get around and break camp."

He was kneeling beside her, staring down
~~~

at her, and something warm went through Hannah. She wondered what it would be like to bed him again, before... The thought excited her. She'd seduce him and then watch him die. What a fitting end to it all. She reached up and pushed a lock of silver-tipped hair from his forehead. "I'm cold, Ramsey."

He was so close to her she could feel the heat of him. It stirred her. She ran her finger down his rough cheek.

"It's early," she said in a soft voice, slipping her hand to his neck and playing with the dark curls that rested above his collar.

Oh, yes. Seduce Ramsey Judd, then send him off forever. A feeling of power came over her. Her hand rested on the back of his neck and she pulled his face toward her and closed her eyes.

But the kiss she'd anticipated didn't happen. Ramsey stiffened. He grabbed her wrist at the back of his head in a vice-like grip and pulled it away. "What the hell you doing, Hannah?"

She blinked up at him. "What is it?" He was staring at her, his eyes like flint.

"I'll be damned if I know. Yesterday you were ready to kill me. And this morning – "

"I was angry. I didn't understand."

"And just like that, you do now?"

"We all make mistakes, Ramsey. Can't we leave it at that?"

The cord in his jaw worked. He threw her hand away. In a hard voice, he said, "Let's get moving."

Damn him! How dare he treat her like this. She watched his back as he dug in the food bag, pulled out a new tin of Arbuckle's Coffee and a can opener. He opened the can and poured a healthy amount into the pot that he'd already filled with water from the river.

Oh, he was despicable. He deserved what he got.

Ramsey took the plates from the rock she had left them on the night before and opened a can of beans.

"Come on, Hannah. The coffee'll be done in a few minutes." He didn't turn around.

She jerked herself out from under her blanket and moved to the edge of the fire.

"Don't make sense," Ramsey said.

"I was just trying to – "

"Bull Brenner works for you. I been thinking about it all night. Nothing makes sense."

Damn that Bull Brenner. How could he be so stupid? Why didn't he just do it and get it over with?

"Can't quite figure it out," Ramsey said. "Purely puzzles me, Hannah."

"If we keep moving, we should catch up with him soon," she said, trying to control her voice.

Ramsey filled the plates with cold beans and sat beside her. She leaned away from him.

"They aren't in front of us, Hannah." He handed her one of the plates. "Cady said Brenner is holed up in a miner's shack the other side of Jackson Bridge. We'll be moving back that direction today."

Hannah's fingers gripped her plate. A little twinge started behind her eyes.

You'll be moving back into the shelter of the woods, Hannah.

We need to stay in the open.

You need a clear shot.

If Bull didn't act soon, it would be too late.

You'll have to do it yourself, Hannah.

And collect the reward. The reward put a whole different light on things.

"Did you hear me, Hannah?" Ramsey said. "I want to go back, see if I can pick up Bull's trail."

Hannah stood. The plate of beans fell from her lap and spilled onto the ground. "No."

"What?"

"We...we should keep moving ahead. If we go back, we could...spook Bull. He could kill Sharon."

"He's back there, Hannah. We'll be putting distance between us and the girl. The closer we are to her, the better chance we have of getting her back safe."

Hannah's temper flared. Her head was beginning to throb. "You don't care a thing about Sharon," she said.

"That ain't true. I care. I just don't think – "

"That's your trouble, Ramsey, you don't think."

"What makes you right, Hannah? Why are you so sure?"

"I know. That's all. We're going ahead."

She started toward her bedroll. "Saddle the horses. I'll get things picked up."

"Hannah – "

"No more!" She faced him. "We're moving ahead. That's the end of it!"

"No, Hannah. We're not. We're going back."

"Goddamn you, Ramsey Judd! You stupid old fool, good for nothing piece of shit!" Her nails dug into the palms of her balled fists. Her head was pounding, now. "All you think about is turning back. You don't care what the note said – that we should keep moving ahead. You only care about yourself. You would risk Sharon's life with your pigheaded notions." Her voice had become loud and shrill. She squinted her eyes against the pain it produced. "I should just shoot you where you stand and haul your body back to town and cash it in. I could, you know. By God, I could!"

Ramsey yelled, "All right, Hannah!"

Hannah shut up. Not a bird could be heard in the pre-dawn quiet. Not even the breeze. Only the bold river rumbling on undisturbed.

"Christ, woman!"

She started toward him. "I mean it, Ramsey –"

"We can't travel the river much longer," he interrupted. "We have to get out of the canyon."

"We'll go over the mountain to Nez Perce, cut down and hit the river near Orofino."

"All right. For another day," Ramsey said. "If Brenner don't make a stand, we're going back."

"We'll turn back when I say turn back."

He grabbed her plate from where she'd dropped it and scraped what was left on it into the fire, refilled it with beans from the can and shoved it at her. "Eat your damn breakfast."

~~~
~~~

Ramsey relaxed in the saddle, his body swaying comfortably with the easy gate of his horse, but his mind was anything but comfortable. Damn the woman. He didn't know if she worried him more when she was mad or when she wasn't. He thought having her mad was the best way to go. At least then he didn't let his guard down. "Are you about ready for a stop?" he said. "We should find camp for the night. The horses deserve a rest."

Without answering, she took off her hat and wiped the back of her hand across her forehead.

It was hot. They'd ascended the mountain at Kamiah, coming out on the prairie above, passed by the towns of Nez Perce and Mohler. Craig Mountain had offered blessed relief from the glaring sun that beat down on them all morning; they'd stopped at Summit midday. But now they were on the river again.

"There's a thicket of willows ahead," he said. "Let's make for that."

They reined to a stop. Hannah took the coffeepot from the pack and started for the river, while Ramsey went in search of firewood. He returned a few minutes later with an armload of dry driftwood. He stopped dead in his tracks.

Damn it to hell, now what?

Hannah stood ten feet in front of him with his own Winchester held tightly to her shoulder, her eye fixed on the sight of the barrel, aimed right at him.

"Hannah..." he choked. A sick feeling formed in his guts. She was going to shoot him this time for sure.

"Shut up and stay where you are. Don't take another step." She lowered the barrel to his feet.

Ramsey sucked in air, then heard the rattle. He peered over his armload of wood. The biggest rattlesnake he had ever seen was coiled directly in his path, too damn close for comfort. And it was about to strike.

Ramsey glanced back at Hannah, watched her finger tighten on the trigger. The rifle went off. The snake's head exploded and the Winchester's slug smacked the dirt at Ramsey's feet.

His heart pounding, he dropped the wood, took off his hat and wiped the beads of perspiration from his brow. "Jesus!" he said, settling himself limply on the ground.

Hannah lowered the rifle.

"I'd hate to have you mad at me. That was some shot."

She didn't smile. "I usually get what I aim at."

"God, I hate snakes."

She leaned his rifle against a large rock, picked the coffeepot up from where she had dropped it and went to the river to refill it.

"Hannah."

She turned.

"Thanks."

She didn't speak again until they had finished eating. Ramsey had walked to the river's edge in the waning light, his hands tucked into his hip pockets. On the opposite bank a black she-bear and her cub had come for water.

"Ramsey," Hannah said, walking toward him, "let's ride on to Orofino in the morning and stay in a hotel. I'd like a hot bath and a comfortable bed."

"It costs money."

"I have the money."

He didn't look at her. "It wouldn't be proper."

"Since when have you been proper?" She was standing directly behind him now, and he stiffened as her hand rested lightly on his shoulder. "We could each have our own room," she said, her voice soft.

He turned slowly. "Hannah..."

She moved closer, wrapped her arms around his neck and pulled him to her.

Now what was she up to?

He didn't pull away. He couldn't. Her fingers caressed the back of his neck, and for the first time in twenty years, she smiled at him. But the smile on her lips didn't reach her eyes. They were stone cold.

What the hell, he thought. He was a man, after all. He put his arms around her waist and she slid in against him. He kissed her.

And then a funny thing flashed before his eyes. A black widow spider and a fly; the spider was sucking the life blood from the fly.

He felt a panic rise in him. The kiss ended. "No, Hannah," he said in a hoarse whisper.

Her lips were parted, her eyes closed. She was the old Hannah again, beautiful and innocent. For a moment, he was almost willing to throw caution to the wind as he bent toward her. Then he stopped.

Her eyes snapped open and he saw the new Hannah, full of hate and anger.

Her smile wasn't successful this time. It turned into a grimace. "Why, Ramsey, if I didn't know better, I'd say you're afraid of me."

"It ain't that," he lied. "We have business to

tend to."

"It's the landlady, isn't it?" She spat the words at him. "You're saving yourself for that fat lump of quivering flesh."

"That's enough, Hannah. I'll hear no more about Mrs. Smith."

"I'm right, aren't I, Ramsey?"

"That's no concern of yours."

Her features hardened. "You bastard." She raised her hand to strike him.

Ramsey grabbed her wrist and held it firmly. "Don't bring my family into this, Hannah. I have a father."

She glared at him. "I should have let that snake have you."

He met her stare. "At least rattlers give warning before they strike."

"I hate you."

"You're a hateful woman."

"What do you mean by that?"

"Nothing." He released her, turned and started away from her.

A sharp, painful blow to his back stopped him. He whipped around, startled, ready to fight, and met Hannah's angry stare. A fist-sized rock lay next to his boot. He looked back at the woman. "Don't do that again, Hannah."

Chapter Eleven

Pleasant had never been on the trail by herself before. It was fearfully exciting, daringly adventurous, even with all the problems she'd encountered so far.

She'd gotten a later start than she'd wished. It took time to lay things out for Olive, then she'd needed to find a packhorse and men's clothes to fit her; she'd needed provisions. She figured she was a full day behind Ramsey and that Larken woman.

The first night, she stayed at the hotel in Grangeville, but the second night had been pure misery. No hotels for her convenience, no houses to seek shelter. She'd waited too late to set up camp, and what little firewood she was able to gather in the dark refused to catch. Her meal of cold pork sat ill upon her stomach, and she tossed and turned all night, with nothing but a heavy quilt between her and the hard ground.

She'd decided to pass through Denver this afternoon, stopped and inquired about Ramsey and Hannah, but no one had seen them. She hadn't come upon any signs of camps along the way, no cold fires. Nothing. It dawned on her that perhaps she'd taken the wrong route. She rode all the way back through Grangeville to Mount Idaho, where she again inquired. Indeed, a man and a woman fitting Ramsey and Hannah's description had been in for supplies the day before. Pleasant was tempted to stay at the hotel in town, but wanted to make up as much time as she possibly could before dark, and rode on.

Tonight she took a different strategy in setting up her camp, allowed herself enough time to collect a respectable amount of firewood and kindle a satisfying flame. She feasted on side pork and fried potatoes and hot biscuits. Quite pleased with herself, she sat in her neat little camp after the dishes had been cleared away, wearing her soft white, flannel nightgown, sipping tea from a china cup.

The rope she had brought along was carefully laid out around a bed cushioned with soft pine bows and moss. She remembered the journey west, when she and Tom slept under the covered wagon. Tom said snakes wouldn't crawl over a rope. She hoped it was true. It had seemed to work last night. It made her feel better, at least.

Her horses were hobbled behind the bushes some distance away; she could hear them chomping grass and moving about. All was well.

A rustling in the brush at the edge of her clearing caused her to stop, listen, and watch. The horses snorted. She expected to see an animal emerge from the trees. Her heart raced, hoping it wouldn't be a bear or a cougar.

Pleasant eyed the blunderbuss that had belonged to Tom, leaning against a tree next to her neatly laid bed roll. Crazy old thing. Tom had shown her the fundamentals of loading it and shooting it, but she'd done neither of those things in all the years since. Would it even function properly, if she needed to use it? Besides, animals were afraid of fire, weren't they? And hers was burning brightly.

No animal appeared, and all was quiet again. She relaxed a little and took a sip of her tea. At the time, her following Ramsey and Hannah Larken had seemed the thing to do.

But now that she thought about it, maybe it was foolishness, being out here all alone in the dead of night.

What in the world would she do when she caught up with them? *If* she caught up with them. She hadn't planned that far ahead. What reason would she give?

How did she know Hannah meant to hurt Ramsey?

Oh dear. Ramsey would think her quite mad.

Pleasant had never been this route. She'd always taken the main road to Lewiston when she'd gone with Tommy, through Denver and Finn and Cottonwood. She'd asked directions in Mt. Idaho and knew that Jackson Bridge lay somewhere ahead of her. Maybe she'd pick up the couple's trail when she got there sometime tomorrow.

A breeze stirred the brush nearby, bringing the lovely smell of wild roses. She'd like to come back here someday, she decided, dig a few of those bushes for her yard. Perhaps Ramsey would help her.

Oh, wouldn't that be splendid? They'd camp right here and have supper together and sip tea. She'd fry a fat hen and put potatoes in the coals of the fire to bake.

A whitetail doe bounded through camp, just beyond the fire. Pleasant's heart leaped to her throat and she nearly dropped her tea cup. She had just settled from the fright when a small spotted fawn followed a few minutes later, its spindle legs spreading in bounding strides to catch up with its mother. Pleasant laughed. She certainly wasn't much of a woodsman, or woods-woman, as the case might be.

It was time for sleep, she decided. She rinsed her cup and saucer with water she'd drawn from the creek earlier, dried them and set them neatly on a tea towel spread on a flat rock for morning.

She was just starting to crawl beneath her clean sheets when she heard another rustling of brush. This time, she didn't start. She was well inside the ring of light from her fire. She felt brave. Nothing would bother her here. It would go away.

But it didn't go away. It sounded like heavy feet on dried twigs. She laid a hand over her heart and turned her head without rising, then gasped. Two men were standing but a few feet from her, grins plastered across their ugly faces.

Pleasant's eyes darted from the men to the

blunderbuss against the tree, then back to the intruders. She felt weak in her knees and her heart was going a mile a minute. She wanted to speak, but fear kept the words from coming out. She could only squeak.

"Well, well, well. What have we here, Jack?" the ugliest of the two men said.

Pleasant's stomach pulled into a tight little knot. She straightened instantly and stared at the men. They were evil looking.

"Ain't this just cozy. It's Mrs. Smith, ain't it?"

Pleasant opened her mouth but couldn't utter a sound. These men obviously knew her, but she'd never laid eyes on them before. The trembling started deep inside her and shook its way up to her throat.

"Look at that, the little lady's speechless."

"W-who are you?" she finally managed to stutter. "What do you want?"

"My name's Bull Brenner, ma'am, this here's my friend, Jack Cady." Bull Brenner winked at her. The man with him stood watching her, the sneer on his lips frightening. "What you doin' away out here all alone, ma'am? It ain't safe."

"I..." She cleared her throat and tried to think of something to say.

"Why, there's bears and cougars and all sorts of things. Outlaws...big bad men. You're lucky we happened along."

"I-I'm on a business trip."

"Business, huh. What do you think, Jack? Is she tellin' the truth?"

"Don't rightly know what kind of business a pretty gal like her'd have out in the middle of nowhere," Jack Cady answered. "Ain't she the landlady at that boardin' house Ramsey Judd lives in?"

"I do believe yer right," Bull answered.

Pleasant jerked at the sound of Ramsey's name.

Bull Brenner's eyebrow shot up. "That's what I thought. Now, ma'am, you just tell me what you're doin' out here."

"I told you. I'm on my way to Lewiston. Business." She'd regained her composer, but the trembling hadn't stopped. "Now if you gentlemen will excuse me, I'm ready to retire."

Bull Brenner laughed. "And right pretty you look, too." He sobered suddenly. "I don't believe a word you say."

"Well, see for yourself. There's my bed all made up."

"I bet she knows something, Bull. She's going to warn Judd."

"Shut up, Jack. What could she know? You go blabbin' your mouth to that bartender at the Lucky Lady?"

"Course I ain't, Bull."

"Bet you said something to that little tart you been beddin' in Indian Bend."

"Aw, Bull."

Pleasant licked her lips. Her throat felt as dry as ashes. Warn Ramsey about what?

"Is that right, ma'am? You lookin' for Ramsey Judd?"

"Of course not. Why would I be looking for Mr. Judd?"

"What do ya think. Shall we trust her?"

"She could be tellin' the truth." Jack Cady scratched his chin.

"What kind of business?" Bull took a step toward her.

Pleasant shrank back. "M-my sister. I have a sister in Lewiston. She's...ill. I'm going to care for her." Pleasant tried to smile, to remain calm, to quit shaking.

"I just don't think we'd better take a chance, Mrs. Smith. You could get yourself hurt out here. You'll be safer with us." Bull bent over her, grabbed her by the arm and yanked her to her feet.

"Take your hands off me!" She kicked the

man in the chins with her bare toe.

Bull laughed and tightened his grip. "We got ourselves a real wildcat, Jack. Come on, ma'am. We don't aim to hurt ya."

"I'm warning you. You'd better let go of me."

"You have me real worried." The man twisted her arm behind her. She cow-kicked, missed. The man wrapped his hand in the heavy braid at the back of her head and held it tight. Pleasant struggled helplessly.

"Saddle her horse, Jack."

Pleasant screamed. From the corner of her eye, she saw Bull Brenner pull his gun from his holster and raise it over her head. Then a searing pain shot through her and darkness descended around her.

~~~

The sun was relentless in the Clearwater. Ramsey and Hannah rode down a long, wide, bolder-strewn flat, closed in by the river on one side and a high cliff, cropped with rocky bluffs, on the other. Only a few scrub willows grew on this particular stretch of the bank. A hot breeze blowing up the canyon carried the overpowering odor of black locust blossoms.

Their smell made Ramsey queasy; sweat poured under his clothes. The old Stetson was
~~~

heavy and hot, but he knew he had to leave it on. The damn sun would fry his brain without it. His feet ached, felt swollen inside his Justins. All he wanted right now was a cool bath, a good meal, and a cheap bottle of whiskey. A soft bed wouldn't hurt his feelings any, either. Orofino was sounding better all the time. A few more hours and they'd be there.

"Let's stop up here and let the horses drink," Ramsey said, lifting his hat and wiping his brow with the cuff of his shirtsleeve. "We could use a cold drink too."

"I'd like to jump right out there in that river," Hannah replied, bracing her feet in the stirrups and lifting herself from the saddle. "My backside feels like it's glued to this damn horse."

"We should move up yonder to the timber. It'll be cooler up there."

"No," she answered stubbornly. "We need to be down here by the river."

"I figure we'll make Orofino just before dusk." Ramsey didn't want to argue with her. She'd been quiet and easy to get along with. He aimed to keep it that way, even if it meant cooking in his own juice for a few more miles.

They reined their horses to the river's bank and dismounted. Ramsey took Hannah's horse and let the animals drink, while Hannah went to the water's edge and washed her face and drank her fill. He allowed the horses to drink a little, then pulled them back. It wouldn't do for them to drink too fast. All they needed right now were mounts with gut cramps.

Hannah finished drinking and took the reins from Ramsey. He removed his hat and doused his head with the cool water, slaked his thirst, then pulled off his boots. Hannah lead the horses back to the water and let them drink more, while Ramsey rolled up his pant legs and waded out to just below his knees.

He felt the whistle of wind close to his ear a split second before he heard the shot. The bullet plunged into the water in front of him. He whirled and saw Hannah standing still as stone. The horses had bolted and charged hell bent down the rocky river bank.

Another shot rang out. Ramsey splashed out of the water. "Take cover, Hannah! We're being shot at!" He dove for a cabin-size boulder a few feet away.

His rifle was in his saddle scabbard, and the Colt was in one of the saddlebags. He watched them disappear with the horses in the distance. His boots were by the river.

Goddamn him for a fool!

He looked around to see where Hannah was. She stood in the same place, the breeze flapping her riding skirt against her legs, staring off toward the rock formation above the river.

"Christ, Hannah! Get down. Whoever it is means business!" A bullet zinged off the rock Ramsey hid behind. Hannah didn't budge. What in the hell was the matter with her?

The next bullet was aimed at Hannah's feet. She jumped as dust and rock particles flew against her legs. Ramsey started from the rock to get to her, thinking she must be in shock.

The look on her face wasn't shock, however. And it wasn't fright. It was pure rage.

She lifted her hand and shook her fist at the cliff. "Goddamn you, Bull Brenner!" she screamed. "Don't shoot at me, you sorry son-of-a-bitch! Shoot at Ramsey Judd!"

Ramsey stopped, moved back to the rock. What in the hell was going on? All of a sudden he felt like he was right smack in the middle of enemy camp.

A man's laughter filtered down from the rocky bluff. "Sorry, Hannah! My aim's off!"

"I'll get you for this!" she called back.

Again the laughter. "The price has gone up," Bull Brenner yelled.

"What are you talking about? We agreed!"

She'd paid Bull to shoot him. Ramsey felt like the biggest idiot on Earth. It made him mad. This whole damn thing had been a trap. Where was Sharon?

"I'll be seein' ya, Hannah," Bull called from the bluff.

"Bull, you come back here! We have things to talk about!"

There was no answer.

"Where's Sharon?"

No reply. Bull Brenner had gone.

Ramsey waited a few long minutes before he ventured out from behind the rock. He stared at Hannah. "What was that all about?"

"What was what all about?"

"If I didn't know better, I'd swear you just did your level best to get me killed."

"Don't be silly, why would I do that?"

"Where's Sharon?"

Hannah stared back at him, her mouth tight, her eyes wild.

"Goddammit, Hannah. I said where the hell is Sharon?"

Hannah turned and stomped off down the riverbank.

Ramsey ran after her, grabbed her arm. She tried to pull free. Ramsey tightened his grip, yanked her around. "You answer me!"

"Go to hell, Ramsey Judd."

Hannah jerked her arm, and he let go of her. She slipped on the smooth rocks underfoot and fell, landing hard on her hands and knees. Glaring up at him through slitted, hate-filled eyes, she snarled, "Don't you touch me again. I'll kill you myself."

"If anything happens to that girl because of your damn craziness, I'll purely throttle you with my bare hands. And that's a promise."

Hannah pulled herself up, held her arm as if it were in pain, whirled and limped away.

"Where the hell you going?"

"To find the horses, stupid," she called over her shoulder. "Or do you aim to walk all the way to Orofino?"

"Just so I get there alive," he muttered to himself. He watched her go. For two bits, he'd leave her here, ride out while the riding was good – when he found his horse. His life wouldn't be worth a plug nickel if he didn't watch his back from eight different directions. But he knew he couldn't do that. God only knew what kind of trouble she'd gotten his daughter into.

Ramsey retrieved his boots and socks, put them on, and took after Hannah. If he rode out now, he'd have her at his back, and he didn't want that. He'd wait, bide his time.

She was still in a fury when they caught up to the saddle horses about a mile down river, holed up in a sumac thicket. The packhorse was nowhere to be found. Hannah didn't speak as she checked her saddle, tightened the cinch, mounted and whipped the mare with the end of the reins. Ramsey dug in his saddlebags, found the Colt and strapped the belt around his waist, tied the holster to his thigh. He checked the cylinder. It was full. Good enough. He wasn't about to get caught at odds again.

It was almost dark when Ramsey and Hannah came to the bridge that spanned the Clearwater River to Orofino. The day had cooled some with the gathering dusk, but it was still hotter than hell. Ramsey was so tired, he felt he couldn't sit his saddle another hour. He needed to rest. If Hannah's hired gun didn't kill him, the trail would.

She hadn't spoken a word to him since they'd found the horses. She'd ridden with her eyes straight ahead, mumbling under her breath. Ramsey was beginning to wonder if the woman wasn't just a tad bit crazy.

He had some reservations about entering a town with her. There'd be a sheriff, and it wouldn't surprise him one bit if she beat a trail there as fast as she could. But, he reasoned, if she'd had a hand in Sharon's kidnapping, like he suspected, he doubted she'd be turning him in.

Not alive anyway.

~~~

Hannah gazed at herself in the hotel mirror and pulled the comb though her long, freshly washed hair. The light from the lamp beside her danced across her face, glistened off her bare shoulders and breasts.

It had been a terrible day, a disturbing one. It gave her a beastly headache, but the hot bath had felt good and she soaked for nearly an hour, letting the steaming water relax her, soothe her until it cooled. The pain in her head was gone now, and she could think clearly.

Bull Brenner had made a bad mistake. Hannah didn't like being crossed. She didn't know yet what he was up to, but it didn't matter. She knew where that cabin was located, and she'd deal with him when the time came. But Ramsey came first. It was quite plain to her now, she would have to attend to the matter herself. And she would. Very soon. If she played her cards right, she'd have the reward money as a bonus. If she was careful.
~~~

Everything had nearly been ruined today on the river. She couldn't remember all she'd said to Bull, but Ramsey was suspicious of her. She would have to win him back, gain his lost trust for a little while longer.

She studied her reflection in the glass. The shadows cast by the flickering light softened her features, made her look younger, she thought. She could still be considered beautiful. He was just across the hall. It had almost become an obsession with her, this game she'd started to play, the seduction of Ramsey Judd. She wanted it more than ever now.

Sharon was safe for the moment. Bull Brenner wouldn't dare hurt her. By the time Bull found out that there was no more money coming, it would be too late for him. She had plans.

But she had to win Ramsey over. One more time, she wanted him to be hers, wanted him to remember her body, take that memory to his grave. The thought made her tingle.

He'd loved her once. He'd told her so. If he hadn't been running from the law, he'd have stayed, he said. Hannah almost believed him.

It was hard for her to feel remorse over any of her actions. It was almost alien to her. In all her life, she'd had very few people she felt remorse for, except her mother – and Sharon, if something happened to her. She might feel remorse for Ramsey, after...

Absently, Hannah dragged the comb through her hair, over and over. It was hard to know what Ramsey was thinking sometimes. They had eaten supper together in the dining room downstairs by candlelight, like lovers. He'd watched her across the table, and in spite of all that had happened today, she had managed to control herself. She'd kept light conversation as best she knew how. But he hadn't talked to her. Not one word did he say to her. He just sat there studying her with those dark, unreadable eyes. It had made her uncomfortable.

Ramsey loved her once. He still had feelings for her, he'd said. He could love her again. She knew he could.

Something like sorrow came over Hannah. It was too bad Ramsey had to die. She still had strong feelings for him. He was right. There was a very thin line between love and hate. Maybe if –

Hannah.

Her long hair tangled and Hannah yanked the comb hard, making her scalp smart.

She smiled at the reflection in the mirror, and the eyes gazed back at her, bright, shining, alive.

She was alive! It felt so good.

Hannah laughed and the sound echoed off the walls of the quiet room. She laughed louder and it made her giddy. In a couple of days she'd have Sharon back. Ramsey would be gone, never to bother her again.

She rose from the cushioned seat in front of the dressing table and wrapped the bath sheet around her. Quietly, she opened the door a crack and peeked out into the hall. Not a soul. Not a sound. Silently, she stepped across the hall to where Ramsey's room was and lifted her hand to knock, then stopped, grasped the doorknob and turned. Her heart pounded. It wasn't locked. He was waiting for her.

Ramsey's room was dark but for the square of moonlight through the parted curtains swaying in the breeze from the open window. Hannah tiptoed to the big bed silhouetted against the light-papered wall. "Ramsey," she whispered.

There was no answer.

"Ramsey." She sat on the edge of the bed next to the bulk of covers and slipped quietly beneath the sheets. "I'm here, Ramsey." He was playing games. It excited her.

Hannah's fingers searched for the soft feel of warm flesh.

"What..." She groped, more frantically, sat up and threw the quilts aside. "The bastard!"

The bed was empty. Only pillows.

Ramsey Judd was gone.

Chapter Twelve

Ramsey left the river and started up the mountain toward Summit, staying to the main wagon road. He didn't like being in the open, but the moon was high to light his way and he could move faster than he could have in the darkness of the trees. He needed to put as many miles between him and Hannah as possible before she discovered he was gone. He hoped that wouldn't be until morning.

He had to find Sharon. He wondered why in the hell Hannah hadn't shot him herself when she had the chance, why she'd gone to all this trouble, hired Bull Brenner to do it. She'd had him in her sights enough times in the past month. Why did she have to go and drag Sharon into it? The woman was just plain sick in the head. That was a fact.

He rode through the night and all the next day, stopping only briefly to let the horse rest. Just before dark, he arrived at Kapelikan's ferry, waited impatiently for it to cross, then passed through Kamiah and started up the hill toward Jackson Bridge. The moon was high again when he finally reined his horse to a stop in a grassy place, hidden by trees, along the banks of the South Fork. He listened and watched, then dismounted, ground-tied the horse and let it drink.

Ramsey removed the light wool, plaid jacket he wore and rolled up the sleeves of his blue denim shirt, washed his face and hands, relieved his own thirst. He wished he had a cup of coffee, dug in the saddlebags for the old jerky stored there and settled under a tree, chewing contentedly until the stringy piece of dried meat was devoured. Then he rolled a cigarette.

He was tired, couldn't remember the last time he had a good night's sleep. He rested his back against the tree trunk, closed his eyes and finished his smoke. He listened to the relaxing lap-gurgle-splash of the water and the tall pines whispering in the breeze. Hoss's bridle jingled as he chomped steadily, hungry after his long ride, feasting on the bunch grass that grew abundant about the clearing.

Ramsey dozed at the edge of full sleep, slipping in and out of consciousness, teetering between dreams and reality.

The horse stopped eating, shook its head, snorted.

Something prickled the hair on the back of Ramsey's neck, and he came wide awake instantly. In spite of the cool night breeze, beads of perspiration formed on his brow and under the week's growth of whiskers on his face. Dappled moonlight through the tree branches danced in the clearing; moon dollars shimmered on the river's surface.

With an uneasy feeling nibbling at his insides, Ramsey straightened his back. His rifle was sheathed on his saddle, the Colt strapped to his leg. He reached down and touched it reassuringly.

He heard the soft whinny of a horse from beyond the privacy of the clearing, the clinking of tack. Hoss nickered, blew softly.

"I hear it." Ramsey stayed calm, spoke from under the brim of his hat still pulled low. "No need to tip our hand 'til we have to."

The horse pawed at the ground and tossed his head again.

"Easy, boy."

Trying not to show concern, Ramsey rose and walked to where the horse was standing, stroked the animal's neck and nervously twitching withers.

Whoever it was, wasn't in any hurry to have his identity known. He wasn't use to being quiet, either, made enough noise to wake snakes. Ramsey eased the rifle out of the sheath. The feel of it in his hands gave him an instant sense of security. He never was one for revolvers, unless there was nothing else handy.

"Whoever it is best be showing himself," he called out in a slow, even voice.

There was more jingle of tack as someone dismounted. Boots shuffled in the loose earth and twigs.

Slowly Ramsey turned to the sound, rifle hipped and cocked. "I don't aim to say it again. Show yourself."

"Mr. Judd?"

"Who is it?"

"Mr. Judd, it's me, Tom Smith."

Ramsey relaxed, lowered the Winchester, the relief almost knocking him over. He shivered, now, as the breeze cooled the sweat on his body. "In Christ's name, Tom, what are you doing out here?"

Tommy Smith stepped from the shadows

of the trees into the moonlit clearing leading a buckskin gelding. "Looking for my ma, Mr. Judd."

He looked tired, his light hair tousled on his hatless head, leaves and pine needles tangled in its mass. The sleeve of his hickory-striped shirt was torn at the shoulder.

"Pleasant? What in blue blazes would your ma be doing in a place like this?"

"Following after you, sir."

"Followin'... What in the hell for?"

"She got Mrs. Jensen to mind the boarding house, took a horse and rode out. Took Pa's old Spencer rifle, too. That thing hasn't been fired in years."

"When?"

"Four days ago. Snuck off without telling me a thing. She swore Mrs. Jensen to secrecy, but Mrs. Jensen got scared when two days passed and Ma still hadn't come home. I made her tell. Ma thinks you're in some kind of trouble."

"That could well be."

Ramsey chewed the inside of his lip. If that didn't just take the cake, he didn't know what did. What had possessed her to do such a fool thing? Not that he wasn't flattered to the core, her caring enough to come looking for him, but that's all he needed was to have Pleasant roaming around out there somewhere slowing him down more. She was probably lost. He'd have to find her, see her and Tom safely on their way before he could finish what he'd come to do. Women, he decided, could sometimes be a royal pain in the ass.

"You come straight from Indian Bend?" he asked.

"Yes, sir."

"Did you see a couple of men?"

"No men. I found Ma's camp a half-day's ride from here. It was deserted. Fire'd been dead for quite a while."

"She can't be far, then. You sure it was your ma's camp?"

"Yes, sir." Tommy's mouth quivered into a nervous grin. "Her tea cup was setting on a rock. The bedroll was one of the quilts from the boarding house. Who else but my ma would have clean sheets and a fluffy pillow way out here?"

Ramsey started to smile, then a sick feeling rolled over in his gut. "You mean she left her grip?"

"Seems so, sir."

Ramsey blew air from his puffed cheeks. One of the horses bit the other and a squeal erupted, then a series of kicks and grunts.

"Knock off the bullshit, Hoss," Ramsey ordered gruffly. "This ain't no time for quarrels."

The horses stomped then stood quietly. He was sorry for the thoughts he'd been thinking a moment ago. Why would Pleasant go off and leave her grip? She could have fallen somewhere, broken an ankle. Or her neck. And it was all because of him.

"Mr. Judd..."

"Something else?" Ramsey looked at the boy.

"Yes, sir. The britches she must have worn were laying all folded neat-like on a rock, along with her shirt and boots." Tommy's forehead creased and there was a worried expression on his face. "I found where it looked like she'd been dragged, Mr. Judd, and some of her hair was caught in a dead tree branch laying on the ground."

Ramsey thought about it for long seconds before it sank in. "You think she's been took?"

"Looked like it to me. Why else would there be drag marks and – "

"Shit!" Ramsey broke Tommy's words off in mid sentence. "That damn Brenner has her." There was no doubt in his mind. He planned to shoot the son-of-a-bitch if any harm came to Pleasant or Sharon. He might shoot him anyway, when he found him, just for the fun of it. And he would find him.

Tommy shuffled his feet nervously.

Ramsey looked at him and said, "Guess we'd better see if we can find her, son."

~~~

Pleasant didn't know how long she'd been unconscious, but when she opened her eyes, it was to a dull throb in the back of her head and a never-before-felt fear in the pit of her stomach. Her hands were bound to the sides of a wooden chair and the spindles dug into her back. Her ankles were spread and secured to the front legs of the chair. Her heart hammered behind her breast as she tried to move but couldn't.

Light came from the sooted chimney of a lone lamp on a rough wood table strewn with several whiskey bottles, most of them empty, in the center of the room. A fire burned in the grate of a stone fireplace where a large black kettle hung from a hook. Pleasant smelled the rancid odor of old meat cooking. The room's single window had no glass, but was covered with some ancient material, gray and tattered, that stirred in the breeze. She saw inky
~~~

blackness beyond.

The floor was littered with debris, and an old wood stove without a pipe took up one corner. Four saddles were pushed against the furthest wall. Three rifles leaned next to the saddles. One of them was the old Spencer she'd been carrying.

Then her gaze rested on a cot where a young woman in a thin, blue calico dress lay, no shoes on her bound feet, her hands secured with rope, her eyes wide and dark and frightened.

Oh dear Lord, it was Sharon Larken!

Pleasant glanced around again. The two of them were alone. She tried to speak, but the words came out in a little croak. She was thirsty, her throat like sand. She tried to summon saliva into her mouth. "Are you okay?" she managed in a rough whisper.

"For now," Sharon replied. "Mrs. Smith, what are you doing here?"

"I came looking for Mr. Judd. He's in danger."

"Yes, I know. My mother hired Bull Brenner to kill him."

"I was right then," Pleasant said almost to herself, "Hannah Larken is behind this whole thing."

There was a noise from outside the cabin and Sharon jumped. "Mrs, Smith," she said, "close your eyes, pretend you're asleep."

Pleasant let her head fall forward and her lids drop just as the door opened.

She heard the shuffling of feet as two men entered, bringing with them the unpleasant, acrid smells of unwashed bodies and rot-gut whiskey. Her nose twitched involuntarily.

"She still out?" It was Jack Cady. "You shouldn't have hit her so hard."

"What difference does it make?" the other man, Bull Brenner, answered. "Now or later, it's all the same to me."

"This is gettin' sticky as hell, Bull. Didn't plan on killin' no women."

Pleasant knew the men could hear her heart. It was hammering loudly in her ears. Her stomach constricted. They were planning to kill her.

"Man or woman, one more don't make much difference. Ya get hung just as high and just as dead."

"I ain't gonna hang, Bull. And I ain't killin' no women."

"You'll do what has to be done so you won't have to hang. If you don't, I'll shoot you myself. I got it all worked out, anyway. Judd'll get the blame and he'll be dead."

"I tell you, I ain't – "

"Oh, quit your whinin'. You got just as much to gain as I do. You saw the assay report on that gold we took out of the cave and the stream. We won't have no worries the rest of our lives."

"What about the girl?"

Bull didn't answer.

"You ain't gonna hurt Miss Larken, Bull."

"Don't know yet."

Pleasant choked.

"I think she's comin' around," Cady said.

Pleasant opened her eyes, raised her head and looked into Bull Brenner's scarred face. She glanced at Jack Cady, then back at Bull. They were both filthy, their heavy flannel shirts streaked with grease, their hands black from days of dirt and grime. She winced as Bull reached out and patted the top of her head, ran a disgusting finger down her cheek.

"Hi there, ma'am. Enjoy your sleep?"

She was too frightened to speak, but she glared at him.

"You stay here and take care of the ladies, Jack. It's time to go and renegotiate with the widda Larken."

"What if she don't?"

Bull glanced at the girl on the cot. "She will."

The man picked up his saddle and rifle and left the cabin.

Jack Cady took a half empty whiskey bottle from the table, uncorked it and took a long swig. He eyed Sharon and Pleasant, crossed the room and sat on a chair like the one Pleasant was tied to, tipped the bottle to his lips again, then corked it. Leaning back and pulling his hat forward, he closed his eyes, his arms resting across his chest, the bottle dangling from one hand.

Pleasant looked across the room at Sharon's frightened eyes. She tugged at her bonds, but the ropes cut into her arms. She had to get free. They were going to kill her. They'd probably kill Sharon too. She had to warn Ramsey.

~~~

On the other side of Jackson Bridge, Ramsey and Tom reined in under a bull pine tree and stood on the stirrups, stretching their legs.

"Better rest," Ramsey said.

"But we gotta find Ma."

"She's where she is, and I don't figure they'll be moving her tonight. Do you know of
~~~

any old shacks around here? A miner's cabin?"

"I don't know this country. I've never been off the main trail."

"Got any grub?"

"No."

Ramsey dismounted and dug into his saddlebags, brought out the bag of beef jerky. "Ain't much," he said, handing a piece to Tommy, "but it'll see us through. The packhorse run off yesterday. Don't even have coffee."

Tommy slid down from his saddle. "Ma's camp is a couple hours from here. Whoever took her didn't bother to take her supplies."

"Then we'll make camp there tonight." He sat himself against the tree, closed his eyes and chewed the piece of leathery meat.

"Mr. Judd?"

Ramsey opened one eye and peeked out from under the brim of his hat.

"Will they hurt Ma?"

His gut tightened. "Can't say," he replied in a controlled voice.

"Shouldn't we go? I mean..."

"Sit down a spell, Tom." Ramsey closed his eye again. "I'm worn out."

"I can't just sit here, Mr. Judd. Not with Ma out there."

Ramsey sat forward, pushed his hat to the

back of his head and pulled his tobacco from his shirt pocket. "Tom, there's a couple men somewhere up yonder that want me dead. Then there's a woman somewhere back there," Ramsey hooked a thumb over his shoulder, "wants me dead too. I feel like I'm between a rock and a hard place. I got a daughter out there somewhere, and now I got your ma to worry about as well. I'm dog tired. I ain't slept in a coon's age. My head's about as foggy as if I'd just swilled a bucket of red-eye. I couldn't fight right now if I had to. If I get killed, they won't stand a chance. Now sit down and rest. We'll be leaving soon enough."

"Your daughter?"

"That's what I said, Tom. Sharon Larken is my own daughter."

"Oh." Tommy sat next to Ramsey, watched him with a curious look in his eye.

Ramsey finished his smoke and closed his eyes, brought the hat down low. He knew Tom wanted more, wanted him to explain Sharon, but he didn't feel like it right now. It was time for thinking, not talking. There was a lot of space out there. It might take days. He needed to get to where Pleasant had made camp. See if he could pick up the trail.

"My ma's kinda partial to you, Mr. Judd,"

Tommy said.

"I'm fond of her too," Ramsey answered without looking at him.

"I mean real partial. I ain't never seen my ma so partial to anyone like she is to you."

Something stirred in the pit of Ramsey's stomach, a good feeling. That was the best bit of news he'd had in a long time.

"I'm real partial to your ma too, Tom. She's a fine woman."

"Sure don't want my ma to get her feelings hurt because of you. Do you know what I mean, Mr. Judd?"

Ramsey peered out from under the hat again. "You going somewhere with this, boy, or just grazing?"

"So what you going to do about Ma?"

"I aim to find her."

"I mean after."

Ramsey closed his eyes again, folded his arms across his chest, relaxed. "I aim to marry her, if she'll have me. That is after I get some business straightened out. Is that alright with you, Tom?"

The boy didn't speak for a long moment, then stretched out on his back, his hands pillowing his head. "That's just fine with me, Mr. Judd."

"Good. Now that that's settled, close your mouth for a spell."

~~~

They reached Pleasant's camp a couple hours past noon. It was just the way Tommy had said it would be: everything laid out neat as a pin, the tea cup turned upside down in the saucer and sitting on a flat rock, her clothes folded next to it.

There'd been a struggle; Pleasant had been dragged to her horse. Worried, Ramsey figured she was probably alive, but may be hurt. He couldn't see the sense in loading her onto a horse if she were dead. He did a thorough search of the area while Tommy drew water from the river and started a fire.

Pleasant's horses were gone, but the pack saddle leaned against a tree, filled with provisions. Hoof prints marked the way the intruders had come and gone. Ramsey followed their trail for a short distance, found it led up toward the brow of a hill and started down the other side, toward a deep canyon. There was no trace of Pleasant's body hidden nearby, thank God.

Ramsey scratched his head. He figured the outlaws' hideout shouldn't be more than a few hours' ride. A good night's sleep and they'd
~~~

tackle it in the morning. Take them by surprise over breakfast.

He and the boy stayed in Pleasant's camp that night, feasted on fresh eggs they found wrapped in cotton and sealed in a coffee tin, side pork and hot biscuits that had been saved from a previous meal. Ramsey swore he'd never tasted food so darn good. Pleasant hadn't packed coffee, but there was tea and lots of it. He and Tom brewed a pot strong and hot.

They cleaned away the supper things and sat beside the fire. The night was cool and quiet. Ramsey gathered wool for some time, then tossed the dregs of his tea cup away and stood. "Time for sleep," he said. "We've got a big day tomorrow."

Ramsey eyed Pleasant's bed lying undisturbed under the tree. It looked mighty inviting. He'd acquired a liking for clean sheets and fluffy pillows.

"Tom," he said, scratching the back of his neck, "you have any problem with me taking that bed over there?"

Tommy suppressed a grin. "Guess not, Mr. Judd."

Ramsey pulled off his boots and crawled under the covers.

"Night, boy," he said.

"Night...old man," Tommy replied slipping into his own bedroll.

Ramsey choked. "What'd you say?"

"You called me boy."

"So I did. I'll have to watch that in the future. Go to sleep, Tom."

Pleasant had done a real good job padding the spot where she'd planned to sleep. The sheets and the pillow still had her scent and it caused a hurting in him, just thinking about her being manhandled by Bull Brenner, maybe injured, damn sure scared to death. Come tomorrow, he vowed, he was going to find her.

That was the last thought he had. He closed his eyes and took one long breath, drifted off into a deep, exhausted, dreamless sleep.

At daybreak, they followed the trail for several miles before it left the timber and climbed toward a rocky bluff. They stopped their horses below the crest and crawled on hands and knees to the top.

Ramsey squinted against the early morning sun, out over the rimrock at a deep ravine, scattered with large outcroppings of rock, sagebrush, and scrubby patches of pine. The silver ribbon of a creek split it in the middle at the bottom. The opposite side of the ravine rose gently to another flat-topped bluff.

Tommy started to stand, but Ramsey pulled him down. "First thing you learn, Tom," he said softly, "don't skyline yourself. Look around bushes and rocks, not over. Understand?"

"Yes, sir."

"Damn good way to get yourself shot. Another thing, if something don't feel right, don't do it. Sometimes your senses know something your head don't."

"Yes, sir."

"We may get into some shooting before this thing is over with. Have a gun?"

"No."

Ramsey reached to his belt and undid the rig, handed the Colt to Tommy. "Put that on. Know how to shoot?"

"Some."

"Good enough. It isn't always a matter of being the best shot. Sometimes it's a matter of knowing when to shoot. Don't unless you have to. Killing a man is something you do when you've tried everything else. Don't aim unless you have the guts to pull the trigger. Don't touch that trigger unless you plan to shoot. It's mighty touchy. Be careful. It's loaded."

Ramsey studied the valley again, starting

at the point at the base closest to him and moving out with each sweep. "Look at things out the corner of your eye, Tom. You can better catch movement that way." He moved down from the crest of the hill, and Tommy followed. "Did you see that little column of smoke about half way to the horizon?"

"No."

Ramsey eased back to the top. "It's there, to the southeast, across the creek. Almost hidden against the haze of the sky. In that stand of scrub timber. See it?"

"Yes, sir. I see it. You think that's where they have Ma?"

"I'd bet on it. Sharon, too. It's chimney smoke. Means there's a cabin."

"Now what, Mr. Judd?"

"We're going down."

They returned to the horses, mounted and started down the steep, rocky trail.

"Mr. Judd, we're going the wrong way," Tommy said after they'd cleared the bluff. "The smoke was southeast. We're going west."

"Never come into the unknown straight on, if you can help it. Always slip in from the side or, better yet, the rear. From what we saw at your ma's camp, there's two men. With luck, that's all who's down there now. One will be watching the women, the other will be lookout. Let's get going."

~~~

Hannah rode with the frenzy of a mad woman, punishing her mare with every mile. She'd been in a rage since she discovered Ramsey gone. Now all she wanted to do was find him and empty both barrels of her shotgun into him at close range. She left her hat at the hotel at Orofino, and her wild, unrestrained hair whipped out behind her. There was a fever inside her. The clothes she wore were damp with perspiration, her head throbbing, heart pounding. The lathered horse wheezed, half wind-broke. Hannah applied her heels to its flanks, lashed it with the reins, leaned forward in the saddle to gain speed. "Go, damn it, go!" Again she whipped the tired mare.

At day break, Hannah arrived at the place where Bull had ambushed them the day before. She slowed. This was a good place to stop. While she rested, she devised a plan. It shouldn't be hard to find Ramsey. He could look for days and never spot that cabin. She'd kill him, then ride on to the hideout and take care of Bull Brenner – and Jack Cady if she had to – get Sharon and take her home. She'd take
~~~

Ramsey's body to Indian Bend and collect her reward.

Maybe the fat little landlady would be there to watch as Hannah led his horse down main street with him lying across the saddle. Maybe she'd make sure the landlady would be on hand to see it. The thought brought some humor to Hannah's mind, some comfort. She calmed herself to a small degree, knowing that by sundown tomorrow, Ramsey Judd would be dead.

But by nightfall, Hannah hadn't found Ramsey or any trace of him. She paused along the banks of the South Fork above Jackson Bridge, washed herself in the cool water, wished she'd brought food with her. The thought of camping for the night here in this spot tempted her, but she knew if she did, Ramsey could put more distance between them. She had to keep going. She remounted and rode steadily. With a brisk breeze pushing her from behind, she cut to the left and took the seldom-used trail that lead to the canyon and the cabin.

Hannah was tired when she crossed the creek at the bottom and made a cold camp. Sleep was long and hard in coming and she lay with empty stomach and hate-filled mind, watching the stars in the clear blackness of the sky over head, listening to a spring-born litter of coyote pups yipping somewhere on the rocky bluff above.

Where in the hell was Ramsey Judd? He couldn't have just disappeared. She was only a few hours behind him. He'd probably rested along the way. She hadn't rested but once. She'd kept moving, pushing hard. She should have caught up with him by now.

He's gone, Hannah.

Maybe he stopped in one of the towns along the way. She cursed herself for not stopping and inquiring after him. But Ramsey didn't like towns. She knew that.

Maybe he's not looking for Sharon.

What if he'd given up the hunt? Gone back to Indian Bend?

What if he's gone to the authorities?

No. He couldn't. He's a wanted man. He wouldn't dare.

You've made a mess of things, Hannah.

Bull Brenner's made a mess of things.

Get Sharon. Go home.

Why couldn't anything ever go the way she planned?

You shouldn't have trusted Bull Brenner. You should have done it yourself when you had the chance. When I told you to, Hannah.

She was going to kill Brenner for this, if it was the last thing she ever did.

Chapter Thirteen

When Pleasant woke from a fitful doze at dawn the next morning, Bull Brenner hadn't returned to the cabin. Jack Cady snored loudly from a bedroll on the floor across the room.

Sharon seemed to be sleeping, her face pale against the dark gray wool blanket she'd been covered with. Cady had taken special care the night before to see that Sharon was as comfortable as he could make her.

Pleasant, on the other hand, had been left tied to the chair all day yesterday and through the night, her only reprieve being a short trip outside on two occasions, when she'd told the man she had to relieve herself. Under his lewd and watchful eye, she'd been forced to hike her night dress and do her business in plain view, the rifle pointed at her back. She'd been terrified to begin with, and this indignity only added to her misery and feeling of helplessness.

Once through the day, Cady had offered her a cup of broth from the kettle on the fire. The rancid smell made her stomach turn and she'd declined. She accepted a cup of the tepid, stale water from a bucket on the floor by the door.

She and Sharon hadn't been allowed to speak to each other, and neither of them had spoken more than a few words to their captor. Pleasant's back ached and she was stiff from sitting. Her arms were almost raw under her night dress where she'd fought against her restraints. She hadn't slept a wink in the hot, airless room, listening for Bull to return, frightened out of her wits that when he did appear, he would shoot her and Sharon.

Jack Cady had kept the fire going all night. The smell from the pot of broth was becoming unbearable, and Pleasant knew if she didn't get away soon, she'd die of the stink and the heat before Bull Brenner had the chance to shoot her.

If only Jack Cady would leave.

Oh God, help him leave.

As if in answer to her prayer, Jack Cady

stirred, rolled over and raised himself on one elbow, glanced quickly at Pleasant, then over at Sharon. His eyes lingered. He didn't speak, but got up and stumbled to the table, uncorked one of the whiskey bottles and took a long swig. He headed for the door, fumbling with the front of his pants.

Pleasant's eyes followed him until he was gone, then darted to the girl on the cot. Sharon's eyes were wide open.

"We've got to get out of here," Pleasant whispered. "If we don't, I swear, I'll die of this wretched place."

Sharon watched the door. "He'll be gone for about fifteen minutes. That's not very much time."

"We have to try. We have to get out of here before Bull comes back. Are you willing?"

Sharon nodded. "But hurry."

Pleasant strained with all her strength at the ropes holding her. They didn't give. Cady had done a good job tying them last night before he went to bed.

It was no use. She looked apologetically at Sharon. "I'm sorry," she whispered. "The ropes won't budge."

Sharon nodded understanding. "Neither will mine."

Pleasant squirmed again in her chair, trying to free herself. There was a loud *crack*. She looked at Sharon, her mouth open. "The chair," she whispered.

Sharon gave a quick nod, sat up straight.

Pleasant wiggled. The seat was loose. Glancing at Sharon, she moved again, deliberately, heavily. The chair cracked some more, tilted slightly to one side.

"One more time," Sharon said. "Oh, Mrs. Smith, you must hurry!"

Again, with every ounce of her strength, Pleasant wriggled in the chair, and the back rungs snapped out. The seat broke away from the legs and twisted loose. Pleasant fell to the floor of the cabin, hard. She shook her feet from the splintered wood, stood, stiff and unsteady. She was free. She threw the rope from her hands.

Heart pounding, Pleasant glanced around the room, spotted a skinning knife on the stones beside the fireplace. She picked it up and hurried to Sharon. "We've got to be quick," she said. "That evil man will be back any moment."

She sawed at the ropes on Sharon's ankles. The knife was dull, but finally Sharon's feet were free. Pleasant worked at the ropes at the girl's wrist until they, too, were free.

"Can you stand?" she asked breathlessly.

"I think so."

Pleasant ran to the window and peeked around the dirty material. Jack Cady was nowhere in sight. "Hurry, dear, hurry."

Almost skipping across the room, Pleasant picked up the old Spencer. Sharon was on her feet. Pleasant handed Cady's rifle to her. Together they hurried to the door, opened it a crack and looked out, then dashed into the early morning light. They ran as fast as they could for the cover of the bushes to one side of the building, Pleasant's long white nightgown flapping out behind her. Sharp twigs poked at her feet, but she kept running. They took a moment, crouching low behind a bush to rest and catch their breath.

Pleasant laid a hand on her breast and puffed. "I wish we could get to our horses."

"It would be too risky."

"Yes, I know."

"Oh God!" Sharon cried. "He's coming back!"

"We have to make it across the yard to the main trail. Wait until he's in the cabin," Pleasant whispered. "Run as fast as you can. If you get ahead of me, don't look back and don't stop. Go to Mt. Idaho. There should be a sheriff there." She hiked her nightgown. "Ready? Run, Sharon! Run!"

~~~

Hannah was just starting up the trail to the cabin when Bull Brenner stepped out in front of her. She pulled back on the reins, causing the horse to rear. Hannah grabbed the saddle horn and hung on. The lathered animal came down hard, danced nervously, eyes wild, nostrils flaring.

"In a hurry, Mrs. Larken?" Bull grinned up at her.

Hot anger at the site of the man rushed up inside Hannah. It felt like her heart was in her head, beating wildly against her skull, like it might burst to be free. "Where in the hell have you been?" she shouted.

"Ain't no way to treat a horse," he responded.

"Where's Sharon?"

"She's safe enough, for now."

"I ought to kill you, Bull Brenner."

"You won't. We got us some talkin' to do."

"Why is Ramsey Judd still alive? Why didn't you get him when you were suppose to?"

"I raised my price."
~~~

"I paid you half already!" she screamed. "We agreed!"

"There's time."

"Time, hell! He's out there somewhere right now. He knows. You won't get another cent from me. Do you hear me? Not another cent. I'll do the job myself. You're fired."

Bull's head tipped back and he laughed loud and hard.

Hannah's fury was like a whirlwind. How dare the man laugh at her. She'd show him. She made for the shotgun in the scabbard at her side.

Bull reached out and grabbed her wrist before she could touch it, pulled the pistol in the holster at his hip with the other hand and aimed it at her. "I said my price went up."

"Let go of me." She twisted loose.

"Get down, Hannah."

She didn't move. She was the boss. She gave the orders. "I told you never to call me that. I'm Mrs. Larken to you."

"We have a lot to talk about...Hannah." He held the revolver level, his finger on the trigger.

Hannah sat her horse and stared at him, a cold edge of fear cutting through her anger. She'd never had a gun pointed at her before. She didn't like it.

Bull stepped back. "Now," he said. "If you ever want to see that little girl of yours again – alive." His face hardened, making him uglier than he already was. "We have a gold mine to talk about."

"You damn crazy fool," Hannah said. "That mine's dead. The gold is gone."

Bull grinned. "The easy stuff. But there's gold there. Lots of it. With the right equipment and man power."

Hannah stared at him. "How do you know?"

"I been up there, Hannah. Took some samples to Grangeville. They're richer'n hell."

"You sorry excuse for a yellow-bellied rattlesnake."

Bull laughed. "That might be," he said. "But I'm gonna be one rich rattlin' son-of-a-mother."

Hannah spit at the ground in front of him.

Bull laughed again. "We could make a deal, Hannah. We could be partners. Maybe even more than partners. You're a right comely woman. We'd be good together. We think alike."

"That'll be a cold day in hell. I'd never take up with the likes of you."

"Seems to me you already have."

"I'll see you dead before you get an ounce

of that gold."

Bull's face sobered. "Sorry to hear you say that." He lifted the weapon, pulled back the hammer. "There's other ways to get that mine. Your daughter might be more cooperative."

Hannah watched his finger tighten on the trigger. Her throat dried. She had to think fast. "Okay, let's talk," she said.

"That's more like it." Bull eased the revolver off cock and relaxed. He was grinning again.

Stupid bastard.

~~~

Pleasant ran for her life. Out of the corner of her eye, she saw Sharon gaining on her. Good.

The distance between them and the shelter of the trees seemed endless.

"Hey! You! Stop!" Jack Cady called from behind them.

Pleasant's heart leaped to her throat. She ran harder. Sharon tripped and went down. Cady's rifle flew from her hand.

Pleasant ran on a few yards, glanced over her shoulder and saw the girl sprawled on the ground, winded. Jack Cady was running toward her. Pleasant stopped.

"I can't, Mrs. Smith," Sharon called
~~~

breathlessly.

"You can."

Sharon pulled herself toward the rifle.

"Leave the gun, Sharon! Get up and run!" The man was closing in. Sharon tried to pull herself up but collapsed.

"Get up, Sharon!"

"Go on, Mrs. Smith," Sharon called back between gasps. "Run. Save yourself."

Pleasant stood watching as Cady reached the fallen girl, picked up the rifle and aimed it at her. She hesitated for a heartbeat, then raised the Spencer to her shoulder.

"I'll shoot you if you harm her!" she yelled at the man.

Cady's rifle swung, the barrel leveling on Pleasant. "Put that blunderbuss down, ma'am."

Pleasant was shaking too hard, the rifle too heavy to draw a bead. Would it fire? It hadn't been used since before Tom died. Was it even loaded? Had Bull taken the cartridge out when she was unconscious?

"No!" she shouted. She had never shot a gun before, much less at another human being. She steadied herself as best she could against her violent trembling.

"Get up, Miss Larken," she heard Cady say over the ringing in her ears. "Or I'll kill your friend."

Sharon tried to move.

"I said get up, damn it! I wouldn't shoot you, Miss Larken. I could never do that. You're too pretty and sweet. I can't let you get away, either. Bull would kill me. But I could shoot her," he pointed at Pleasant with his rifle, "if I had to." He looked at Pleasant. "Ma'am, I'm warning you. Put that thing down."

Pleasant's throat felt parched, her lips dry as paper. She had nothing to lose. She kept the barrel of the Spencer up.

Jack Cady tensed, readied. "Please, get up. I don't want to shoot no women."

Pleasant drew a deep breath, closed her eyes and applied pressure to the cold steel beneath her finger. If she didn't, she'd die. She knew it. She had to do it. A false calm settled over her. She couldn't miss at this range, could she?

"Cady! Drop the rifle!" The man's voice came from the trees at the edge of the clearing.

Jack Cady's rifle blast broke the stillness. And then another shot from the opposite direction.

Pleasant opened her eyes. Jack Cady lay sprawled on the ground, face down. He lifted himself, tried to crawl, then fell back. A shiver shook his body, then he was still. Everything was still. No sound except the echo of rifle fire reverberating through the trees.

Pleasant stood staring, the Spencer still clutched tightly in her hands.

~~~

Hannah heard the exchange of fire from up the trail. So did Bull. He took his eyes from her and looked over his shoulder.

Quick as lightning, Hannah dug her right heel hard into her horse's flanks, jerked the animal's head around. The horse sidestepped, danced in close to Bull. Hannah slammed the sole of her boot a smashing blow to his face.

Bull dropped his gun, flew backwards, and landed staring at the sky a few feet away. Hannah grabbed the shotgun, pulled back both hammers. The horse stomped nervously and Hannah tightened her knees to its sides for balance. She took deadly aim at the prostrate man.

"Get up, Bull."

Bull raised himself, blood streaming from his smashed nose, collecting in his thick mustache. More blood oozed from the deep cut in his lip.

"Those shots came from the shack," he said, wiping his mouth with the back of his hand.
~~~

"There's trouble."

"You buzzard-faced crow bait," she said through clenched teeth. "You got trouble right here. Get up."

Bull staggered to his feet. A gray fear spread over his mangled face. "Now, Hannah – Mrs. Larken – let me go. I gotta get back to the cabin."

"I'm tired of messing with you." She fired both barrels.

The blast nearly unsaddled her. The horse spun and screamed. Hannah grabbed the reins just as she was thrown from the horse's back. She hung to them as the horse tossed its head, tried to rear, and brought its hooves down inches from Hannah's shoulder. The leather lines nearly pulled from her grasp.

Finally, Hannah calmed the wild-eyed mare enough to get to her feet and pick up her gun.

Bull Brenner lay in the trail ten feet from where he'd been standing. He was still, blood spilling from the large gaping hole in his chest.

Hannah didn't have time to take pleasure in the sight of his open, dead eyes. She put her foot in the stirrup and managed to mount the mare as it spun in a tight circle. "Hee-aw!" She kicked the horse, whipped it with the reins.

The mare shot forward, its hooves striking the man in the trail as it passed over him.

~~~

A tall man Pleasant had never seen before emerged from the timber across from the cabin, a black hat pulled down low on his forehead. A silver star was pinned to the front of his denim shirt. He walked toward them, and Pleasant felt herself begin to tremble with renewed vigor.

Sharon pulled herself to a sitting position and stared at the newcomer. She gasped and cried out, "Joe!"

The man dropped his rifle and ran toward her.

"Joe," Sharon cried. "Joe."

He knelt and pulled her into his arms, held her close.

Pleasant watched on, dumbfounded.

"How did you find me?" Sharon cried, looking up into his handsome face.

"Shhh," he whispered. He laid a hand at the side of her head and pulled it in against his chest. You're safe. I'm here."

Pleasant's knees felt weak. She dropped the Spencer and let herself go down, covering her face with her hands as she went.

"You okay, ma'am?"
~~~

Pleasant looked up. The man was watching her. "I...I think so."

"Can you walk?"

"As soon as I quit shaking."

"I'm Joe Keys."

Pleasant's lips trembled into a smile. "I'm certainly glad to meet you, Mr. Keys. My name's Pleasant Smith."

"Let's get back to the cabin." He walked to where she was still sitting and held out his hand, helped her up, then retrieved the rifles from the ground. "Can you manage these, Mrs. Smith?" he asked, handing her the rifles.

"Yes, I think so." Pleasant let him stack them like cord wood across her outstretched arms. Joe picked Sharon up effortlessly and carried her past the fallen man.

"I heard them talking, Joe," Sharon said in a weak voice. "Mama killed – "

Another blast exploded like a cannon from down the main trail.

Pleasant's heart stopped. "My Lord, what was that?"

Joe halted. "A shotgun," he answered, then hurried toward the cabin, Sharon still in his arms. "Come on, Mrs. Smith. I want you both inside. I'll have to go investigate."

Ramsey, she thought. The earth tipped

under her feet. The rifles she carried crashed to the ground. She felt herself falling. Darkness crept in about her.

~~~

Birds flew up from the scrub brush beside the trail Ramsey and Tommy traveled. The horses snorted and Ramsey pulled to a stop. "Rifles," he said. "From the direction of the cabin."

Tommy looked back at him, eyes wide with fear.

Ramsey didn't answer the question in the boy's expression. He urged his horse forward; Tommy didn't move. Ramsey looked over his shoulder. "Come on, Tom. We can't be but a few miles."

Tommy nudged weakly at the horse's flanks and followed after.

They rode in silence, forded the wide creek at the bottom and moved on up the other side of the canyon. Ramsey's teeth ached from the firm set of his jaw. If either of those women were harmed in any way...

For the second time in his life, Ramsey Judd was in a killing mood.

And then another blast split the air, to the left of the cabin this time. It was louder than the two preceding shots, the echo rattling
~~~

against the canyon walls.

He glanced nervously at Tommy. Tommy's eyes were big, his face pale.

"Mr. Judd..."

"Keep moving, Tom."

"What was it?"

Ramsey felt the panic crawling up his spine. He urged his horse to move faster. He had to get to the cabin. He hoped to hell it wasn't to late.

"Mr. Judd, what was it?"

"It was both barrels of Hannah Larken's 16-gauge."

"You said she was behind us."

"She damn sure was. She must have passed by our camp last night."

"But, sir, the horses. They'd've raised a fuss."

"Not last night." Cold fingers of fear clutched at Ramsey's stomach. He'd slept sound. Too damn sound. "She could have passed right under our noses and not even known it herself."

"Why's that, Mr. Judd?"

"The wind was riding with her, blowing from the west. It was at her back."

"You mean she snuck right past while we were asleep?"

"She didn't know," Ramsey answered. "If she had, I wouldn't be here to talk about it."

~~~

Hannah came to the clearing, saw the man lying in the dirt outside the cabin. Shotgun in hand, she slid from the saddle before the horse stopped moving. "Sharon!" she screamed.

The lathered horse trotted to the trees, stood with its head hung low, breathing hard.

"Sharon! It's Mama." She ran for the cabin door.

It slowly swung open, and Joe Keys stepped out.

Hannah raised the shotgun and aimed it at him. "What are you doing here? If you've harmed my girl..."

Sharon emerged from the open door, followed by Pleasant Smith.

Hannah eyed the three of them, her attention momentarily caught by the woman in the white night dress. What in the hell was she doing here?

Joe took a step forward. Hannah acted instinctively, tightening her grip on the gun. "Don't come any closer. Sharon, get behind me. I'm taking you home."

Sharon didn't move, just stared at her mother.
~~~

"Sharon, baby, come on. I've saved you."

"Mama," Sharon breathed. "Mama, how could you?"

"It's alright, sweetheart. Everything is going to be okay." Hannah tried to smile reassuringly. Her hands were shaking. "Mama's here."

"Put the gun down, Mama."

"Get behind me, Sharon."

"No."

Hannah stared at her. "What did you say?"

"I said, no, Mama." She stepped between Joe and Hannah. "You've done enough. Don't add to it. Put the gun down."

Joe took a step forward, laid his hand on Sharon's shoulder and pulled her back. He faced Hannah.

"I'll kill you," Hannah said to the man. "Let my daughter go."

"She's free to do what she wants, Mrs. Larken. I'm not stopping her."

"Come on, Sharon."

The sound of horses hooves caused the party to glance up. Ramsey Judd and Tommy Smith slid off their saddles and hurried toward them. A little gasp escaped Pleasant's lips.

Tommy went to stand between his mother and Sharon Larken.

It's him Hannah! It's him!

Hannah swung the shotgun. "Drop the rifle, Ramsey."

He let the firearm slide to the ground. "So this is it, is it?"

Hannah looked at him through squinted eyes. Her head had begun to throb. The walls of her vision closed in around him. "This is it. I've waited a long time."

"You're really going to do it this time?"

"I really am."

Ramsey took a step toward her. "I'm ready. But first, I have to say something to Sharon."

"Shut up, Ramsey."

"No. If I'm gonna die, I'll have my say." He glanced at Sharon, then back to Hannah.

Hannah tightened her grip, her finger firmly on both triggers.

"Please, Mama. Don't do this," Sharon cried again. "Please, please, put the gun down. You've killed enough."

"No, Sharon." Hannah looked at her daughter.

She knows.

She mustn't know. Hannah couldn't let her. "I haven't – "

"You put a pillow over Grandpa's face. You murdered him."

"No, Sharon."

"Bull Brenner told Jack Cady. I heard him. It's true, isn't it, Mama?"

"Sharon, I – "

"Isn't it, Mama?"

"He was old and sick. I was tired. He was a terrible man. He killed your grandmother."

"Grandma hanged herself. Grandpa told me before he died."

"She didn't belong here," Hannah said. "She was a fine lady."

"Grandma was crazy. Insane. Grandpa feared she'd even killed her own son."

An old forgotten memory flared up in Hannah's mind. The woman, her mother, mixing the heavy dose of laudanum to give to the ailing, fussing little boy. He'd been ill for most of the trip, crying at night, keeping the family awake, wearing his mother down. And the grave where they laid him hours later.

"And Papa," Sharon continued. "The Indians didn't kill Papa. You did. You shot him and blamed it on the Indians. Bull Brenner saw you."

Hannah shook her head, brought herself back to the present. "Sharon – "

"You hired Bull Brenner to kidnap me, and to kill Ramsey Judd. Why, Mama, why?"

"You don't understand."

"I need to know why."

Hannah gazed into her daughter's sad angry eyes.

So much a child can't understand about life.

So much to learn. "Sharon, honey..." Hannah licked her lips. Her throat felt like she'd swallowed barbed wire. "I'll explain everything. When we get home. I'll tell you everything you want to know. Get away from that man. Come with me."

"No, Mama. I can't."

Hannah shifted her gaze back to Joe. "Then I'll kill him too."

Ramsey took a step closer.

Hannah!

Chapter Fourteen

The clearing was charged, like a violent storm ready to break. Hannah's face was an unreadable mask, her body tensed, her feet braced, the shotgun steady and aimed at Ramsey.

"I'm warning you, Ramsey. I'll shoot. So help me God."

She glared at him through icy eyes. All other eyes were glued to her.

"I know, Hannah." Ramsey watched the wretched woman before him. She looked like a mad woman. She *was* a mad woman. He felt something. He didn't know what it was. All he knew was that he had to help her out of this mess. He didn't want her to bring more trouble down upon herself.

Hannah was sick. He knew that now. Why

he hadn't seen it before, he'd never know. He should have.

"There's no doubt in my mind," he said quietly. "I don't rightly believe God'll have a hand in it, though."

"You're a wanted man, Ramsey, a dangerous man. There's a price on your head. I can kill you and get away with it. There's a reward."

Unconsciously, he moved his toes in his boot. The wad of paper was gone.

"That's right, Hannah, honey." Ramsey's voice was low and calm. Steady. "There is. I don't blame you for wanting me dead. It wasn't right what I did. But if you shoot me, someone here's going to shoot you. I don't want that to happen. I don't want you to die."

Her tongue darted over her lips. The barrel of the gun wavered, then steadied. "I'll take my chances," she said, her voice weaker, trembly.

Ramsey had to buy time. He had to find a way to get to her. Stop her. "Before you shoot me, can I talk to Sharon? Our daughter?"

Ramsey heard the intake of breath from behind him, but didn't take his eyes off Hannah.

"I'd purely like to tell her how much I love her. How sorry I am that I didn't stick around and be a proper daddy to her, take care of her and her mama. I'm truly sorry for that, Hannah. Truly I am."

Hannah's expression changed. For a moment, he saw something in her face, a glimmer of something old and almost sweet. A ghost of a smile played on her lips, then died away, replaced by confusion, bewilderment.

This could be it. She was weakening. Ramsey held out his hand. "Come on, honey. Come over here. Everything is going to be okay now."

She glanced at the group of people standing beside the cabin, then back at him. She relaxed ever so slightly, took one hand from the shotgun and moved it, like she might be reaching out to him. Then she stiffened, clutched it tighter.

She was waging a battle, he knew, with that unknown thing inside her. He had to help her fight it. Help her defeat it. "Hannah, love..."

The softening of her features again, the wistful quality in her expression. "Oh," she whispered. "Oh, Ramsey, I love you."

"I love you, too, Hannah." His voice was choked. He meant it. That's what he was feeling. He did love her. Not the way a man loves a wife or a sweetheart, but he loved her.

"You do?" She was like a little girl, almost innocent.

It was time. Ramsey started towards her. He needed to get to her now. "Of course I do, Hannah. You're the mother of my daughter. Our beautiful daughter, Sharon. Shall we put that gun down now and go for a walk? Talk about it?"

It was too late. Something behind her eyes snapped. The spell was broken.

Her eyes wild, she took several steps toward him, the gun wavering in front of her. "You!" she screamed. "You – liar! Sharon! Don't listen to him. Don't listen to him, child."

Ramsey made his move. He lunged at Hannah. Hannah stepped back, snagged her heel on a rock on the ground behind her. She started to go down, caught herself and pulled on both triggers at the same time.

The blast was deafening.

Hannah jerked, then crumpled to the ground. The shotgun fell heavily beside her.

Ramsey stood dazed, petrified to the spot, his ears ringing. What in the hell happened? He waited for Hannah to move. She didn't. His feet were like lead weights as he forced them forward, looked down at the lifeless face, the sightless eyes, the red stain forming on the front of her shirt over her heart.

"Aw, Christ." He fell to his knees beside her. "Hannah!"

Ramsey only remembered twice in his life when he'd felt so sad and helpless, a hurt so deep and painful it overwhelmed him. The wife and son he'd lost, and the death of his brother.

For a moment, he was back on the banks of the Mississippi and it was Jared lying on the ground before him.

He lifted Hannah gently into his arms and held her close, rocking her back and forth. He couldn't stop the tears that flooded his eyes and coursed hotly down his face.

He should have known.

Dammit. He should have known.

He'd heard her fire the shotgun earlier. Both barrels. She hadn't taken time to reload. Confused and sick, he looked up half expecting to see Johnny Bowler standing a few feet away.

Tommy Smith stood, hands empty at his sides, a stunned look on his face. Beside him, Pleasant's stricken expression, her eyes momentarily colliding with Ramsey's. She lowered her gaze, stared down at her hands clasped in front of her.

Ramsey's eyes moved to his daughter.

Sharon held the Colt revolver in both hands, arms stretched out in front of her, face drained of color, her eyes blank, staring. The young man that Ramsey didn't recognize stood beside her, his face registering shock.

Ramsey lowered Hannah to the ground, breathed deep, put forth every effort he could manage, and raised himself to a standing position.

Sharon dropped the revolver, turned and walked to the row of trees at the edge of the clearing. The man started after her.

"Wait," Ramsey said softly. "Let me."

He followed his daughter. She was sitting on a fallen log. He quietly sat beside her.

"It had to be done, Mr. Judd."

Ramsey found his voice. "We do what we have to do, Sharon."

"You're really my father?"

"I am."

"I see."

"I had to go away. I didn't know about you."

Sharon heaved a long sigh and raised her eyes to look at him. "Did you really love her, Mr. Judd?"

"Yes, Sharon. I loved her. Maybe not the way she wanted me to, but I really loved her."

"Can you forgive her?"

"We all need a little forgiveness."

"I loved her." Sharon dropped her gaze, stared at her fingers entwined on her lap, twisting them until the knuckles were white.

"I know."

"Mr. Judd – " She bit her bottom lip. "She wasn't always this way, was she? You knew her. Was there good in her?"

"She loved you. That was good."

"No. It wasn't good. Not the way Mama loved."

Ramsey wanted to touch his daughter, comfort her. He didn't know how. He didn't know her. The pain on her face wrenched at his heart. He couldn't think of a thing to say.

"Will you leave me, sir? I need to be alone."

Silently, Ramsey rose, the helpless feeling weighing him down. He left her sitting there and walked back into the clearing. The stranger was dragging Jack Cady away to the side of the cabin, out of sight. Tommy and Pleasant had gone inside.

Ramsey removed a blanket from the bedroll on Hannah's horse and spread it out on the ground next to her. He knelt and brushed the hair away from her face and closed her eyes.

Poor, sick Hannah. She wasn't to be hated. Life had made her the way she was. Life and the legacy obviously left to her by her mother. Ramsey had played a part, too. He was guilty as hell. He killed her, he knew, just as if he'd pulled the trigger himself.

The stranger joined him as he was laying Hannah on the blanket. He knelt and helped Ramsey wrap her, then found rope and secured the blanket in place. Together they lifted her over the back of her horse.

"What happened, here?" Ramsey said quietly. "How'd Sharon get that gun?"

"I didn't have time to do a thing. She grabbed that revolver out of Tommy's – " The man wiped his face with his hand. "I couldn't stop her."

Ramsey drew a long breath. "She wouldn't have had to done it. The shotgun was empty."

"No need to tell Sharon that, is there?"

"No," Ramsey answered. "No need."

"My name's Joe Keys, by the way."

"How'd you come to be here?"

"I was in the saloon in Indian Bend. It was all over town. Some woman at the boarding house told one of the boarders Sharon had been kidnapped. I've been sweet on Sharon for a long time. Hannah fired me because of it. I rode back to the ranch to make sure it was true. Bull Brenner was gone. No one had seen him for a couple of days. I put two and two together, followed a hunch. It was a long shot. He use to stay here when he went hunting."

"Hannah wanted me dead pretty bad."

"Hannah Larken was a strange one. Didn't want anyone close to Sharon."

"Bull turned the tables on her."

"Bull wanted that mine of Hannah's. I'd heard him talking about it often enough." Joe took makings from his pocket and rolled a cigarette, handed the makings to Ramsey. "I worked for Hannah long enough to get to know Bull pretty well."

"You heard that shot a while ago?" Ramsey asked, rolling a smoke for himself. "What you make of it?"

"Figure we'll find Bull back along the trail somewhere," Joe answered. He struck a wooden match with this thumbnail. Cupping his hands around the flame, he lit his own smoke, then Ramsey's.

"That's the way I figure it, too," Ramsey said, sucking the smoke into his lungs.

"I'll deputize a couple men when we get back to town," Joe said, "have them go looking for him. No need to do it now. I have to get

Sharon squared away."

"Deputize?"

"I was sworn in a couple weeks ago in Indian Bend."

For the first time, Ramsey noticed the star on the front of the younger man's shirt. "You're the sheriff, then?"

"When Hannah gave me the ax, I needed to do something. They needed a sheriff and I needed a job."

"You heard what Hannah said about me?"

"I did. Figured we'd get a chance to talk about it."

"I'm tired of running, Joe. I just want to get it over with."

"What are you wanted for?"

"Desertion. Civil War."

"What side?"

"Union." Ramsey dropped the cigarette at his feet, ground it out with the heel of his boot. He told Joe the story. "I'll give myself up when we get back to town," he finished.

"No need. I know where to find you. Let me get in touch with the war department. That was twenty years ago. Maybe they've forgotten about you."

"The government don't forget."

Joe slapped him on the back. "Right now,

lets get these people out of here. They've been through enough."

A saddled, bald-faced sorrel without a rider wandered into the clearing, staying close to the edge of the trees, reins dragging. Ramsey glanced at Joe. "Kind of cinches it, doesn't it? I'll lay odds that's Bull's horse."

"I'm inclined to agree with you."

"Joe," Ramsey paused at the door to the cabin, "I was wonderin'. What's your intentions where my daughter's concerned?"

Joe's mouth quirked into a grin. "Honorable, sir. I wish to marry her."

"Best go to her, son," he said, opening the door. "I have a feeling she's gonna be needing you about now."

"Can you take the bodies back to town?" Joe asked. "I don't want to cause Sharon any more pain than I need to. I'll take her out one of those back trails."

"I can do that. No sense sending anyone for Bull, either. I'll send Tom and Pleasant on with you, pick up Brenner's body and bring him along."

"I'd be obliged."

Ramsey was tired when he entered the cabin. He felt like he'd been over fifty miles of bad road, all up hill. Pleasant sat on a bench beside the table and Tommy sat on the one across from her. They were both silent.

"Can you be ready to leave soon?" He directed his words at Tommy, but didn't take his eyes off Pleasant.

"The horses are out back," Tommy answered. "I'll get them saddled."

"Good. Do that now, please. I need to speak to your mother."

Tommy rose quickly and left. Ramsey gazed at the woman across the room from him. She watched him, lips parted, eyes big and round and soft.

He didn't know what he wanted to say, what needed to be said, but knew he had to say something to her, needed her to understand. His emotions were running wild, constricting his throat. He wanted to yell at her for being there, but was damn glad to see her. He needed to look at her. He was about as mixed up in his head as he'd ever been. He took off his hat, worked the brim with his fingers and cleared his throat.

"You okay?" he asked.

"I'm fine. How's Sharon?"

"Taking it pretty hard."

"Yes, I'm sure."

"I'm sorry, Mrs. Smith," he said. "Sorry as

hell."

"So am I, Mr. Judd."

Ramsey knew he'd lost her. He'd lost everything a few moments ago: Hannah, his daughter, and now this woman. He didn't blame her. He'd done it to himself. Ran away from everything he'd ever loved. Now he'd stopped running, but it didn't much matter. It was too late to change things.

Pleasant waited quietly, an expectant look on her face.

"You got something else to put on?" he asked.

The color rose to her cheeks. "No."

"Don't matter."

The room was still for several seconds while Ramsey searched for words that wouldn't come.

"Mrs. Smith, I need you to understand those things I said a bit ago...to Hannah, I mean."

Pleasant gave him a trembling smile. "I understand, Mr. Judd. Of course you'd feel something for Mrs. Larken. She's the mother of your child, after all."

I do – I did, but not the kind of feeling that – "

"Yes," Pleasant said. "It's kind of like that

unexplainable love we have for lost souls. Is that what you're trying to say, Mr. Judd?"

"Yes, ma'am. That's it."

Again, an awkward silence settled in the room. There was more he should say. He fought for what it might be and finally gave up, clamped the hat back on his head. "I'm sending you and Tom on ahead with Sharon and Joe. I have some business to tend to." He started to go, then turned. "That was a damn fool thing to do, Mrs. Smith."

Pleasant's chin quivered. Her eyes filled with tears.

"Ah, damn, ma'am. Don't cry." Ramsey was across the room in three strides. He took her hand and pulled her up to him.

A little sob escaped her. Ramsey wrapped her in his arms and stroked her hair. "Don't cry, Mrs. Smith." He could feel the heat from her body under the thin fabric of her gown, the trembling inside her. "What's the matter? Were you hurt?"

"No," she said on a hiccup.

"Then what is it?" He stepped back from her and looked into her face.

"Oh," she said, gazing up at him, tears slipping down her cheek. "Mr. Judd, I'm just so glad you're alive. I was so afraid – "

"Ah." Ramsey brushed a damp, stray strand of hair from her temple, then bent low and placed a soft kiss on her lips. They were warm and yielding and his mouth lingered, tasting the salt from her tears, then pressed harder.

Feelings exploded inside him. For a moment, he almost forgot what had happened a few minutes ago. Forgot all the troubles that might lay ahead. All he wanted was Pleasant. She was his world. Nothing else mattered.

Ramsey broke the kiss and stepped back.

"I love you, Mr. Judd," she whispered.

"You can't go in there, Sheriff," Ramsey heard Tommy say from outside the door. "Mr. Judd is talking to my ma."

"I love you, too, Mrs. Smith."

They gazed at each other for a long moment, and he knew she did understand. How could he have ever doubted her? He knew there weren't anymore words necessary. What needed to be said was said.

"They're ready to leave," he said. "It's over. Best be going home."

Chapter Fifteen

Ramsey rode into Indian Bend, leading the three horses with their grim cargo. Physically and emotionally drained, every bone in his body ached, and there was a heaviness in his heart he couldn't seem to shake. It had been a damned long week; a lot had happened. All he wanted was to sit in Pleasant's kitchen and let her soothe away his worries, like she had a way of doing. But he couldn't. Not yet. He still had a long way to go.

He rail-tied the horses in front of the sheriff's office, just off the main street, and wearily walked inside the small, board structure. It was hot. A potbelly stove stood in the middle of the room with a coffeepot steaming on top, the smell telling Ramsey it had been there for a while. The walls of the room were cluttered with posters, bulletins, and notices. Three wooden chairs sat along one wall, next to an empty gun rack. Tommy Smith sat in another matching chair behind the only desk, his long legs stretched out on the papers strewn over its top, his head back, mouth open, arms across his chest, sound asleep.

"Tom."

The young man jerked to wakefulness. "Mr. Judd."

"Where's Joe?"

"He took Miss Larken home. Told me to wait for you here."

"What's he want done with the bodies?"

"Joe said you was to take Brenner and Cady over to Doc Cobb's. He's the undertaker, too. He wants Mrs. Larken took to the ranch. Doc Cobb has a pine box waiting, if you could manage it."

"How's your mother?"

"Fine, Mr. Judd. She's real tired. Mrs. Jensen's with her."

"You tell her I'll see her tomorrow afternoon, you hear?"

"Yes, sir, I will."

Ramsey left, delivered Cady and Brenner to Dr. Cobb, tied the wooden coffin onto Jack Cady's horse and rode from the town, ignoring the few people on the nearly deserted street who stopped to stare at him as he passed.

Clouds had gathered in the west, and Ramsey knew they'd be getting some weather before morning.

It was almost midnight when he reached the ranch. There was the welcome smell of rain in the air as he stripped his horse and rubbed it down in the make-shift barn Hannah had used since hers had burned. Then he gently lifted Hannah's wrapped corpse from the ruined little mare's back, relieved that the stiffness of death had left her, the rigor mortise having worn off with the passing hours. He also knew that he'd have to work fast. Putrification wouldn't be long in starting now.

He pried the lid from the box with an iron bar and looked inside. His heart sank at the starkness of the interior. Just bare boards. No lining of any kind. Nothing to rest her head upon.

Cold, he thought, shivering. Hannah will be cold. He knelt and began undoing the knots securing the wrappings around her, thinking as he did that the blanket would be too dirty to use for lining. He had to find something. He couldn't leave it this way. It wouldn't be fitting. Hannah deserved better, didn't she?

"Mr. Judd."

Ramsey looked up. Sharon was standing in the doorway, holding a basin of warm water. Under her arm was a bundle wrapped in a clean, hand-stitched quilt. Her face was pale and she looked like she'd been crying.

"You needn't do this, Sharon. Leave the stuff, I'll take care of it. You go back to the house and get some sleep."

"No," she said. "I have to. Will you help me?"

Ramsey nodded and worked some more at the knots.

They didn't speak as they washed Hannah's body, combed her hair and dressed her in the brown skirt and blue shirt Sharon had brought.

"She was quite beautiful, don't you think, Mr. Judd?" Sharon gazed down on her mother lying quietly, peaceful for the first time either of them could remember, in the coffin they'd lined with the quilt.

"Yes," Ramsey said in a quiet voice. "She really was, Sharon."

"Good night, Mr. Judd."

"Good night, hon."

Ramsey picked up the soiled clothes and wrapped them in the wool blanket, put them in the corner of the small shed to dispose of when the sun came up. Then he nailed the lid into place, closing the pine box for eternity.

The barn had grown warm and he welcomed the fresh air as he stepped outside. A few cold, wet, heavy drops of rain had already begun to stir up the dust at his feet.

Ramsey lit a lamp in the bunkhouse. Three men snored in cots at one end. One of them was Joe Keys. Quietly, Ramsey found an empty bed, flopped into it and slept the night through.

The morning of Hannah's burial broke dark and dismal. The clouds had moved in and hovered low over the family cemetery on her mountain. It was raining hard by the time Ramsey and Joe lowered the casket into the freshly dug grave beside Hannah's mother. The burial was attended by five people: Sharon, Joe Keys, Ramsey, and the two ranch hands. There was no eulogy, Sharon said, because her mother hated preachers and didn't believe in God and the hereafter, so it would have been a waste of time.

Sharon scooped up a handful of wet earth and threw it into the hole. It hit the wooden box holding her mother's remains with a soft thud. She wiped her muddy fingers on the black skirt she wore, then silently turned away. Ramsey and Joe watched her back, straight and rigid, as she headed down the hill through the rain-soaked grass toward the house.

"Can you take care of this, Joe?" Ramsey asked.

Joe nodded, picked up a shovel and tossed it to the hired hand standing nearest to him. He picked up another and they began filling the grave. Ramsey started after his daughter.

It was the first time he'd ever been inside the house that Pete Lacey built. He hesitated, started to knock, but didn't and entered. It was quiet. Too quiet. He passed through the plain but clean kitchen and found Sharon, shivering, sitting in a wing-back chair in the front room, before the cold grate. Her wet, dark hair was matted to her head, her face ghostly white, dark smudges under her eyes. Her clothes clung to her like a wet cocoon.

She was grieving, he knew, and he should leave her to it, but he wanted to be close to her, comfort her if he could.

"Would you like a fire, honey?" he asked softly, standing in the doorway.

Sharon didn't speak, stared straight ahead. Ramsey could hear her teeth chattering.

"Why don't you change out of those damp

clothes while I get some wood?"

Still, Sharon didn't answer. Ramsey wondered if she was aware he was even there. He moved quietly across the room, took a lap robe from the settee and wrapped it around the young woman, his hands lingering, pressing gently against her shoulders. Then he left to find kindling.

He'd hoped that fatherhood would be a natural instinct kind of thing, he'd just know what to do and what to say. But it didn't work that way. He was on his own, with no experience. He found himself appreciating more his own father, the way he handled the toughest situations. Ramsey had taken it for granted.

When the fire was blazing, chasing the chill from the room, he went to the kitchen, started a fire in the cook stove and pushed the tea kettle into place, found tea and prepared it. He took the pot and two earthenware cups back to where his daughter was sitting, silent and withdrawn. He filled one of the cups and placed it in her icy fingers, then sat in a rocker next to her with a cup of his own.

The room was almost dark enough to justify a lamp, but Ramsey lit none. The steady ticking of the old clock on the mantel registered the minutes of silence that stretched out between him and his daughter.

Funny, Ramsey thought, how the sound of rain hammering a tin roof can close out the rest of the world, and a cup of tea can warm from the inside out like nothing else. He looked around him. The room was cozy, more Sharon's personality than Hannah's, he was sure, the dark logs of the walls, chinked with mud and dried grass, glistening with bee's wax even in the dimness, and splashes of color on the worn, but serviceable furniture from throws and crocheted fusties on the backs and arms.

Sharon moved for the first time, lifting the heavy cup to her lips, sipping, then lowering it. She swallowed, then sighed, shook herself, like suddenly awaking from a doze. "What do I call you, Mr. Judd?" she asked, watching the leaping flames licking at the round, larch log he had laid there.

"What do you want to call me?"

"I can't call you Papa. I had a papa that raised me. I loved him very much."

"I understand. You could call me Ramsey."

"That doesn't seem fitting either. And Mr. Judd seems awfully formal." She turned her head slowly and looked at him. "I'm terribly confused."

Ramsey lowered his gaze, looked into his cup, watched the amber liquid as he swirled it with the motion of his wrist. "I can understand how you might be. Guess I'm a little confused by it all myself."

"What am I suppose to do now?" she asked.

Ramsey looked back at her, held her unhappy, confused gaze. "Go on with your life, Sharon. You're young."

"What life? I had no life, except for Mama. She's gone, Mr. Judd."

"I'm sorry about your mama."

"It's done. I can't dwell on it or I'll become as crazy as she was. She was crazy, wasn't she?"

"You have the ranch," he said, not wanting to give the obvious answer.

"This place? I hate this place. I've been a prisoner to it all my life. When I was a girl, I use to dream of how it would be when Mama died. When I'd finally be free of it. Does that sound terribly wicked?"

"What about Joe?"

"What about Joe?" she said.

"You're planning to wed. Anyhow, that's what he says."

"We were. But not now."

"What makes now different?"

"Mr. Judd, I can't marry Joe. What if I become like my mother and my grandmother? What if I have children? Would they be like that? I can't take the chance. Don't you see? It would be too risky."

"Does he know how you feel?"

She turned away, back to the fire. "We haven't talked about it." She took another quick breath. "I've decided to go away. Far away."

A sick, panicky feeling swept through Ramsey. He hadn't thought of her leaving him. "Where, Sharon? Where would you go?"

"I don't know. Maybe east. There's a whole box of money in Mama's bedroom. Enough to take care of me for a long time."

"What would you do in the East? Do you have family?"

"Not that I know of. I don't know what I'll do. But I have to get away from here."

"Running away isn't the answer."

She looked at him again, her eyes hardened now. "You did."

Ramsey felt the truth of her words hit home like a hammer on a flat nail. "Yes," he said, leaning forward, his arms on his knees, both hands wrapped around the mug. "And look where it's gotten me. I missed out on what should have been the best part of my life. I missed out on you, Sharon."

"Why did you? Run, I mean?"

"You heard what your mama said. I'm wanted by the law. When I should have stayed and faced up to my mistakes, I ran. I planned on making that right now, but it's a little late."

Sharon lowered her gaze. "I'm sorry," she said softly. "That wasn't fair."

"It was the truth."

"I've been thinking it over," Sharon went on. "I want to sell this place. Where I go and what I do...well, I'll decide when the time comes. But I do want to get shed of this ranch. There's nothing for me here. Too many memories." She took another sip of her tea. "And I don't want Joe to know. Not right now, at least."

"He loves you very much."

"He thinks he does. But if I turn bad..."

Ramsey chewed the inside corner of his mouth. There could be some truth in what she said, he supposed, but somehow he doubted it.

"If you were going to turn bad, you'd have done it by now," he said. "I don't think there's much danger of that happening."

"And my children?" She looked him in the eye again. "Can you say it won't happen to my children?"

"No. I can't say that. No one can. Not even you, Sharon. Life is kind of like poker, I guess. We gamble. We can't live our lives being afraid of the risks."

"When the risk involves innocent children?"

"And what if you play the hand wrong, Sharon? Throw it in when you're holding a full house? Walk away figuring someone's holding a royal flush, not knowing for sure if you won or lost?"

"I played poker with my grandfather when I was a little girl, Mr. Judd. I know the game." She paused. "Would you like to buy me out?"

The question threw Ramsey for a moment. "Me? Good Lord, girl. I don't have a pot to – I don't have money to buy you out."

"The ranch is showing profit. I was up half the night going through Mama's books, waiting for you. That's one thing she did well. She kept her books up to date. You could work it, pay me a percentage of the gross income until it's paid for. I don't need the money all at once. Like I said, there's a small fortune in Mama's chest. The only stipulation is that you can't do anything with Mama's claim until the land is yours."

"What if I go to prison?"

"Then it would be paid for when you get out. You could have someone run it for you."

"I'm not a young man, Sharon. If I go to jail, I could be dead when I get out."

"Now who doesn't want to take risks?"

She held his gaze, her jaw firm, her expression determined. Much like her mother's, Ramsey thought.

"I want to sell. I want to sell to you. Do you want it or not?"

Ramsey ran his fingers through his hair, scratched the back of his head. Hell yes, he wanted it. But he wanted Sharon with it. It would be a good place to spend his old age. A living for him and –

She made it sound so damned easy.

"And if I say yes, then you're going back East and I won't see you again. I can't do that, Sharon. Hell's fire, girl, I can't do it."

"And if you go to prison, you won't see me anyhow. I'd say the cards are dealt. You going to play or throw in your hand?"

Ramsey thought about it for a long minute. Any way he went, he could come out on the losing end. "If I say no?"

"Then I'll sell to someone else. They'll open that old mine of Mama's and Lacey's Mountain will be gone."

"And you'll leave anyway, one way or another?"

She gave a sly smile. "I said I haven't decided what I'm going to do."

"And if I say yes?"

"We'll be bound to keep in touch no matter where I go or what I do. You'll owe me money for a long time."

"You're a shrewd little business woman, Sharon."

"Well, what's it going to be?"

"And Joe?"

"Joe has nothing to do with this. I want to sell."

"Will you talk to him?"

"I will."

Ramsey grinned. "I'm in," he said. "But you have to go see a lawyer, get it down on paper legal like, just how it's going to work, in case I am gone for a spell. Don't pack your bags right away, okay? I'd like to get to know you first. You might even learn to like me a little."

"I'm renting a small place in Indian Bend." A slight smile pulled at her lips. "I'll be there for a while."

~~~

It was late that evening when Ramsey and
~~~

Joe rode into Indian Bend together. Ramsey said nothing of the conversation he'd had with Sharon. He wanted to in the worst way, wanted to tell Joe to convince her to stay, to marry him. But he knew it was none of his business.

"I took the time to send a telegraph yesterday, before I went to the ranch," Joe said as they stopped at the door of his office. "I should be getting an answer back shortly."

"Guess we'll know soon then."

"We should. Go home and get some sleep. I'll let you know."

"Thanks, Joe. I appreciate it."

Ramsey rode on to the boarding house and put his horse away, then walked to the kitchen door like a man with a purpose and rapped.

Pleasant answered, the worried expression on her face instantly erased by the site of him, high color rising to her cheeks.

Ramsey took her in with his eyes, from the top of her golden head, to the white apron over his favorite pink calico dress, right down to the tips of her high-buttoned boots. Damn, she was pretty. It was good seeing her safe and sound, standing here in her own kitchen. He grinned and breathed deep, savoring the sweet smell of lavender that seemed to follow her everywhere she went.

"Evening, ma'am," he said, removing his hat.

"I've kept your supper warm, Mr. Judd."

She held the door wide and he stepped in. He felt awkward somehow in her presence, but she went about the business of removing his plate from the warming oven and made tea in a china pot. She turned from her work, saw him still standing in the middle of her kitchen.

"Please, sit down," she said with a smile. "It's ready."

"Thank you, ma'am. Mighty kind of you."

"Oh, Mr. Judd," she said, wiping her hands on a towel. "It was no trouble. You look tired."

"Guess I am a little," he replied, taking his seat at the freshly laid table. "It's been a long day."

Pleasant was quiet now. She watched him pick up his fork and dig into the plump dumplings swimming in thick chicken gravy on his plate. "I have apple pie for desert."

Ramsey grinned. "Sit down, Mrs. Smith, please. Talk to me."

Pleasant slid onto the chair across from him. She waited for him to chew and swallow what was in his mouth. He looked up, winked, and took another bite, enjoying his food. He was aware of the expectation on her face, the anxious way she watched him, waiting for him to say something.

What he wanted to say was of a serious nature. He couldn't just blurt it out. It took some thought. He had to get it right the first time, couldn't be floundering for words. So he kept her waiting, fidgeting with the tablecloth, fussing with the stray strands of golden hair at her neck, until he had taken the last bite of pie and washed it down with tea.

"Mr. Judd, I thought you wanted to talk."

"I do, Mrs. Smith. But right now, looking at you is mighty pleasing."

Pleasant blushed crimson, lowered her gaze.

"You heard Hannah, didn't you?" he said, becoming serious. "I'm wanted by the law."

"I found the wanted poster on the floor of your room."

"It was a long time ago, ma'am."

She looked up at him. "Why did you do it?"

He rolled the last of the food from the crevices inside his mouth with his tongue, took another swallow of tea. She had a right to know. She'd be the hardest to try to explain it to. He hoped to hell she'd understand.

"I got tired of the killing," he said softly. "Couldn't take it any longer."

"That was a bad time, Mr. Judd. Brothers against brothers, fathers against sons, neighbors against neighbors. I can see where it would make you feel that way. We were all glad when it was over."

He wondered if he could leave it there. If he needed to tell the whole story. He watched her, held her eyes with his. She didn't waver.

He opened his mouth to speak again.

"No," she said. "You needn't explain. Not tonight, Mr. Judd. We can talk about it another time."

"Does it change things with you and me?"

"You've proven what kind of a man you are. It doesn't change things."

Ramsey breathed a sigh of relief. "Ma'am, I been thinking about this for a long time. I'm not going to mince words. I got something to say – to ask of you, and there's no since beating around the bush." He pushed his chair back from the table. "I been bouncing around from pillar to post for twenty years. Not a thing to show for it. Up until now, I couldn't even boast a steady income. Been making my way with odd jobs and lucky poker hands. I've even been known to raid a hen house or a garden patch or two."

Pleasant waited. Listened.

"Ma'am, I've made a lot of mistakes along the way and I'm aiming to set those mistakes to right. That could take time. I don't know what's going to happen down the line, but I – "

"Mr. Judd, for someone who doesn't beat around the bush, seems to me you're doing a lot of stamping right now."

"Yes, ma'am. I'll get to the point."

"Please do."

"I just bought a ranch, Mrs. Smith."

"You've what?"

"I bought the Larken place from Sharon. It'll be a good living. Course I have to pay for it, but even at that, I can support you now."

"Mr. Judd, what are you trying to say?"

"That is if I don't go to prison, in which event, I'd have to leave you and – " He stopped, looked at her, suddenly lost for words. How could he expect her to wait for him? This was a fool notion he was having. Maybe he best forget it.

The tea kettle on the cook stove hissed steam. The rain had begun again and it pattered gently on the window behind the lace curtains.

"Joe's been sending some telegrams. He should know in a day or two how I stand with the War Department." Again Ramsey stopped talking. He gazed at the flustered face across from him. This was not going exactly the way he'd planned. "Ma'am...I – "

"Yes, Mr. Judd? Go on."

"Ah hell, ma'am. Would you consider marrying an old broken down saddle tramp like me?"

The most beautiful smile Ramsey had ever seen spread across Pleasant's face. Her hand went to her throat and she breathed a long breath, let it out slowly. "Why, Mr. Judd," she said, "I thought you'd never ask."

"Well, I just did. So what's the answer? Do you need time to think on it? You want to wait until Joe gets some news?"

Pleasant didn't hesitate a moment. "Yes," she said.

"I understand. Don't blame you one darn bit. I have no right to ask you to be my wife knowing I might be locked up for a spell. That's okay, Mrs. Smith."

"I'll marry you, Mr. Judd."

Ramsey looked at her. His mouth was open, but he couldn't shut it.

Pleasant giggled.

Had he heard her right? "You just said – "

"I said yes, Mr. Judd."

Ramsey got up from the chair, nearly

knocking it over in his haste to get around the table, down on one knee, take her hand in both of his big ones and put it too his lips. "I swear, you've purely made me the happiest man in the whole damn state. Er...excuse my words, ma'am."

He stood, bringing her with him, pulled her to him and kissed her hard on the mouth.

Pleasant laughed behind the kiss. Ramsey pulled back, looked at her wide-open eyes and laughed too, then led her around the kitchen in a kind of music-less, happy little two-step, twirled her under his arm and brought her back to him.

This time the kiss was serious. He was sure the toes of his boots were curling up from it. One thing he did know for certain: there was a hardening in his crotch that pushed fiercely against his rough denim trousers.

Pleasant pressed herself tighter against him. "Oh, Mr. Judd," she whispered, pulling her lips from his and brushing them against his ear. "This could be very serious."

"Yes," he whispered. "I should take my leave before it's too late."

Neither moved away from the other. They stood locked tightly in each other's arms.

"I'm afraid it's already too late," she said.

"If that wonderful part of your anatomy isn't tended to, why, my dearest darling, it could break off and we'd spend our whole married life wondering what it would have been like."

Hell. Ramsey was convinced.

"That would be a shame, Mrs. Smith." He nibbled the top of her ear. "Purely a shame."

Peasant reached behind her and took his hand from her waist. "Come with me, Mr. Judd. We'll take care of that right now."

~~~

Early next morning, almost before the sun was up, a blushing Peasant threw a robe over her naked, newly aroused body, tied it securely about her waist and answered the persistent knocking at the front door. Joe Keys smiled back at her.

"Morning, ma'am. I'm looking for Ramsey. I checked his room. He wasn't there. It's rather important and I thought maybe – "

"Oh, dear me." She felt the heat rise up from her stomach, into her neck and ears and to her cheeks. She laid a hand on her hot face and opened the door wider. How could he have known Ramsey would be here? "Do step in, Mr. Keys."

She was shaking from embarrassment as she went into the bedroom and closed the door,
~~~

leaned her back against it and stared at the undressed man with the cocky grin on his face, leaning on one elbow in her bed.

"Mr. Judd, it's Joe Keys. How do you suppose he knew?"

"Don't you fret, Mrs. Smith." Ramsey swung his long legs over the edge of the bed and retrieved his pants from the crumpled heap of clothing he'd dropped in hasty recklessness the night before. "You go to the kitchen and build us a cup of coffee. I'll take care of Joe."

"Oh," she cried, the back of her hand going to her forehead. "Mr. Judd, I certainly can't go back out there."

"Now go on, darlin'." Ramsey pulled the suspenders over his bare torso. "You'll have to get use to waking up with me in your bed."

"After we're married, Mr. Judd. What must that man be thinking of me?"

"He probably thinks you're a mighty attractive woman and that ol' Ramsey's a damn lucky man. Go on now." He was laughing at her.

Pleasant took a deep breath, darted out of the bedroom, and almost ran to the kitchen, not even glancing at the tall young man still standing beside her door. She built a fire and made the coffee, shaking so badly she nearly dropped the pot three times. She heard the soft murmur of men's voices from the front part of the house, then heavy foot steps. Ramsey, barefooted and no shirt, entered the kitchen with Joe.

"It's okay, Mrs. Smith," Ramsey said to her back. "Joe has agreed to be my best man."

"Oh, Mr. Judd, for heaven's sake!" Now she was embarrassed. She bustled about, gathering cups and the sugar bowl and a pitcher of cream from the cold box on the back porch, and set them on the table. "Your coffee is nearly done. I'll get dressed and leave you to it."

"No," Ramsey said. "I want you to stay. This involves you, too. Sit down, Mrs. Smith."

Pleasant grabbed a towel from the counter, lifted the heavy coffeepot from the stove and filled the cups, then they all sat down together.

"I'm sorry, ma'am," Joe said, his own face a bright shade of pink. "I had no idea I'd find Ramsey down here. I just figured you might know where he was."

"It seems you were right, Mr. Keys."

Ramsey chuckled. "Ain't she the prettiest thing you ever saw first thing in the morning, Joe? Her hair all mussed like that and her face shiny and bright as a dew-kissed apple?"

"You stop that, Mr. Judd!"

Joe cleared his throat. "What I came for was, I got an answer to that telegram I sent last night."

"Already?" Ramsey said.

Joe smiled. "It's later in the day there than it is here. I got good news and bad."

"I'll take the bad first," Ramsey replied, lifting his coffee cup to his mouth.

Pleasant held her breath, braced herself. Bad news. She must be ready for the very worst. Oh please, God, she thought, not too bad. Please. She knew she might lose him. He'd told her that. And she'd accepted it. But now, how would she handle it if he had to go away from her – maybe for years?

"There was a fire in the records room in Washington a few years ago," Joe said. "A lot of old documents were destroyed."

Ramsey cocked an eyebrow, a grin pulling at one side of his mouth. "And the good news?"

"As far as the War Department is concerned, Ramsey, they never heard of you before."

"Oh my word," Pleasant breathed in relief. "That is good news." She looked at the men. "I think, isn't it, Mr. Keys? What exactly are you saying?"

"It means simply that there are no outstanding warrants against Ramsey Judd. The war's been over for a lot of years. Ramsey's crime isn't worth the paperwork."

"You mean – " Ramsey said.

"You're a free man." Joe grinned. "The folks in Washington couldn't give a hoot for you. Does that hurt your feelings?"

"Well, I'll be go to hell."

Pleasant closed her eyes and thanked the god she had just prayed to. Ramsey was safe. He wasn't going away. Then she glanced at the clock. "You'll be going somewhere, Ramsey Judd," Pleasant said, standing. "I hope not to hell, but you can't stay here. And you, too, Mr. Keys. I'll have three men and a boy down here for breakfast in another hour and I'll not have the likes of either of you sitting around in my kitchen. Now get, both of you."

"Not even hitched yet, Joe, and she's bossing me around like she owns me." Ramsey grinned, got up from the chair. "I'll just be fetching my boots, if that's okay with you, ma'am."

Pleasant picked up the towel from the counter and threw it at him.

Joe stood. "Now, when's the wedding?"

Ramsey looked at Pleasant. He was still

grinning. "I took advantage of this dear lady last night, pure and simple. Best be making an honest woman of her as soon as possible. Besides, she told me I couldn't wake up in her bed again until after we've wed." He cupped his hand around his mouth, winked and leaned toward Joe. "Then I get to call her Pleasant," he whispered loudly. He put his hand down. "Today at one o'clock. Sound okay to you, Mrs. Smith?"

Chapter Sixteen

"Hell, Ramsey. I don't know what to do." Joe put his end of the hewn log in place and straightened, wiped his brow with a red bandanna he'd taken from his hip pocket. They'd been working since sunup on the walls of the new barn Ramsey needed to finish before winter. It wouldn't be a large affair, big enough to stable several head of horses, and the cow, and a loft for hay. But Ramsey was soon realizing that it would be one hell of a big job. At the rate he was going, it would take a couple years to finish.

"It's been two months since Hannah died and she's just as pig headed as she was when it happened," Joe went on. "Don't seem to want a damn thing to do with me."

"Give her time, Joe." Ramsey lifted a water

jug to his lips and let the tepid liquid slide down his throat. He wanted to tell Joe what was eating at Sharon, didn't really know if he should. Seemed to him like a daughter should be able to confide in her father and not have to worry about it. "She's having a hard time of it right now." He handed the jug to Joe.

Both men were bare to the waist, muscled from hard work, their skin, bronzed by the mid-August sun, glistening with perspiration.

"Did she flat tell you no?"

"Not exactly. She just said she needed more time to think on it. She has this fool notion that she needs to be free for a while. I just can't figure her out."

"She was under her mama's thumb for a long time. Maybe she wants to try her wings before you go clipping them again." Ramsey hadn't intended for the words to be sharp, but that's the way they came out.

"I don't aim to clip her wings," Joe snapped back. "I just want to marry her."

"Sorry, Joe. Didn't mean it the way it sounded." Ramsey was protective where Sharon was concerned. Maybe too protective. That's probably what Sharon didn't need right now. And he was still fighting the battle of whether he should level with Joe, tell him the fears she'd confided in him.

Joe didn't answer. He tipped the jug up and took a long drink.

Ramsey hefted the double-bit ax lying on the ground beside him and swung it at another log, notching it to match up with the one it would lay on. "Women get some funny notions once in a while. She'll come around."

"Ever since she moved into that old room of yours, she's been about as independent as a lone she-wolf."

"Pleasant has a mind of her own, too. Those women have been thick as thieves since Sharon moved in. Sharon helps her in the kitchen, fixing meals, helps with the books – "

"That's what I mean, Ramsey, she don't have any time for me anymore."

"Pleasant hasn't got too much spare time for me lately, either. Last night, late, she was going over the ranch accounts with Sharon."

Ramsey finished the notching and they lifted the log in place. It was a perfect fit.

"What do you suppose they're up to?" Joe asked, stepping back and looking at their work.

"Don't know that they're up to anything. Maybe they just like each other's company."

"Nope. There's something in the wind. I feel it in my bones."

"How's Tom working out?" Ramsey picked up the ax again.

"Best damn deputy I could have hired. He's got a real way with people, Ramsey."

"He liked getting out of the boarding house. It was time for him to be on his own. Felt he needed to stay and help his ma – until I came along."

"Speaking of Tom, I best be getting back to town. He'll be wanting to call it a day. He's kind of sweet on the little Johnson girl. Been calling on her almost every evening."

"I'm going to call it quits here, anyhow. I'm taking a load of supplies up to Rock Creek and check on the sheep. Maybe you could stop by and tell Pleasant I'll be a little late. She ain't going to like it much. I've been late every night this week."

"I can do that."

"Appreciate your help, Joe."

"That's okay. I'll be back in the morning."

The sound of a wagon on the road leading to the house caused the men to turn.

"What in the hell?" Ramsey pushed his hat to the back of his head. "That's Pleasant driving that wagon."

"She's got it loaded to the nuts," Joe said.

"Christ, now what's she up to?" Ramsey

hurried to meet her, opened the gate and swung it wide, allowing her to drive the old dilapidated freighter pulled by a team of strong work horses through. Joe was right behind him.

"Where'd you get that wagon, Pleasant?" Ramsey asked. "And whose horses are those?"

Pleasant didn't speak a word, just flicked the lines and pulled past him, stopped in front of the back door.

"What are you up to, woman?" Ramsey called.

"I'm moving in, Mr. Judd," she said, jumping down from the seat and working the ropes that secured the canvas over her load.

"You're what?"

"I sold the boarding house."

"You what?"

"Help me with these ropes."

Ramsey fumbled with the ties. "Mind telling me what this is all about?"

"I sold the boarding house."

"You said that. Why'd you sell the boarding house?"

"Because I wanted to sell the boarding house."

"Why'd you want to – Hell's fire, Pleasant."

"Keep your tongue, Mr. Judd. If you're

going to be a rancher, then I'm going to be a rancher's wife. You're never home anymore. You're always up here."

"I've got work to do. It takes a lot of work to run a sheep ranch."

"I know that. That's why I sold the boarding house."

"Who'd you sell it to?"

The ropes were loose. Ramsey drug the canvas off the wagon. Pleasant took a box from the back.

"Get that big crate, right there, will you, Mr. Judd? And be careful. It contains china. Joe, be a dear and bring that one next to it, please."

Ramsey picked up the crate and followed her into the house. "Who'd you sell it to?"

"Sharon."

Joe was just coming through the door. He dropped the box on the kitchen floor. "Sharon?"

"Sharon?" Ramsey echoed.

"Be careful with those things," Pleasant ordered. "If one piece of my mother's china gets broken, I'll have your hides." She looked around. "That girl was right. This is real nice. I'll have it snug and cozy in no time."

She walked into the front room, leaving both men staring after her with their mouths open.

"Ramsey," she called. "You and Joe can take that bed on the wagon upstairs and put it in Sharon's room. Tear Sharon's down. It goes back to town. Hurry and finish unloading the wagon. She said she has some things already in crates up there. Load them up. Then you'd better be on your way, Joe. She's going to need your help. Will you please return the wagon to the livery?"

The men looked at each other.

"Move," she said coming back to the kitchen. "Time's wasting. Oh yes, Mr. Judd, Sharon said to tell you...actually, she said 'tell *Father*,'" Pleasant smiled, "she's decided to play her hand. She said you'd know what she means."

~~~

That evening, Ramsey and Pleasant sat in the straight-back chairs Ramsey had carried out to the porch that stretched across the front side of the house. A cool breeze bringing the smell of Autumn stirred through the trees bordering the yard. Ramsey packed tobacco into the bowl of his new pipe that Pleasant had bought for him at Henry's Mercantile in town and lit it. Then he wiggled his toes in the comfortable pair of genuine leather slippers
~~~

she'd ordered from the Sears and Roebuck catalog.

Life was good.

"It's pretty here, Mr. Judd," Pleasant said, gazing out over the rugged landscape.

Ramsey reached out and gathered her hand from her lap. "It's a might prettier now that you're here. I'm going to bring that porch swing up from the boarding house. Is that okay with you?"

"You know what I'd like to do?"

"Now what would that be?" He pulled on the pipe and sent a cloud of smoke curling into the breeze.

"For Thanksgiving, I'd like to invite Sharon and Joe and Tommy and the men from the boarding house for dinner."

"Pleasant, there's not a doubt in my mind, you'll do what you take a good notion to do."

"You're not angry with me then?"

"No, I'm not angry. Shocked would be a better word. Wouldn't've dreamed you'd be wanting to live way up here."

Pleasant smiled. "Wouldn't work out well, having two households. Besides, I really did want to get out from under the boarding house. Sharon will do well."

"Did she really call me Father?"

"Yes, she really did. We've had a lot of talks, Sharon and I. Can you keep a secret, Mr. Judd?"

"Been known to." He grinned at her.

"There's going to be a wedding in the family very soon."

"I was hoping. Poor ol' Joe's been about half out of his mind with worry."

"She just needed time. That was pretty hard on her. The way it happened and all. Poor Hannah."

"Well, it's done and over now." Ramsey drew on the stem again. "We best put it behind us."

"You're right, dear."

"I'll see if Joe would mind bringing our mail up once a week," Ramsey said.

"Oh, dear me." Pleasant reached into the pocket of her skirt. "I nearly forgot. This came for you today." She handed Ramsey a long white envelope.

Ramsey removed the pipe from his mouth. "What's this?"

"I posted a letter for you the morning you went with Hannah. That's the answer, I think."

He looked at the name scrawled neatly in the top left corner of the envelope. A warm feeling formed in the pit of his stomach and spread upward. "I'll be damned."

Elizabeth Judd, Cincinnati, Ohio.

Who's Elizabeth Judd?"

"She's my mother," he answered in a soft voice. "I didn't even know if she was still alive."

Crickets chirped from the bushes at the side of the house, and an owl hooted from the woods. Ramsey held the letter loosely in his lap. What would his mother have to say to him after all these year? He was afraid to find out.

"Aren't you going to open it?"

He hesitated a few seconds longer, the pipe clamped tightly between his teeth, then carefully tore the end and pulled out the folded paper inside, opened it and read.

My dearest son Ramsey,

How long I've waited for your letter. I've missed you so much, son. Yes, your father knew about Jarred. We were presented with a medal by General Grant at a special ceremony right here in Cincinnati. A young man named Johnny Bowler came by our house right after Jarred was killed. He told us what happened. He stayed on to help your father about the farm. Such a nice boy, hard worker. He became like a third son to us.

Ramsey stopped. A mixture of guilt, remorse, and homesickness stabbed at him. He fought the emotions building in his gut, swallowed hard against the lump in his throat, blinked his eyes to stop the tears that were trying to push their way to the surface.

Ramsey, dear, he continued, *your pa died ten years ago. His heart gave out on him. Johnny and I laid him to rest in the little cemetery on the hill overlooking the farm. He was proud of his sons to the very end. Both of them.*

The lump in Ramsey's throat tightened. Grief overtook him. He put the fingers and thumb of one hand hard against his eyes briefly, then continued reading.

Johnny and his wife, Carolina, and their four children, two boys and two girls, live here at the farm with me now. I turned the place over to him right after your father died. He's done a good job through the years. I know you won't mind. I've left the farm to Johnny after I'm gone. It's all done up legal at the courthouse.

Son, I'm sending a letter I've kept for years. I received it right after the war. I didn't know where to forward it, but I hung onto it in hopes someday you'd return. I long to see you again, hope I get to before I die. I'm old, 75 my next birthday in August, but I'm in good health and will be able to wait a little longer.

Come home, son, if you can.

Deep and endless love, I remain your ma,

Elizabeth Judd

Ramsey clutched the letter in his lap. His breath caught in a quiet sob and his shoulders heaved. He hadn't cried since the death of his brother. He didn't try to stop the tears, let them flow freely down his face.

He should have gone home. It should have been him who buried his father, him who looked after his mother. He'd failed them. Now it was too late and there wasn't a damn thing he could do about it. He'd thought about Johnny a lot through the years, and they hadn't been kind thoughts.

"Are you okay, Mr. Judd?" Pleasant asked.

Ramsey couldn't answer.

"Mr. Judd?"

He handed the letter to her and she read it silently.

"Oh, Ramsey," she choked. "Such a wonderful letter."

He wiped his face, unashamed, with the palm of his hand, reached in the envelope and took out another folded piece of paper. It was from the Department of War; its contents pertained to general amnesty for war criminals. One paragraph stood out from the rest:

Come in, surrender, and be paroled; fail to surrender and be regarded as an outlaw, and when captured, be treated like one.

Ramsey handed it over to Pleasant. If he'd stayed and faced the music all those years ago, he wouldn't have had to live the way he had. Life taught dear lessons, he thought, if he'd a mind to learn them.

He was sorry for the turns his life had taken. Sorry for the things he should have done but didn't. There was no going back. The past was the past, and it was too late to try to make up for it. He guessed a man had to do a lot of riding, take a lot of bad forks in the trail, do everything he'd done to get where he was at this moment. And right now, Ramsey knew he was where he needed to be. He was here with Pleasant. His daughter was a few hours away. Taking those two things into consideration, there wasn't much room for regret.

"You really need to visit your mother, dear," Pleasant said softly, reaching out and laying a hand on his. "You know that."

"Don't see how I can." He took a handkerchief from his pocket and wiped his face, blew his nose. He was okay now. "I have to get that barn up."

"You're making do."

"Yes, we're making do, using one of the sheep sheds." He shoved the handkerchief back into his pocket. "But the sheep will be coming down from high pasture in another couple of months. I'll need all the space I can get. I've got the hay stored in another one of the sheds until I get the loft finished."

"There must be a way."

"I'd still like to know who burned that damn barn," Ramsey said almost to himself.

"Life has to keep a few secrets, Mr. Judd."

"I suppose you're right."

"If you don't go, you'll hate yourself for the rest of your life. If you don't do it now, you never will."

"It takes time to cut logs, Pleasant."

"Why don't you purchase lumber?"

"I can't afford to buy lumber. Not for a year or two at least."

"You married a woman of means."

"I can't use your money."

"It's our money now, Mr. Judd. And besides, Sharon gave me a more-than-fair price for the boarding house. Buy the lumber. Hire the hands you'll need. Let them build the barn. You're getting too old for that kind of work anyway. You go see your mother."

Ramsey sighed. "Yes, I'd like to see her...and Johnny, too. Sounds like he stayed and did what I should have done."

"Then do it."

He looked at her. "Would you go with me?"

"Who would look after the house?"

"The house can take care of itself for a while. That hired help you're set on can tend to the cow and the chickens."

"It's settled?" she asked. "We're going?"

Ramsey grinned. "I love you, Mrs. Judd."

Pleasant beamed. "Well, then," she said, standing and smoothing the apron about her middle. "This calls for a celebration. I have just the thing. You wait right here." The screen door squeaked as she opened it. "I have dried apple pie cooling on the counter."

"When did you have time to make apple pie?"

She giggled and turned back. "Oh, Mr. Judd, I love you and all your foolish questions."

Ramsey watched her. She was watching him, too. He grinned and raised an eyebrow at the pretty little flush that touched her cheeks. He had a feeling she was thinking the same thing he was.

You know, Pleasant, of all the things I like about you, apple pie has taken second place on my list. I can think of another fine way to celebrate."

The flush deepened and her smile

widened. Pleasant held out her hand to him. "You silly, wonderful man," she said. "That apple pie can just wait."

Tina Spencer

Acknowledgments

I would like to thank all the people who helped me in the beginning, my friends at the University of Idaho, to Rubell Dingman for her write-up in the *Argonaut Campus News*. Thank you to Tim Curry for his help with computer matters that would still have me stumped if he hadn't come to my rescue. And of course to cousin Cindy, forever and always. Also, thank you, Jack Hiday, for all the work you did on getting just the right book cover. You are an artist.

And I'd like to give honorable mention to my friend Rich for sharing in the fun.

Tina Spencer

Tina Spencer

About the Authors

Tina Spencer lives in Troy, Idaho, where she's called home for fifty years. In 2008, she retired from the University of Idaho dining services in Moscow, Idaho, where she served as barista in campus coffee shops for eighteen years. Her father was born and raised in, and has strong ties to, the Salmon River country where this book started. He talked fondly of the area and told lots of stories of his boyhood growing up.

Writing in the spirit of adventure and happy endings, Pacific Northwest author Cindy Hiday has won numerous honors, including first place in the Kay Snow Awards for fiction from Willamette Writers. Her humorous literary novel, *Father, Son & Grace* (republished as *Destination Stardust*), is a five star Reader's Favorite and local book club choice. When she isn't writing, Cindy enjoys growing her own produce, hiking old-growth forests in search of the next waterfall, and strolling long, sandy beaches.

Visit www.cindyhiday.com.